Katy Evans's *USA Today* and *New York Times* bestselling series strips away everything you've ever believed about passion—and asks the dangerously enticing question, "How real is what you feel?"

Praise for Katy Evans and

MINE

"Steamy, sexy, intense, and erotic, *Mine* is one that will have you hanging off the ropes. And begging for more."
—Alice Clayton, *USA Today*
bestselling author of *Wallbanger*

"SEDUCTIVE, WILD, AND VISCERAL."
—Christina Lauren, *New York Times*
bestselling author of *Beautiful Bastard*

Praise for Katy Evans and

REAL

Remington Tate, the unstoppable bad boy of
the Underground fighting circuit has finally
met his match . . . in Brooke Dumas.

"A scorching debut."

—Christina Lauren

"I have a new book crush and his name is Remington Tate."
—*Martini Times*

"Remy is the king of the alpha-males."
—*Romance Addiction*

"I loved this book. As in, I couldn't stop talking about it."
—*Dear Author*

"Kudos are in order for Ms. Evans for taking writing to a whole
new level. She makes you FEEL every single word you read."
—*Reality Bites*

"Remy was complex and his story broke my heart . . . made me cry! Katy Evans had me gripped and on the edge of my seat through the whole story. . . . Without a doubt I absolutely fell in total LOVE with Remy."

—*Totally Booked*

"Edgy, angsty, and saturated with palpable tension and incendiary sex, this tale packs an emotional wallop. . . . Intriguing."

—*Library Journal*

"Unlike anything I've ever read before. Remy and Brooke's love story is one that has to be experienced because until you do, you just won't get it . . . one roller-coaster ride that you'll never forget!"

—*Books over Boys*

"Some books are special. . . . What a rare gift for an author to be able to actually wrap your arms around your readers and hold them. Katy Evans does just that."

—*SubClub Books*

"Wow—Katy Evans is one to watch."

—*Wicked Little Pixie*

ALSO BY KATY EVANS

Real

Mine

REMY

katy evans

G

Gallery Books

New York   London   Toronto   Sydney   New Delhi

G

Gallery Books
A Division of Simon & Schuster, Inc.
1230 Avenue of the Americas
New York, NY 10020

First Gallery Books trade paperback edition November 2013

GALLERY BOOKS and colophon are
registered trademarks of Simon & Schuster, Inc.

For information about special discounts for bulk purchases, please contact Simon & Schuster Special Sales at 1-866-506-1949 or business@simonandschuster.com.

The Simon & Schuster Speakers Bureau can bring authors to your live event. For more information or to book an event contact the Simon & Schuster Speakers Bureau at 1-866-248-3049 or visit our website at www.simonspeakers.com.

Designed by Davina Mock-Maniscalco

Manufactured in the United States of America

10 9 8 7 6 5 4 3 2 1

Library of Congress Cataloging-in-Publication Data is available

ISBN 978-1-4767-6446-7
ISBN 978-1-4767-5566-3 (ebook)

to my husband, you know the million reasons why

REMY PLAYLIST

"IRIS" by Goo Goo Dolls

"I LOVE YOU" by Avril Lavigne

"KISS ME" by Ed Sheeran

"WILL YOU MARRY ME" by John Berry

"EVERYTHING" by Lifehouse

SEATTLE

There will be hundreds of days in my life that I won't remember. But this is one day that I will never forget.

Today I marry my wife. Brooke "Little Firecracker" Dumas.

I promised her a church wedding. And a church wedding is what she'll get.

♥ ♥ ♥

"I SWEAR IF you frown any harder at the door, it's going to collapse under your stare," my PA, Pete, calls from the couch.

I swing around to where he and Riley have been watching me pace around the living room of Brooke's old Seattle apartment. Apparently those two are amused as fuck by me. Dipshits. I don't see what's so amusing. Turning back to the bedroom door, I continue pacing.

For the life of me, I can't imagine what's taking her so long. It's been exactly fifty-eight minutes since she locked herself up in our bedroom to get ready, when Brooke—my fucking Brooke—usually gets dressed in five.

"Dude, it's her wedding day. Chicks take a lot of time to get prepped." Riley thrusts his arms out in the air in a gesture that implies *That's life!*

"Like you're an expert now," Pete jabs.

"It's the dress!" Melanie, Brooke's best friend, says, exploding out of the master bedroom with a trail of white stuff that looks like a veil. "It has all these buttons . . . and what are you three doing here anyway? Remington, I talked to Brooke about it. You guys should leave and we'll meet you at the altar."

"That's fucking ridiculous," I say, laughing. But when Melanie keeps staring at the three of us, and especially me, with an expression someone might use on a couple of dogs they want to scat, I scowl and head to the bedroom door.

I curl my fingers around the doorknob and speak through the closure slit. "Brooke?"

"Remy, please don't come in here!"

"Come to the door, then."

When I hear shuffling, I press closer to the edge and drop my voice so the dipshits on the living room couch don't hear. "Why the fuck can't I see you right now, baby?"

All this entering and exiting the room by Melanie, with me separated by a locked door from my soon-to-be wife? I don't like it. And separated despite the fact that she's supposed to be getting dressed for *me*.

"I guess because I want you to see me walk up to you," she whispers.

God, that voice, right there. Makes me want to throw the door down and kiss the hell out of her, then do stuff to her under that dress she's trying to put on—the things that husbands do to their fucking wives. "I will see you walk up to me, baby, I just want to see you now too. Open the door and I'll do your buttons."

"You can undo them later and then do *me*." The cheeky statement is followed by a soft "Gaaah," like someone—a very little someone—is amused about something on the other side of this door.

"Excuse me, Riptide," Melanie says as she returns, and waves me away from the door. "You boys should head out to church. We'll see you there in thirty minutes."

I scowl when she slides inside the bedroom like a goddamn worm through a tiny slit, preventing me from so much as glimpsing Brooke. Using much the same method, the much-larger Josephine steps out with something squirming against her chest. My son looks at me from the crook of her arm and falls still; his lips are curled in such a way that he almost wears the same amused expression Pete and Riley do.

He takes the hand he's got stuck inside his mouth and slaps it flat and wet to my jaw. "Gah!" he says, then squirms and flings himself to me.

Catching him, I nuzzle his stomach and growl, which elicits another "Gaaaaaah!"

When I lift my head to look into his eyes, he's fucking delighted. And so am I, but I growl again like I'm not and grumble at him, "You think I'm funny?"

"Gaaah!"

His eyes are all mischief. His head is smaller than my palm as I cup it and buzz the fuzz on the top of his head. My four-month-old, Racer, the son Brooke gave me? He's the most perfect thing I've ever done in my life.

I never thought I'd have something like him. Now my life revolves around *this* dimpled squirrel, who pukes on all my fucking T-shirts, and my Brooke. And, god, where do I start with her?

Pete slaps my back with a loud *thunk*. "All right, dude, you heard them. And watch it—he's going to get all that baby stuff on your suit!"

Clamping my jaw, I pat Racer's head and he grins at me. He has one dimple, not two. Brooke says it's because he's only half mine. I contest he's all mine, and so is *she*.

Smiling back at him, I return him to Josephine, who assures me, "Go peacefully, Mr. Tate, I've got this."

She's supposed to be a bodyguard, but I don't know what the hell she is now. She strolls outside with Racer and does some nanny work too. He sticks his fingers into her hair and pulls and she even seems to like it.

After a glance at the kitchen clock, I level my gaze at her. "I want her there in fifteen minutes," I say, and she nods.

A limo is waiting for my bride, but Riley's got the keys to Melanie's convertible, parked just outside without the top down. We all leap inside. I drop down on the front passenger seat and then stare up at the window of our temporary apartment. I can't understand what the big fuss is about wedding-dress buttons. As far as I'm concerned, I should ride, in the car, with my wife, to the fucking church, where we marry. Period.

"Rem. It's not like she's going to leave you standing at the altar, man," Riley says, laughing.

"Yeah, I know," I whisper, turning back around. But sometimes I just don't know. Sometimes all my chest feels knotted and I think about waking one morning to find Brooke and my son gone, and dying is too easy to describe what I want to do.

"Twenty-eight minutes, she'll be walking up to the altar in white, just for you," Pete says.

I stare out in silence.

Brooke has been excited about this all month. Wondering if this, if that, if a cake, if not a cake. I'd say yes to anything that made her voice more excited, and she'd kiss me like I like. So now she seems in control, getting dressed, ready for her day, and I feel like a mess because she'd said she didn't mind us driving together to the church. And then her best friend put stupid-girl ideas in her head. I ride alone. To a church I never go to. To marry my wife. She's right behind us, but I'm not good. I'm fucking anxious and this is an anxiety that would have been appeased if she'd opened the door and just looked at me with those gold eyes—my mind would have gone still and all the roiling in my chest would have gone quiet.

But it's not happening.

Now I have twenty-seven infernal minutes to go . . . and my mind is playing tricks on me like it does when it starts swinging like a pendulum, and the only way I can seem to stop it is with her.

Tapping my foot, I stroke the ring in my hand. Then I pull it off and it helps to see her name on its inscription: TO MY REAL, YOUR BROOKE DUMAS.

THE DAY I SAW HER

The Seattle crowd roars as I come trotting out onto the Underground walkway.

Far at the end and directly in my line of vision, the ring awaits. Twenty-three feet by twenty-three feet, four ropes parallel on each side, four fucking posts, and that's about it.

That ring is a home to me. When I'm not on it, I miss it. When I train, I think about it.

Every step I take in its direction pumps me up and gets me going. My veins dilate, my heartbeat works to feed my muscles. My mind sharpens and clears. Every inch of me readies to attack, defend, and survive—and give these people the thrill they're all yelling for.

"Remy! I love you, Remy!" I hear them yell.

"I'll suck your cock for you, Remy!"

"REMY, POUND ME, REMY!"

"Remington, I want your Riptide!"

Stretching out my fingers, I grab the top rope and jump over it into the ring, taking a look at the people surrounding me. The lights are shining. My name is on everyone's lips. And all their excitement and anticipation spins around me in a fun little whirl-wind. They're yelling and waving pink shit at me. They want me up here. Right here. Just me, some asshole opponent, and our fists.

I whip off my robe and hand it to Riley, my friend and Coach's second, while people rise to their feet and scream louder as I turn to acknowledge the crowd. They're all standing. All looking at me like I'm their God of War and tonight is the night I will give them vengeance.

I fucking love it.

I fucking love those yells, the women screaming about the kind of shit they want me to do to them.

"Remy! *Remy!*" a crazy-sounding female shouts at the top of her lungs. *"You're so fucking hot, Remy!"*

I turn in amusement, and my gaze runs down the crowded aisle and snags on her. The one with long mahogany hair, and amber eyes, and pink, plump lips that immediately part in shock. I feel stupefied.

My instincts kick in, and I take in the stranger with one quick sweep. She's young, athletic, and dressed demurely, but there's nothing demure about the way she runs her wide, disbelieving eyes all over me.

Holy god, I feel like she's just run her tongue all over my cock.

When her eyes lock on mine, I raise a brow in a question, silently asking her, *Did you just shout at me or not?*

Her cheeks flood a nice shade of pink, and I realize it was her friend who yelled, her friend who pales compared to her. This one doesn't strike me as the kind to be courting the attentions of someone like me. But she's got all my hunter buttons engaged, and now I want her and I'm going to have her.

I wink at her, but I can instantly tell she's not feeling playful. She looks appalled.

"Kirk Dirkwood, the Hammer, here for all of you tonight!" the guy with the microphone yells.

My lips curl as I turn to watch Dirkwood hop into the ring and remove his cover, and I flex my arms and curl my fingers until my knuckles pop out. My body feels good—every muscle is warm and ready to contract. I know I'm good as fuck, but I want *this* girl to know it. I'm feeling very, very possessive, and I don't want her to look at anyone but me. I want her to see I'm the strongest, the fastest. Hell, as far as I know, I want her to think I'm the only man in the whole damn world.

Kirk is big and slow as a snail. He throws the first punch, but I can see it coming from the moment he even starts thinking about moving. I duck and come back with a punch that knocks him to the side and rocks his balance. She's watching me, I know it. The heat in her gaze makes me fight harder and faster. Hell, I own this ring. I love everything about it. I know its dimensions, the feel of the canvas under my feet, the heat of the lights on me. I have never lost a single Underground fight. People know that no matter how badly I get beat up, I always get back up and finish the battle on my terms.

But tonight? I feel *immortal.*

The crowd starts chanting my name.

"REMY . . . REMY . . . REMY."

It's my ring. My crowd. My fight. My fucking night.

Then I hear that voice again. Not *her*, but the woman she came with. "Ohmigod, hit him, Remy! Just knock him dead, you sexy beast!"

I oblige and knock Kirk down on the canvas with a hard thump. Yells erupt all over.

The ringmaster grabs and lifts my arm, and I swing my head to look at her, curious to see the look on her face. I'm panting and possibly bleeding, but none of that matters. All that matters to me is checking her the fuck out. Did she fucking see how I knocked him out? Is she even impressed, or not?

She returns my stare, and my gut twists all around. God, she's making me hard. She wears these nice clothes, and I swear she's the classiest thing I've ever seen in a place like this. Still, whatever she's wearing, it's too much and needs to come off.

"REMY! REMY! REMY! REMY!" people yell.

Their chants grow in intensity while her startled golden eyes devour me like I'm devouring her.

"You want more Remy?" the announcer happily asks the crowd. "All right then, people! Let's bring out a worthier opponent for Remington Riptide Tate tonight!"

Hell, they can bring out anything they want, man or monster. I'm so primed, I could take a couple at once.

In my peripherals, I've got her pinned down, nice and tight. In that frilly shirt. Those body-hugging pants. I've already cataloged her at about 120 pounds and five feet seven, at least a head shorter than me. In my head, I'm already measuring her breasts in my hands and tasting her skin with my tongue. Suddenly, I notice she whispers something to her friend, rises to her feet, and takes off down the aisle.

"And now, to challenge our reigning champion, ladies and gentlemen, is Parker 'the Terror' Drake!"

I stare in disbelief as she walks off, and a knot coils tight around my gut as the rest of my body tightens in preparation to chase.

The crowd comes alive as Parker takes the ring, and all I can do is watch her leave my arena while every molecule in my body screams at me to go get her.

The bell rings, and I don't play the little feinting and waiting game that me and my opponents always do. I stare into Parker's face and give him a look that says, *Sorry, dude,* and go straight for the *slam* and knock him down.

He falls splat and doesn't move.

The crowd is stunned into silence. The announcer takes a moment to speak as I wait, frustrated as fuck, my heart pounding in anticipation as I wait for Parker to stay down and the counting to begin.

It begins.

Come on, motherfuckers . . .

I'm fucking winning the championship this year and I won't be disqualified . . .

Just call it a knockout and let her hear . . .

TEN!

"Holy cow, that was fast! We have a KO! Yes, ladies and gentlemen! A KO! And in record time, our victor once again, I give you, Riptide! Riptide, who's now jumping off the ring and—*where the hell are you going?*"

The crowd goes crazy as I land on my feet on the aisle and their screams follow me all the way to the lobby. They are screaming for me while my body is screaming for me to catch her. *"Riptide! Riptide!"*

My heart pumps like crazy. She's walking fast, but I'm fucking running. Every one of my senses demands I chase, capture, and have this girl. I grab her wrist and spin her around.

"What the—" she gasps, her eyes wide in shock.

She's so beautiful my lungs freeze. Smooth forehead, long lashes with spiky tips—those gold eyes, that dainty nose, and those marshmallow lips. I need to taste that like yesterday. My mouth waters as a wild, primitive hunger opens up inside me.

"Your name," I growl. Her wrist is tiny in my hand, fragile, but I'm not about to let go. Oh, no.

"Uh, Brooke."

"Brooke what?" I snap, tightening my hold.

Her scent works me into a lather. I need to find the source of that scent. The back of her ears? Her hair? Her neck?

She tries to pry her hand free but I tighten my hold because she's not going anywhere but my bedroom.

"It's Brooke Dumas," a voice behind me says, and then the crazy friend who was with her throws off a number, which my idiot brain doesn't grasp, for I'm still hung up on her name.

Brooke Dumas.

My lips curl as I meet that pretty gold gaze. "Brooke Dumas," I say gruffly out loud, slow and deep, my tongue twisting around the name as I savor it. Such a strong, classy fucking name.

Her eyes widen in shock—and she gives me a hungry, doe-eyed look that lets me see she's a little excited but a little afraid.

It makes me crazed. I need to touch, smell, taste, claim. I burn with the need to tell her she should be afraid of me, and at the same time, all I want is to pet my hand down her long hair and promise her I'll be her protector.

Yielding to the impulse, I slide my fingers into the nape of her neck, fighting to be gentle so that she won't run, while only one thought remains in my head: *Take. Her.*

My gaze never leaving hers, I set a dry kiss on her lips, slowly, trying not to scare her, but just so she knows who I am, and who I will be for her.

"Brooke," I say against her soft lips, then I draw back with a smile. "I'm Remington."

Her eyes meet mine, and they're metallic gold and liquid with something I recognize as wanting. My smile fades as I look down at her mouth again. It's so pink and soft I bend my head to take it even more deeply. My blood rushes through my veins as her scent drowns me. I want this woman. I can't wait one more second without tasting her, taking her.

One second she's warm and trembling in my arms, quietly tipping her head back for more, and the next, the crowd engulfs us and some fucking lunatic is screaming in my ear.

"Remy! I FUCKING LOVE YOU! Remy!"

Brooke Dumas seems to snap into motion and quickly squirms free.

"No." I reach out to snatch up a piece of her white shirt. But she and her friend wind through the throng like wiggly little bunnies, and I'm in the crowd stuck with two fans who—

"Riptide, my god, please let me touch your cock."

"Riptide, you can take us both together!"

As they rub their hands down my abs, I think, *FUCK!* and pry their arms away, then I charge after her. When I reach the elevator, the gate is shut and I hear her noisily ascending up to street level.

"Remy!"

"Remington!"

Growling in anger, I slam my palm to the closed door, then dodge an incoming group of fans and bulldoze my way back into the locker room.

I don't know if I'm angry, frustrated, or . . . I don't know. Where the fuck is she going? She was looking up at me like she wanted me to eat her; I don't even understand fucking females and never fucking will. Scowling as I charge to get my stuff, I slam my fist into a locker.

"Take care of your knuckles, Tate!" Coach snaps as he gathers all my things into a red duffel.

I loathe being told what to do. So I slam my other fist into another locker and dent it like I did the first, then I glare at the old man and grab my headset, my iPod, and a sports drink. Following my crew out to our Escalade, I'm pissed as fuck at myself for letting her go. I try saving her number on my phone, at least the few digits I remember.

"That KO was unbelievable, dude, you knocked him down within three seconds!" Riley says, laughing.

I stare out the window at the lights of Seattle and tap my fingers on my knee.

"All right, so what was that all about? Are we going to discuss the elephant in the car?" asks Pete from up front. "The one with the long hair? You seemed hell-bent on chasing, Rem?"

"I want her watching my next fight." The car falls silent when they realize I'm fiercely hung up on her.

Pete sighs. "All right, I'll see what I can do. We also got you a couple of girls."

"A good assortment," Riley adds. "A blonde, a brunette, and a redhead."

And as soon as we get up to the suite, there they are. They're waiting for me. Three girls with different-colored hair, waiting in next-to-nothing clothes, ready to fuck the Riptide.

Their eyes light up when they see me.

"Get rid of them," I flatly say, then shut myself off in the master bedroom.

Showering in record speed, I then pull out my laptop and look up *Seattle, Brooke Dumas* for the rest of her number.

Grabbing my headset, I cover my ears with my Dr. Dre headphones and play loud music while I search, search, search, and then—

Bingo.

Scrolling down, I scan several articles about Brooke Dumas. One claims she's a sports rehab specialist who interned at a Seattle academy. Prior ones mention her being a track athlete. A sprinter. Odd things happen in my chest. I reread that part, and, yeah. A sprinter.

Now I understand why she's so lean, athletic, and fast. But she has some curves, the kind of curves I've never seen on a sprinter before. I curl my fingers into my palm as I replay how her small, perky breasts rose and fell as she looked up at me. My mouth waters as I remember the way she smelled. *Fuck me.* On YouTube, I find a video of her during some sort of tryouts. My heart starts whacking hard again when I pull off my headphones and click Play. She wears little shorts. Her hair in a ponytail. And I see her long, lean, muscled legs. My cock swells, and I shift uncomfortably and bend to get a closer inspection as she gets into position. The group shoots off. She starts fast—

Then one of her legs buckles. And she falls. She lays there, on the ground, and starts sobbing as she struggles to stand.

My chest does something weird.

Shit, she's crying so much her body shakes with it.

Forming fists, I watch her try to hop out of the track on her own, while the asshole spectator who recorded the video just keeps repeating, "Man, her life is over," again and again.

Camera zooms in on her tear-filled face, and I quickly pause the screen and stare at her. Brooke Dumas. She looks just like she did today, but a little younger, and a whole lot more vulnerable. There's a little dimple in her chin from her expression, and those gold eyes are so drowned in tears, I can barely see their pretty whiskey color. I start to read the comments beneath the clip, of which there are quite a few.

> **Iwlormw:** *Rumors have it she'd been doing cross fit against the advice of her coach and had already tweaked that knee!*

> **Trrwoods:** *That's what happens when you don't prepare properly!*

> **Runningexpert:** *She was good, but not that great. Lamaske would've still kicked the shit out of her in the Olympics.*

My stomach boils.

I watch the video again, and my stomach boils even more.

With an angry growl, I toss my sports drink across the room and hear it slam against the wall. I want to destroy everyone making fun of her.

She'd stood there tonight in my arena, trying to raise her walls up to me, and she'd looked proud as a warrioress, like she hadn't already endured the world watching her fall once already. My chest twists so hard, I can't breathe right again, and I growl and slam my laptop shut.

Pete raps his knuckles on my door and pushes it open a little. "Rem, you sure you don't want to partake?"

He widens the gap and gestures at the trio of women behind him, their expectant eyes peering into my bedroom. They collectively sigh and one murmurs, "Please, Riptide . . ."

"Just once?" says the other.

"I said get rid of them, Pete." I crack my knuckles, then my neck. The door closes and a sudden quiet settles in the suite, until Pete comes back and pries the door open again.

"All right, dude. But I really think you should've gone for them. . . . Anyhow, Diane wants to know if you want dinner in here."

Shaking my head, I carry my iPad to the dining room and settle down to wolf down the contents of my plate on autopilot while Pete makes some phone calls confirming our hotel reservations in Atlanta next week.

While I'm eating, all I see are gold eyes, and parted lips, and the way Brooke Dumas looked at me, like a doe who's just realized there's one predator after her that won't give up until she's caught.

I want to make her mine.

Mine.

I want to smell the fuck out of her 'cause it gets me all cranked up and nothing has ever cranked me up like her scent just did. I want the joy of looking at her and touching her and I want. To make. Her. *Mine.*

Grabbing my iPad, I look her up on the Internet again as I chow, stopping on a picture from her sprinting days. She's like a gazelle, and I'm going to be the lion that catches her.

"Pete, you think I need a sports rehab specialist?" I ask.

"No, Rem."

"Why not?"

"You're an asshole, dude. You hardly let the masseuses massage you for more than twenty minutes."

"I need one now." Pushing my iPad over to him, I tap the screen and signal to the name below her image. "I need that one."

Pete lifts an interested eyebrow. "You do. Do you?"

"I need a sports rehab specialist on my payroll. I want her to tend to me every day. In whatever ways they do."

He smirks. "They don't do blow jobs, I'll tell you that."

"If I wanted a blow job, I could have had three just now. What I want . . ." Once again, my finger taps over her name. "Is *this* sports rehab specialist."

Pete's eyebrows fly up to his hairline, and he leans back and crosses his arms. "What exactly do you want her for?"

I chomp down the rest of my food, then take a long gulp of water so I can speak. "I want her for me."

"Rem . . ." he says in warning.

"Offer her a salary she can't decline."

Pete answers me with a puzzled silence. He seems taken aback and is trying to make sense of me. He's looking into my eyes, and I can tell he's observing whether they are black or blue.

I'm not black. So I wait quietly. He sighs, slowly jots down her name, and speaks cautiously. "All right, Remington, but let me say, this has *Bad Idea* written all over it."

Shoving my plate aside, I lean back and cross my arms.

My head betrays me half the time. One day, it tells me I am god. The other, it tells me that I not only rule hell, but I invented it. Does Pete think I give one fuck about what *his* own head thinks about *my* idea? I don't listen to my head anymore. I listen only to my gut.

"I want her watching me fight Saturday," I remind him as I get up and shove my chair back under the table. "Get her the best seats in the house."

"Remington . . ."

"Just do it, Pete," I say as I cross the living room back to the master.

"I already have the tickets ready to go, dude, but it's hard enough keeping Diane from knowing of your . . . er, issues. It's going to be even harder to keep it from someone like this sports rehab specialist."

I prop my shoulder at the threshold of my bedroom and think about that. I lower my voice. "Make her sign a contract, so I have guaranteed time with her. And stabilize me the instant I start losing my shit."

"Remington, just let me get some other girls—"

"No, Pete. No other girls."

I shut myself in my room and grab my headphones, then just lie there with my iPod in my hand, staring at it.

What will it be like if I make her mine?

I don't delude myself into thinking that she will accept me, but what if she does? What if she can understand me? The way I am? The two parts of me? No. Not two parts. Every. Single. Fucking. Part. Of me.

My gut tightens as I remember the way her eyes shone when she looked at me. The way they softened after I kissed her and she looked into my eyes, wanting more of me.

I have never seen a look quite like that before. I have been wanted by thousands of women. Nobody has ever looked at me with such open, frightened longing as her.

She was not frightened of me. She was frightened of "it." This same thing clenching my gut that has me all tangled up. Every cell in my body is buzzing with awareness. Every inch of my skin is awake. My muscles feel primed like they do when I'm ready to fight. Except I'm not ready to fight now. I'm ready to go get my mate.

God help her.

❤ ❤ ❤

THE SEATTLE CROWD is wild tonight. Backstage, the noise reverberates between the walls, bounces off the metal lockers in the room where I prepare with some of the other fighters. I watch Coach bandage the fingers of one hand, and all I can think of is how Brooke Dumas is out there among the spectators, sitting in one of the seats I bought for her.

I'm so jacked up I feel like I'm plugged into a fucking electrical outlet. Blood pumps heady through my veins. My muscles are loose and warm and ready to contract and strike anything in my path. I'm ready to put on a fucking show and there's one girl, one lovely girl, that's got me tied up in knots, that I want to see me fight.

I hand Coach my other hand and stare at my bare knuckles as he shoots off the same instructions he always says.

My guard . . . patience . . . balance . . .

I zone out, letting his words slip through me and into my subconscious, where they belong. Right before a fight, I find a calm. I can hear all the noise but listen to nothing. A clarity comes with fighting. Every detail sharpening in your mind.

This sharpness and awareness makes me lift my head to the

doorway. She stands there like out of some childhood dream, looking at nobody but *me*.

She wears a pair of white jeans and a pink top that makes her skin look even tanner than it is and so damn lickable my tongue hurts inside my mouth. Neither of us so much as twitches as we stare.

Hammer steps into my peripherals, and when I see him head straight for her, my anger ignites.

With deadly calm, I grab the tape from Coach and throw it aside as I stalk over to her. Then, I position myself directly behind her and to her right, taking my spot in a way that lets the dipshit Hammer know I was *born* to be here. Beside, behind, and by her.

"Just walk off," I warn him, my voice low but lethal.

He doesn't seem inclined to listen, instead narrows his eyes in contest. "She yours?" he asks with narrowed eyes.

Nodding, I narrow my eyes and let my gaze burn into him. "I can guarantee you, she's not *yours*."

The asshole leaves, and I notice Brooke doesn't move for a long second, as if she doesn't want to step away from me in the same way I don't want her to go anywhere. Holy god, she smells good.

I drag her scent to my lungs like a junkie, and suddenly every inch of my body wants to cup her hips and draw her into me so I can scent her more. She turns her head to mine and softly murmurs, "Thank you," but quickly leaves. I duck my head and haul in as much as I can before she walks away.

I remain standing there, feeling dizzy, my shorts ridiculously tented.

"Riptide! Hammer! You're up next!"

Exhaling as I hear my name, I glance narrowly at Hammer across the room, who seems amused as fuck that I am clearly in deep shit with this girl.

He's in even deeper shit with *me*.

"Remington . . . are you listening to me?"

I whip around to Coach, who's fixing that last bandage he couldn't secure. I keep glaring at Hammer as Riley extends my satin robe, and as I ram my arms into the sleeves, I decide Hammer better be prepared to vacation in a coma for a while.

"I said don't let that bastard get to your head." Coach knocks his knuckles to my temples. "And that girl neither."

"That girl's been in his head since the first fight here," Riley tells him with a smirk. "Hell, he wants to carry that girl around with him like an accessory on tour. Pete is drafting the contract as we speak."

Coach pokes a finger into my chest and I feel it almost bending. "I don't give a shit what you're planning to do tonight with the girl. You keep your head in the fight going on *right now*. You got that?"

I don't answer, but obviously I get it. I don't need to be told these things. Half a fight is in your head. But Coach likes feeling useful, so I just roll with it and trot out. I've fought all my life to stay sane. To keep focused, driven, and centered. But tonight, I fight to show one woman my worth.

I climb onstage and go to my corner, and I can hear the crowd going wild. Makes me smile.

At my corner, I yank off my robe and hand it to Riley, and the public goes even wilder when my muscles are on display.

They shout my name and I let them know I fucking love it, chuckling with them as I stretch out my arms and let them know I'm soaking it in. Every second it takes for me to do my turn, my heart pumps, and pumps, and pumps in exhilaration, because I feel gold eyes on my back, almost burning through me, making me want more. More than what I get here, from this wild crowd. More than what I've ever been given in my life.

Dragging in a breath, I keep turning in her direction, my gut already tight with the sheer anticipation of looking into her eyes. I want her to be looking at me when I turn. I know it's going to give me a rush. Her attention gives me a rush. The way she smelled in the locker rooms—so fresh and clean—still heats the blood in my veins. I don't know what it is about this woman but all I've been able to think of since the first moment I spotted her is hunt. Chase. Claim. *Take.*

"And now, I give you, the Hammer!"

I smile as Hammer is announced, and finally, I slide my gaze to where it wants to go and there she is. Jesus. There she is. And she's just like I wanted her, looking at me.

She sits there, tense and lovely, with her hair down her shoulders and her eyes wide and expectant. I know she was waiting for me to turn. I can almost see her pulse quicken—mine does. I don't know what this is. If it's fake. If it's real. If she's real. But I know I'm leaving this city soon, and I won't be leaving without her.

Hammer comes into the ring—*my* ring, where I've never let any other motherfucker finish standing—and I jab a finger in the air toward him . . . and then I point at her.

This one's for you, Brooke Dumas.

Her eyes flash in disbelief, and I want to laugh when the blonde friend beside her starts screaming. The bell sounds, and my muscle memory takes charge as I position my guard, bounce on my toes, and do my thing.

We go toe-to-toe. I feint and Hammer swings, opening his side. So I jab his ribs, feel the satisfying punch race up my arm, and we bounce apart. Hammer is stupid in the head. He falls for all my feints and never covers right. I ram him hard enough to make him bounce on the ropes and drop to his knees. He shakes his head and hops to his feet after a moment. I *love* this. My heart pumps slowly. My every muscle knows where to move, what to do, where to send my power—right from my center, up my chest, shoulder, down the length of my arms, to the tips of my fucking knuckles that hit with the force of a charging bull.

I take him down, and then I do the same with the next foe. And the next.

A powerful energy takes over me as I fight, and I fight knowing that Brooke Dumas watches me. If there's anything in my head other than winning, it's that I want her to think inside that lovely round head of hers that she has never, *ever*, seen a man like me.

By the time the tenth guy falls, sweat coats my chest, and as the ringmaster raises my arm, I'm anxious to see the look in her eyes. I want to see that she liked it, that she—like everyone else in this room—thinks I'm the shit. Our eyes lock, my gut goes hard and twisted and wild with desire, and I smile at her as I try to catch my breath.

When the ringmaster releases my arm, I cross the ring, jump over the cord, and land in the aisle, watching her part her lips in shock as I come over.

People go crazy when I go outside the ring, and they're losing their shit right now.

The whole room screams with their applause and cheers. And I know they all can see where my gaze rests and where I'm headed.

"Kiss his heart out, woman!"

"You don't deserve him, you bitch!"

"You go, girl!"

I smile down at this woman who has stolen my thoughts, and as I wonder if she wants me to, she looks pleadingly up at me, almost begging me *not* to kiss her here. My blood simmers as I remember her lips on mine, but it won't be happening again.

Not until you're ready, Brooke Dumas.

I bend to her and scent her hair, whispering at her temple, "Sit tight. I'll send someone over for you."

I back off before I lose it, and climbing up into the ring, I steal one last look at her. My chest does all kinds of strange things when our eyes lock.

"*Riptide, people!*" the announcer screams.

The yells feed me. I suck them in with a smile, full of pride and satisfaction. I can see in every one of these people's eyes that I'm the man. But I want to see it in her eyes. That. I'm. The Man.

The man who wants to be Hers.

❤ ❤ ❤

THERE'S NO TIME to wait for Coach to rehash what I did. I pummeled ten dudes to the ground and I'm fucking tired. But—at the same time—I'm wired as hell.

"Well done, boy. I'm gonna send a pair of masseuses to work on you," he says once we're in the locker room, and slaps my back.

In silence, I grab a pair of Gatorades to replenish my minerals and head out to the car with my duffel, knowing Pete and Riley will bring her to me soon. I want her.

At the hotel suite, my cock is hard and fully standing when I shower and I have to turn the knob to cold—ice-cold—as the water runs down my body. Dragging in a breath, I close my eyes and plant my hands on the wall as the water calms me.

But, god, the way she looks at me, the way she smells . . . Come tomorrow, when she works for me, I can smell her anytime, if I want to. And I want to.

When I come out of the shower in a towel, a pair of massage therapists have been let in by Diane.

"Food's hot now, Remy," she calls from the kitchen.

"Not now." I grab an ice pack from the fridge and several

more Gatorade bottles and then settle down at the foot of the bed, my muscles worn. My face hurts and I slap the ice pack on the sore as the women start working me. They massaged me last time and immediately get to work on my arms and shoulders while I intently wait for a certain signal from out in the living room.

And then I hear it.

Anticipation curls around my gut and I train my eyes on the bedroom door. Pete strolls inside in his best PA mode, and something tangles in my chest when I see her following him.

Brooke Dumas.

God, she scrambles my head.

Her legs look lean and endless in those tight jeans she must use butter to slide into, and the soft-pink top she wears is the same exact shade of her lips.

I like the shade of her hair, dark and seductive and sun-lightened with just a hint of copper, and I like the small earrings on her ears. She's wearing hardly anything fake. No watch. No bracelets. Just the small earrings, and her lips are shiny with something. The rest of her is fresh and natural as a flower, but not even flowers smell as fucking good as her.

She's checking out my bare chest, and I concentrate on not blinking in order not to miss the way her cheeks heat up and her eyes fill with lust. My body tightens with need. I haven't had anyone in days, and I'm not used to any sort of abstinence. It's simple to me: if I want it, I indulge. Hungry? Eat, asshole.

But all I want to eat now is *her*. I wish her hands were the ones on my shoulders. . . . No. I want my hands on her small shoulders. But I want them most on her clothes, ripping them away so I can see her.

When Brooke stares at me, and then the therapists, in slight confusion, I slap the ice pack down, finish my Gatorade, and toss it aside.

"Did you enjoy the fight?" I ask.

She startles slightly at my voice, which is gruff with dehydration and exhaustion, and my lips curl into a smile.

I want to run my fingers over her skin. She was a runner, and that flesh has seen the sun. It looks as warm as her eyes and the faint light streaks in her beautiful dark hair.

She's silent as she contemplates the question. Like it has an answer other than the one I've always received, which obviously is yes.

Isn't it?

"You make it interesting," she finally answers.

I'm slightly thrown. So, she's not a fan of mine? "Is that all?" I prod.

"Yes."

The hands on my back and shoulders become annoying, and I roll my shoulders to jerk them off. "Leave me," I command the women.

The women head out—and she's alone with me. In my suite. My bedroom. Inches from my bed. Inches from *me*.

Once again, I'm hard as stone. I remember she'd been sitting with two women and a man who seemed protective of her. *Yeah, thanks for protecting her, dude, but I'm taking it from here.*

"The man you're with . . . Is he your boyfriend?"

Amusement sparks in her eyes and I think I see a slight curl to the corners of her lips. "No, he's just a friend."

"No husband?" I keep prodding. Possessively, I study her ring finger and see how slim and delicate her hands look.

"No husband, not at all."

The air is static. My entire body is ready to fuck her. Just being near her feels sexual. "You interned at a private school rehabbing their young athletes?"

She looks surprised, her eyes sparking with curiosity and disbelief. "You looked me up?"

"Actually, *we* did." Pete and Riley come into the room, and her attention swings away from me. But mine doesn't shift. I know what they're going to say already. I told them what, exactly, they would propose today.

Miss Dumas . . . I'm sure you're wondering why you're here, so we'll just cut to it. We're leaving town in two days and I'm afraid there's no time to do things differently. Mr. Tate wants to hire you. . . .

She looks so surprised that I smile inside, even as my insides go tense. I don't want her to say no. She surprised me today, denying she liked my fight. If she says no to this too, I'm not going to take it so well.

The tension escalates when she frowns after Pete's explanation that I want her to travel with me from site to site. I don't like the way her eyes darken.

"What is it, exactly, that you think I do? I'm not an escort," she says.

Okay, so she doesn't look as excited about the job as I'd thought she would be. Wary, I settle back down on the bench seat and watch her, torn between amusement and frustration at the way things are developing. Both Pete and Riley burst out laughing at her comment; I don't.

"You're onto us, Miss Dumas. Yes, I admit when we're traveling, we find it convenient to keep one or several special friends of Mr. Tate's to, shall we say, accommodate his needs either before or after a fight," Pete laughingly explains.

Her left eyebrow shoots up and now I want to laugh at how these idiots paint me. But, hell, if she thinks my being friendly with the ladies is something bad, then wait until she hears about the worst part of me.

Suddenly, this whole scene is just not amusing at all. If I go manic before I can ever get close to her, I'll be completely fucked. But I also can't just take her to bed and let her go; I don't want to let this one go.

"A man like Remington has very particular requirements, as you might guess, Miss Dumas," Riley tells her. "But he's been very specific in the fact that he's no longer interested in the friends we had secured for him during our trip. He wants to focus on what's important, and instead, he wants you to come work for him."

She glances at Riley, then Pete, and then at me, and she looks puzzled, which is cute.

Pete flips through the folders. "You interned at the Military Academy of Seattle in sports rehab for their middle graders, and we see you've graduated only two weeks ago. We're prepared to hire your services, which will cover the duration of our eight cities we have left to tour, and Mr. Tate's continued conditioning for future competitions. We will be very generous with your salary. It's very prestigious to tend to such a followed athlete and should be impressive in any résumé. It might even allow you to be a free agent if in the future you decide to leave."

She blinks and seems completely disconcerted. "I'll have to think about it. I'm not really looking for something away from Seattle long term."

She glances at me, somehow hesitantly and even confused. "Now if that's all you wanted to say to me, I'd better get home. I'll leave my card on your bar." She swings around and heads for the door.

For a moment, I stare at her retreating back, disappointed as fuck.

I've been planning this for days. I've been wondering what it would be like to have her with me every day. I've been stone-hard to the point of pain imagining what her hands on me will feel like. . . .

"Answer me now," I say, my voice harsher than I anticipated.

"What?" She pivots around in surprise, and I pin her down with my eyes and silently will her to fucking understand that I'm trying to do a good thing here, to get to know someone—to get to know *her*—and I don't want her pissing on it like it's nothing. Like I'm used to doing this sort of shit for anyone.

"I've offered you a job, and I want an answer."

A leaden silence descends.

She stares at me, and I stare back just as fiercely, the air charged around us.

I've wanted nothing but to kiss her since the first night I saw her. I only gave her a peck, just so she knew I was going to have her. Now I wish I'd stuck my tongue inside so I could have appeased this wild craving to know what she tastes like. I want to know *all of her*, every scarred little piece of her knee, to the perfect contours of her face, to the way she thinks. And whether she wants to or not, I want her to know *me*.

She seems to drag a breath for courage before she starts nodding. "I'll work with you for the three months you have left to tour, if you include room and board and my transportation, guarantee me references for my next job application, and let me promote the fact that I've worked with you with my future clients."

Her answer takes me aback, and when she swings around to leave, I quickly stop her by saying, "All right." When she turns, I glance at the guys. "But I want it on paper she's not leaving until the tour is over."

I get up and head over to her.

She watches me approach with those alarmed doe eyes again; they are soft as a deer's, but far prettier. Her breasts rise and fall, and I like that she knows. She knows something is going on here. She's confused that I didn't pursue her like she'd thought, but that is all right. Because my pursuit will be slower now, and deeper, so that in the end I can take her, fast and hard, like I'm used to taking everything in my life by force. But she's so special, I want to reach the very core of her being before she's mine. And when I'm there, and she's soft and yielding to me, I'm not going to let her go.

Holding her gold gaze, I squeeze her hand gently, whispering, "We have a deal, Brooke."

TO ATLANTA

There's an image in my head of Pete and Riley arriving at the airport without Brooke Dumas, and I don't like it. Pacing the length of my jet, up and down, I ram my hands into my jeans and peer out the window, but there's still no Pete or Riley or Brooke Dumas.

I pull my hands out and crack my knuckles.

"Save it for the ring, boy," Coach grumbles, flipping through a sports magazine, and I flex my fingers and inhale deeply. I need to train. I've needed to train longer, harder lately. I'm horny as fuck and just thinking about her gives me a hard-on.

From the bar, I grab a bottle of water, down it slow and cold, trying to relax. Then I go take a seat on the bench and put on my headphones. I scan my songs and look for something fast and hard, select it, and let it blast in my ears—then I see movement up in the front of the plane.

All my insides go still.

Nothing does that to me but looking at her.

And, yep, I'm looking.

My eyes feel out of control as they run up and down her body while Pete introduces her to Coach and Diane. My heart starts pumping blood to the south of my body, and the music blasting into my ears is forgotten. She doesn't see me yet, but I see her. Every inch of my rapidly swelling cock is aware that she's near.

Her round butt is encased in a knee-length skirt. My eyes run down her lean, toned calves and her pretty ankles to her feet in plain ballet-type shoes. An image of those ankles locked at the small of my back as I thrust into her body flashes through me. I fist my hands at my sides and force myself to exhale, but my blood is still prepping me to mate with her.

I watch as Pete finally directs her in my direction, and every primal instinct inside me stirs as she starts down the aisle toward me. A blush reddens her pretty tan skin. It colors her face and spreads down her throat and dips into her cleavage, and I want to pull open the buttons of her top and see if she's blushing all the way to the tips of her pretty little tits. God, I want to hold those little tits and take them in my mouth, and most of all, I want to see the expression on her face while I do so.

Pushing the thought aside, I pull off my headphones, turn off my iPod, and stare at her face. She's not only beautiful as fuck, but she's excited, her eyes shining into me.

"You've met the rest of the staff?" I ask her, my voice gruff with arousal.

"Yes." She smiles, a genuine smile that goes all the way to her eyes as she takes her seat and neatly straps on her seat belt. Her soft, smoky voice has a strange, calming effect on me. But my dick is still pressing hard against my zipper, and I have no idea what I'm going to do with it for the next couple of hours.

"Did you hire me for a particular sports injury or more as prevention?" she asks.

More so I could claim you. "Prevention," I whisper.

She chews on the inside of her cheek as she surveys me, and she has no idea that as she measures the breadth of my chest, my arms, and my torso, I'm struggling hard not to lean down and kiss her lips.

"How are your shoulders?" she asks, looking quite the professional little thing. "Your elbows? Do you want me to work on anything for Atlanta? Pete tells me it's a several-hour flight."

Yeah, it will be, and I'll probably have blue balls by the end, but what the hell. I want her to touch me bad enough that I stretch out my arm and offer her my hand.

She seems slightly surprised but takes it in both of hers; I don't expect the way my gut tangles at the contact. Her body warmth blends with mine when she opens my huge hand with her little fingers and starts rubbing my palm, searching for knots. Her fingers are strong, but soft, and her touch is torture to my libido but too close to heaven to stop.

"I'm not used to such big hands. My students' hands are usually easier to rub down," she tells me animatedly.

Soft fingers scrape across the calluses in my palms as we talk about her students, and how I condition eight hours a day.

"I'd love to stretch you when you're done training. Is that what your specialists also do for you?" she asks.

I nod, and my mind instantly goes to the YouTube video I've been watching nonstop. I really fucking wish I'd been there so I could crush the asshole woman's video camera with my hands.

"And you? Who pats your injury down?" I ask as I signal to the knee brace that peeks from under her skirt.

"No one anymore. I'm done with rehab." She raises a brow and looks alarmed. "You googled me too? Or did your guys tell you?"

I googled you, and I wanted to punch my fist through a wall, then go get you and carry you off that track and lick your tears dry.

Pulling free of her hand, I realize I'm the one who wants to do the touching here, so I signal at the knee. "Let's have a look at it."

"There's nothing to see." She doesn't seem delighted about the attention, but ends up lifting her knee anyway. I seize it with one hand and rip open the Velcro, instantly spotting the scar cutting across the joint.

I hold her knee in my hand, and I stroke my thumb across, noticing her slim, muscled thighs, the tightness of her quad muscle. She's strong and lean, but lithe, like a cheetah. I want her. Refusing to stop touching her, I explore her marred skin and she bites her lip and exhales.

"It still hurts?" I gently ask.

She nods and explains that it's a double injury. She tore her ACL first six years ago, and then again two years ago.

"It hurts not to compete anymore?" I prod.

Her expression softens when she holds my gaze, and something, something invisible, tugs me to her even as I watch her lean the slightest fraction closer to me. "Yes. It does. You'd understand, right?"

Slowly I lower her leg, and instead of nodding, I stroke my thumb across her knee, so she knows that I do understand. More than she knows. We both watch me caress her, and, god, it feels so right I want to drag my finger up the inside of her thigh and under her skirt, so before I follow the impulse, I pull back and stretch out my free hand, gruffly telling her, "Do this one."

Testing the territory, I slide my arm along the seat behind her as she takes my hand and starts working it. My nostrils twitch at our closeness; she doesn't pull away. She smells . . . of soap and some sort of berry shampoo, plus her own female scent is sweet and warm in my nose. She probes and searches and I open my eyes and watch her face, soft and yet concentrating. My heart pounds faster.

She moves to my wrist, and she twirls and then probes into my forearm, and when she closes her eyes with a look of utter concentration and pleasure, I want to groan and tease and laugh at her and kiss her all at the same time. She looks young and innocent, and my hunter-gatherer instincts are in full force. I've hunted her and now I want to gather her to me. . . .

I decide to touch her. Tease her. I want to make her smile. Hell, I want to see her smile at *me*.

I cup the nape of her neck and I lean in. "Look at me."

She opens those gold eyes, lowers my hand, and smiles in bemusement. Fuck me standing, but she was getting worked up with me and every inch of my body knows it.

"What?" she asks.

"Nothing." I smile, but I'm hot and bothered and delighted, all at once. "I'm very impressed. You're very thorough, Brooke."

She grins almost innocently. "I am. And wait until I get to your shoulders and back. I might have to stand on you."

She amuses me. So much I poke her biceps with my fingers. Then her triceps, and I say, "Hmm," and when I place her hand around my biceps, her eyes flare wide. I love it. I know she likes how big and hard it is, but she pretends otherwise and playfully responds, "Hmm."

We laugh. We're laughing when she seems to realize Pete and company have fallen quiet and are watching us.

She pulls something out from her bag, and I glare at Pete, silently telling him, *Back off, bozo!*

She clears her throat and sets an iPod and headphones on her lap. Curious, I snatch up her iPod and connect my headphones and start going through her music, handing her mine in return. She has tons of recent songs and some earlier older ones I recognize. She drops her headphones and grabs her iPod back, returning mine.

"Who can relax to that?" she protests.

"Who wants to relax?" I taunt.

"I do."

I give her back my iPod. "I've got to have some easy listening for you. Listen to one of mine and I will listen to one of yours."

I scan my iPod, sure of the song I want. I don't regularly listen to it, but the times it comes on shuffle, I hear every fucking word, and now the need to play it to her is becoming more intense by the second.

A song plays for me from her library, and it's sassy, but I'm mostly watching her listen to the one I picked for her.

She ducks her head to cover her profile with her hair. Her hand trembles on the iPod.

I can't take it and lean forward to catch her expression.

I keep listening to the song she played me. How she won't write me a love song. That's okay. She's still playing me one, really.

My lips twitch and I chuckle, but she ducks her head to her lap as she listens to the rest of the song.

My smile fades, my body tight. Fuck, I want her. I want her to get it. I want her to get me.

She listens quietly to "Iris" from the Goo Goo Dolls, then she slowly removes her headphones and returns my iPod. "I wouldn't have guessed you had slow songs in there," she murmurs, talking to my iPod as she returns it.

I keep my voice low so that only she hears. "I have twenty thousand songs—everything is in there."

"No!" she automatically protests, then checks my iPod and notices it's true. God, she's adorable.

"Did you like it?" I quietly ask her.

She nods.

Her cheeks are flushed, and it takes all my effort not to kiss her. Instead I search for another song on my iPod and pass it over to her, playing "Love Bites" to her so she hopefully gets an idea of how very much I want her.

PRESENT

SEATTLE

It's not really fun to ride in a convertible when you're stuck in traffic," Pete muses as we hit some traffic and sit there like mannequins in a storefront.

The people inside the cars around us are staring. "You're breaking a couple hearts just sitting there, Rem," Riley chuckles from the back and angles his thumb over at a car filled with coeds.

They start squeaking when I look at them, and my guys laugh.

Turning straight ahead, I curl my fingers into my fist and slip my ring back on, then I survey my knuckles. I'm so ready for the season. Brooke is already packing for Racer. Seems like the plane luggage is going to be full of baby stuff, strollers, and everything Racer has invaded us with since he was born. I'm fucking anxious to have Brooke just for me for a night where she doesn't need to hurry out of my arms and tend to him.

"Hotel suite ready?" I ask Pete as the traffic finally starts easing.

"Yep."

"My iPod?"

"Yep. Took it this morning, and headphones."

"Every detail to the T as discussed?"

"*Everything*," Pete says.

I raise a brow at him, but he starts to drive forward, leaving me musing on the word *everything*.

I can't wait to take her in my arms.

I can't. Fucking. Wait. To marry her again.

The first time I married her, it was in City Hall, now we'll be in a real church.

I wanted to ask her to marry me with a song after last season's final, but Racer decided to drop by early, and I ended up proposing with Brooke in the beginning of labor in my arms, breathing in short, panting breaths of pain. "The song was supposed to ask you to marry me, but you'll have to settle on me doing the asking," I'd whispered, looking intently into her eyes. "Mind. Body. Soul. All of you for me. All of you mine . . . Marry me, Brooke Dumas."

"YES!" she'd cried, laughing, and crying. "Yes yes yes," she'd repeated, and I'm so fucking glad she kept saying yes because I couldn't hear it enough. I'd wanted to win the championship for her. I wanted to feel worthy of her. Right then and there, with that one word, she made me feel like I was.

And hours later I was half mad with pain watching her give birth, and I barely thought I could take it when I heard the first cry of our—*our*—baby. I wanted a girl as perfect as Brooke, and instead, she gave me something I never knew I wanted: something perfect that looks like me.

ATLANTA

The heavy bag swings. Slam. Wham. It swings, side to side, as I drive my fist into the center and follow with my left, then my right. Slam. Wham. Thunk. Slam.

Coach tells me I'm showing off, and I'm not going to waste my words and explain to him the ways I intend to *keep* showing off my moves in front of her.

I picture Scorpion, my mortal nemesis's face, in the center of my bag and wham. Bam. *Thunk.*

When I boxed with professionals, everyone wanted my ass. I was younger, faster, and stronger—you're not taught this shit. You have a good fist, or you don't, and fists were all I had. But when I look at Brooke, I'm aware of another use for my hands, how their palms and the tips of my fingers want to trace every inch of her slim, lean, little body.

"What is Remington having for breakfast?" she asked Diane this morning as she walked into the suite.

I perked up at the table, and when Brooke noticed, she smiled and said, "Good morning, Remington."

The way she says my name feels like a lick across my body.

"Good morning, Brooke," I rumbled.

Pete and Diane observed us in noticeable amusement.

Once Brooke had brought her plate over to the table and sat on the opposite side of where I was, I watched her slide the fork into her mouth and suddenly became so thirsty that I jammed a carrot into my mouth. She licked the corner of her lips, and I wanted to go over there and haul her down with me, on my lap, lick up the flavors from her mouth.

I leaned back as Pete told me something, and I wanted to toss all the plates aside and spread her on this table, get her ass in my hands, lick my tongue across her spine and up to her neck while my fingers worked all the soft and wet spots of her. I grunted at the thought.

"What?" Pete says.

She looked up at me.

I scowled at Pete. "What?" I said.

He shook his head and stood while Diane asked Brooke something about how she dealt with all these men. When she laughed at that, my body tightened and I stared. Her throat curved back, her ponytail falling. I wanted to pull it down as I tipped her head back and kissed her.

"You done?" Riley asked from the door. *You done ogling her?* I could see him think.

Scowling, I grabbed my stuff as we headed off.

Now I've been pounding the bags—all of them—as fast and hard as I can, and I still can't get rid of all this extra energy. Pausing for a moment, I look at her on the sidelines, hot as fuck in her tight exercise gear and ready to put her hands on me. I want them so badly, tonight I want to keep her for hours in my room, working on my body.

On *me*.

Hours later, I'm prepped and primed by the time I'm in the Underground locker room.

My body engages when the announcer calls, *"Remington Tate, Riiiiiptide!"*

Screams burst across the arena, rushing through me. I trot outside, and I know exactly what to do when I hit the ring. I draw it out for the crowd tonight, and I take my time tossing my robe aside and making my turn, amused by the screams, the kisses flying at me, the banners.

"And now, the famed and acclaimed Owen Wilkes, the 'Irish Grasshopper'!"

Grasshopper heads for the ring, and while the crowd takes him in, I look at Brooke. She sits with her dark hair down while the corners of her sweet, little mouth are curled upward for me, and for as long as I've lived, I've never seen something so pretty from up here.

The bell snaps me back to attention.

I head to center. Grasshopper is in my peripherals, jumping side to side like a fucking springboard. He'll wear out soon. I wait and watch him. I see my opening on his side. I swing, slamming my fist into his gut, knocking him out.

"Remyyyyyyy!" people scream.

The line of opponents keeps building as I fight my way to the Butcher. He's twice my weight and three times as wide, but nobody cares about that. He draws blood, and so do I.

He takes the ring with the agility of a meatball. Then he looks at me. I look at him.

The bell rings: *Ting.*

We take positions and eye each other over our knuckles. Butcher is known to wait boxers out, but I'm impatient to get things going. My knuckles knock into his jaw several times; I start with easy, quick hits, then I edge back and Butcher comes at me with a solid punch to the side that rocks me back a step. It takes me a moment to get back in position. I inhale through my nose, then my arms shoot out and I bury my fists, one after the other, into Butcher's flabby stomach. I back off and watch him swing, and instead of covering, I take the hit. He slams me again.

"*Boo! Boohooo!*" the crowd shouts. I see his fist coming at me again, and I catch it with my face. My head swings and blood flies from my mouth. That's better.

Straightening, I lick up the metal taste in my mouth.

He slams me down to one knee.

The screams intensify, and I know the entire arena must be looking at me, but I'm only aware of *her* eyes on me. I jump back to my feet and wipe my bleeding lips. Endorphins kill the pain. I glance at her, but the look on her face gives me pause. She's white as paper. Hell, she looks ready to bolt. I'm so damned puzzled by the worry in her face, I take another punch. This one rocks my balance and before I know it, I'm bouncing against the ropes, something I never do.

"*REMY . . . REMY . . . REMY!*" the crowd starts chanting.

I'm caked with sweat and my mouth is still bleeding when I straighten and notice Brooke is not even watching me fight anymore. She's dropped her head and stares at her lap.

Fuck.

Yeah, that's the way to impress her, you fucking dickhead.

Clamping my jaw, I straighten and glance into Butcher's keen brown eyes. "Playtime's over," I growl, and I swing out one of my most powerful punches, feeling the crack of his ribs under my knuckles. He crashes like a dead weight on the mat, and the crowd comes alive with a roar. "*Yeah!*" I hear the collective yell, then the chant, "*REMY! REMY! REMY!*"

I stand by as the counting begins, and a knot of frustration and disappointment tightens in my chest when Brooke still doesn't look at me. Finally, the announcer's voice bursts through the speaker as the ringmaster comes to raise my arm. "Our victor, ladies and gentlemen! *Riptide!* Rippppppptiiiiiide! Yes, you hungry ladies out there, scream your hearts out for the baddest bad boy this ring has ever seen! Rippppppppptiiiiiide!"

The crowd starts shrieking my name, and I quickly jump off the ring and grab a Gatorade from the bucket at Coach's feet.

"Remington," he snarls.

I shake my head and stalk down the walkway. I could tell by his tone that he wanted to have words, and I'm not in the mood to get my head chewed off in front of Brooke.

Back at the hotel, back in my room, I drop down on the bench at the foot of my bed and wait, sipping my Gatorade, replaying the pretty smile she gave me before the fight.

By the time she walks into my room, I'm so impatient, it feels like I've waited for this girl all my life. Our eyes lock, and the hunter in me goes wild. Her cheeks are flushed, and her legs long and endless in those jeans she wears. I want those legs and those arms around me, that mouth under mine, whispering my name. Fuck me, *when* can I have her? I loathe thinking I'm going to make her mine and the day my dark side catches up with me, she'll be gone, her walls will be up and she won't let me in, and I will be forever every woman's adventure. A sex god and a plaything. Nobody's real. Nobody's choice. Nobody's anything.

"Like the fight?" I ask her.

"You broke the last one's ribs," she tells me, breathless.

I drain my Gatorade and send the bottle spinning across the floor as I force the knots in my chest to loosen. "Are you worried about him, or me?" I can't believe I'm fucking jealous of the Butcher.

Her lips pull at the corners. "Him, because he's the one who won't be able to stand tomorrow."

Then—finally!—she comes and does what I secretly wanted her to do. She kneels between my thighs and starts to smear a thick, shiny paste over the cut on my lower lip. I get instantly hard. Her sweet scent teases my nostrils, and I force my body not to move a single muscle so she doesn't stop what she's doing.

God, she smells like a fucking angel.

"You," I hear her suddenly admit to me, her voice a soft whisper. "I worry about you."

I stare at the top of her head and want to bury my nose in all that dark hair and sniff her until the world ends. She covers up the salve tin and remains on her knees and seems to consider what to do next. I want her hands all over me, so I wrack my brain to find the source of my biggest discomfort, other than my dick.

"I messed up my right shoulder, Brooke."

A spark of concern flashes in her gaze, and when she notices my smile, she rolls her eyes at me and sighs. "With a bulldozer like you, I knew it was too much to hope you'd survive this night with just a cut lip."

"Are you going to come fix it?"

She pushes to her feet but huffs as if she doesn't want to. "Of course. Someone has to."

I'm amused by her, how she acts tough and sassy with me. I like it.

She heads to the back of the bed and grabs my shoulders in her hands. She prods expertly into my tissue, and when she hits the spot, an annoying pain starts to awaken. I zone out of there and focus on the feel of her cool, little fingers.

"That ugly bastard landed a pretty hard one here. He landed *a lot* of hard ones. Does it hurt?" she whispers. She eases on her investigations for a second, then she pushes even deeper.

She's pushing so hard, a fractionally amused part of me wonders if she wants to make me sound like a pussy and say, *Yes*. "No."

"I'll rub you down with arnica, and we'll do cold therapy."

She sounds businesslike as she works some nice-smelling oil into my skin. I hear the slick sounds as her touch slides over my skin, and I imagine turning around, lowering her down on my bed, and being the one who drags his hands all over her. Being the one who finds a slick spot that makes noise when I rub my fingers across.

"Does it hurt?" she asks.

"No."

"You always say no, but I can tell this time it does."

"There are other parts of me that are hurting more."

"What the hell?" The door of the suite slams shut, and Pete storms into the master bedroom squealing like a freaking banshee. "What? The *hell*?" Pete demands.

A couple of seconds later, Riley joins the party. "Coach's in a snit!" he rants. "What we all want to know is, why the fuck are you letting your ass get kicked?"

Brooke's hands stop massaging my shoulders, and I swear to god, I want to pound their faces in for taking those hands away from me.

"Yes or no: You let him get in on purpose?" Riley demands.

I don't answer.

But the look I'm sending in their direction is so clear, only a wall would not understand my fucking meaning—to piss *off*!

"Do you need to get laid?" Pete asks, glaring as he signals down at my lap and the painful, pulsing erection she just gave me. "*Do* you?"

Brooke mumbles something under her breath, and the moment she leaves, Pete fixes his attention on me. "Dude, you can't let them do this to you just so you get her hands all over you. Look, we can arrange some girls. Whatever it is you're doing, you can't play these damned games like a normal person. You're just torturing yourself, Rem. This is a dangerous thing you're doing with her."

My heart is pounding in anger and frustration. She. Is. Mine. Mine to take. Goddamn them for making me feel like I'm not worthy of her.

God.

Damn.

Them.

"You bet all your money on yourself this year, remember that episode?" Pete asks me, like I'm a fucking moron and don't remember the million other times he's told me this in a panic. "Now you need to defeat Scorpion at the final *no matter what*. And this includes her, dude."

Teeth clenched, I keep my voice low as I fight to keep my temper in check, but my god, I want to punch them. Scorpion is a walking corpse. Nothing on this earth or on this planet will keep me from busting his face open and taking the title that belongs to *me*. He ruined my life once and that's fucking enough for me.

"Scorpion's a fucking dead man, so just back off."

"You pay us to prevent this shit, Remy," Pete counters, jerking on his tie as he paces around.

I rise to my feet and look at Riley, then wait for Pete to stop pacing and look at me. They're my guys. My brothers. I pay them a lot of money to keep me from doing shit, and to keep me from screwing up. But I'm not screwing up with Brooke. Jesus, I haven't set a fucking finger on her even when the thought of her under me is taking chunks out of my brain. I softly growl, "I've got. It. Under. Control."

Shoving past them, I go grab my sweatpants and a T-shirt, then slam into my bathroom to change. I find Brooke in the kitchen, talking to Diane, and the mere sight of her round butt is a friendly greeting to my dick. Under control my ass. I'm a walking tornado of lust and it's all because of her.

Stepping close behind her, I seize her wrist and tug her around to look at me. "Do you want to run with me?"

I want to be with her. Alone.

If I can't fuck her yet, I want her close. I want her in my space, so deep that soon I want her space and mine to be the same—to be buried to the hilt in her, and she's wrapped, hot and wet, all around me, and we're just Brooke and Remington.

I can tell she's alarmed by the tumultuous energy around me, and I can't help but notice how cautiously she inspects my bruised chest.

"You need to eat, Remy," Diane chides from the corner.

Smirking at her, I grab a gallon of organic milk from the counter and down it, then wipe my mouth with the back of my arm.

"Thanks for dinner," I say, then I glance at Brooke, lift one eyebrow, and wait for her to answer.

The lady takes her sweet time.

"Brooke?" I prod.

Scowling thoughtfully, she keeps glancing at my chest. "How do you feel?" she asks, studying me with a keen, doctorly look I used to get at the Institute.

"I feel like running." I peer into her gaze and dare her to deny that she wants to be alone with me too. "Do *you*?"

I count up to eight heartbeats, and she still hesitates, driving me insane, until she finally nods. "Let me grab my sneakers and put on my brace."

I nod, and my mouth waters as she walks out of the kitchen to go change. God, this girl is going to be the death of me.

We run along a well-lit dirt trail that's scattered with trees. As soon as we start, I pull my hood over my head to keep it warm and pump my fists in the air to keep the blood in my muscles rather than where it goes to when she's around. The air is cool. She wears running shorts and a top that hugs her curves, and in my peripherals I see her breasts bouncing, her butt firm as her long legs take those sprinter strides.

Drives me fucking crazy.

"So what happened to Pete and Riley?" she asks.

"Out looking for whores."

Her eyebrows go up as I keep punching into the air. "For you?"

"Maybe. Who cares."

Her ponytail bounces and swishes side to side, and I like it. I like the way she measures her stride to mine, how our feet hit the dirt at the same time.

We pass a couple of other runners on the trail, but we keep going. Brooke is fit and fast. I've never had a training buddy, but I swear I could get used to this. To running with her.

We covered four fast miles easily before she stops and sets her hands on her knees and waves me forward. "Go on, I'm just gonna catch my breath, I'm getting a cramp."

I search into my hoodie's front pocket and pass her an electrolyte pack, then I bounce in place to stay warm and thrust my fists alternately in the air as her marshmallow lips part and she slides the pack over her tongue.

Fuck.

Me.

Standing.

All my blood rushes to my groin.

I've seemed to stop bouncing.

I don't believe I'm even breathing.

Fuck me, she's tonguing that packet right in front of me, and

I'll be damned if I don't just stand here and watch like a dickhead. "Any left?" I ask.

She hands it over. I can't help but notice she watches me as intently as I just did her as I push it into my mouth. This is what I want to do to you, I think as I look at her. This is what I want to do to your tongue, Brooke.

Sucking the remaining gel out of the packet, my body tightens when her taste slides through me. The packet has never before tasted like this. Sweet, but sweeter. It's so fucking warm, and I'm so turned on, I suck every last drop as I look at her. Her lashes are lighter at the tips, and they sweep upward as she forces her gaze from my lips, to my eyes. Eyes that I'm fucking swallowing her with.

God, I want you. I want you now. I want you tomorrow. I want you the instant you're fucking ready for me.

"Are they right? What Pete said? Are you doing it on purpose?"

She holds my stare with curious intent, and I'm trying to get my head straight, still rubbing my tongue on the packet. I've never waited so long to claim something I want, and I've never wanted anything like this. It's driving me insane and crazy. Her breasts look perfect in her running gear. Her ass. Her legs. She's delicious and I'm hungry. I am so fucking hungry for her.

"Remy, sometimes you break something and you never get it back. You *never* get it back." Her voice falters, and she glances at the street and passing cars for a moment.

And just like that the lightness of tasting her is gone and my chest feels heavy. The YouTube video plays in my head and the instinct to protect her from everything they said and everything they called her only frustrates me because I can't do shit.

"I'm sorry about your knee." I'm not good with words, but as I slam-dunk the packet into the nearest trash can, I wish I were.

I wish I could tell her how I feel thinking about her crying and helpless. I'm going to fucking protect her from now on if it's the last thing I do on this planet.

"It's not about my knee," she counters. "It's about you not taking your body for granted. Don't ever let anyone hurt you, don't *ever* allow it, Remy."

I shake my head to appease her but scowl when I think of not ever getting hit again. She will never understand how much I crave her to touch me. Not only sexually. Her touch does crazy shit to me. I'm sick for it. I'm . . . sick.

Fuck me. She's so beautiful and I'm so broken.

"I'm not, Brooke," I gruffly tell her. "I just let them get close enough I can fuck them over. Little sacrifices in search of the win. It gives them confidence to get a couple of punches in, then it starts getting to their head, that I'm easy—that I'm not like they've heard I am—and when they get drunk on how easy they're pounding Remington Tate, I go in."

Her eyes brighten beautifully. "All right. I like that so much better."

We keep running, our feet hitting the dirt, our breathing equal. Right here and right now, I'm just a guy running with a girl and, holy mother, how I want her.

"I think I quit. I'm going to be so sore tomorrow, I'd rather hit the sack now than require you to carry me to the hotel later," she tells me.

"I wouldn't mind."

In the hotel elevator, several other people board with us, and instinctively I pull my hoodie lower over my head.

"Hold the elevator!" a couple shouts, and Brooke presses the button until they hop in. I grip her hips and pull her close to me once they board. Then I drop my head, close my eyes, and smell her. My body heats instantly, and I get so worked up, I imagine peeling off her top and scraping my palms over her skin until I've got her breasts nestled in my hands. . . .

"You feel any better?" she asks, her voice somehow different from usual.

"Yeah." I duck my head even closer, and I want to kiss the back of her ear. Edging closer, willing her not to pull away, I put my mouth a hairbreadth away from her skin. "You?"

The scent she wears right now makes my mouth water. Sweat is the best fucking accessory on her. She's sweaty and delicious and I want my tongue on her neck. My hand clenches on her hip, and I have to force myself to release her as we stop at our floor and step off the elevator. She steps into her room, then I head to mine, and soon I stand under my showerhead, making the water as cold as it can get and opening my mouth so the water hits my tongue, which still fucking tingles after tasting the electrolyte packet she did. I curl my hand around myself and close my eyes. Fuck, I want her. I want this in her. In her and on her.

I squeeze my length and then angle back so that the cold water runs over my body and cools me down. It doesn't. So I have to think of my parents. The final. Scorpion. And finally I'm cool enough to soap up myself.

When I step out to dry, I hear female voices outside. Easing into a T-shirt and sweatpants, I head down the hall to the kitchen. "Hey, Rem, look what we got for you," Pete says from the living room, and he spreads his arms out.

Two girls stand there.

"Remy," the blonde gasps.

"Riptide," the redhead says.

Clamping my jaw, I shake my head and go grab my headphones from where I'd left them this morning on the dining table.

"Come on, dude, they're putting up a show just for you." Riley follows me to the kitchen, where I pull out a coconut water from the small fridge.

"I'm not in the fucking mood tonight."

"Fine. You crave something else. That's okay. Just chill out with us, man."

Sighing, I drop down and sip my drink as the girls start some sort of dance. One sits on my lap. The other dances on top of the coffee table. She's got all the right things, and she's readily displaying them for me. But what I want to see is Brooke in her exercise clothes, with her brace, her little boobs jumping up and down as she runs. No. What I want to see is Brooke bare-butt naked for me. I want her eyes to shine with desire. I want to know the size, shape, texture, and taste of her nipples, and I want to goddamn sink every part of myself, my cock, my tongue, my fucking fingers, inside her pussy and I want it to be *wet*.

Fuck me, I want it to be so wet, I want to *hear* it.

There's a knock on the door.

"What's the matter?" the girl on my lap pouts. "A little birdie told us you wanted to play with us, Remy."

"Yeah?" Riley asks to whoever is on the other side of the door.

I stiffen when I hear a muffled voice, and my cock shoots up like steel when I realize it's Brooke.

"Who is it?" I ask as Riley shuts the door. I shove the chick off my lap and stalk over.

"Brooke seemed to lose something."

"What did she lose?" I'm sure as fuck she must have seen the dancer, and I'm sure as fuck I don't want her thinking I'm putting my hands on anyone but her.

"I don't know, dude! She made a mistake!" he cries.

I charge to the door, and when there's no sign of her outside, I start down the hall to her room. I reach the doorknob and engulf it in my palm, and I swear it's still warm. I lean my forehead against the door and my heart pounds as I strain to hear something inside, but there's no noise.

I stand there like a fool. Thinking about her breath as she ran with me. The way her ponytail bounced when her shoes hit the dirt. The sight of those pink lips around the electrolyte packet in the way I want them around me.

I don't know how long I stand there, but I'm there when an old couple walk past and stare at me in pity, like I'm some poor fuck kicked out of his own room. Hell, I wish that was my room. I head back to the suite, rescue my headphones from the blonde's butt, then I head to my room. The guys keep partying outside. They're disappointed, and I know, but I don't care. I slip on my headphones and stare up at the ceiling as the music starts. I got banged up today. I put my body under immense strain; I don't feel it. All I feel is this fucking ache inside me that I somehow want her to magically fill. I'm hard and throbbing and wondering if she wants me, if she gets wet when she thinks about me.

The guys think I'm obsessed with her, that I'm going to get manic any second now and once again fuck up my entire life like I always do.

They're so right, I don't even laugh anymore when they warn me.

❤ ❤ ❤

I HAD A wet dream.

I woke up in the middle of the night, thrusting the mattress, growling her name. I didn't let myself come. I snapped awake, punched the pillow, roared in frustration, and filled the tub with cold water, then sank myself in and stayed there until the sun rose.

I've never been a merry dandelion in the morning, but today my bad mood and my sexual frustrations hang over me like a cloud with fucking thunderbolts in my head.

My sparring partners? These guys have tits and a vagina. They can't take a good sparring session, and Coach? He's in a snit when I knock them both down.

"These are sparring partners, Tate! If you'd only stop knocking them down and just have fun and work on your moves, you'd still have someone to train with today. . . . Now we've run out and you have no one to practice against anymore."

"Then stop giving me little pussies, Coach," I angrily spit. "Send Riley up here."

"Ha. Not even if he were suicidal. I need him *conscious* tomorrow."

"All right, Rem, I've got a little something for you," the man in question suddenly calls, clapping on the side. "I know for sure he's not going to knock this one out, Coach," Riley says, and then he signals happily at Brooke.

I notice Brooke—Brooke Dumas, of all people—is climbing into the ring with me. I want to laugh. It's like matching a kitten to a lion, but I don't laugh because she's wearing a black Lycra sort of outfit that molds to her every fucking curve. My eyes sweep over her and my entire body seizes. She starts to approach, swinging her hips and looking fierce, like she plans to inflict some damage on me.

I like her so much, my fucking chest hurts looking at her.

I like her eyes, her mouth, her smile, the things she says. I like her white, little teeth, her slim, small, strong hands. Her lean runner's legs. The shade of her skin, sun-kissed and lovely. I like the ways she wears her hair. I'm attracted to every inch of this woman and every day is a challenge to keep my hands to myself when my gut screams at me to *Take. Her.*

"Don't smile like that. I can knock you down with my feet," she warns me.

She's so cute, I can't stop smiling. "It's not kickboxing. Or are you going to bite too?"

She swings her leg out and I deflect it easily with one arm, lifting one eyebrow. Well, well, well, now. She's pissed at me?

She kicks again, and I deflect, then watch her circle me and jump up and down as she warms up. Clearly, she's attempting to weave, and she's not only pretty good—she looks so damned good doing it. I want to stand here all day and let her weave around me and even punch me if she wants. She tries a test punch. I'm too well trained. My body moves on automatic. My arm flies out to catch her full fist in my palm.

"No," I softly admonish, and curl my fingers over hers and tell her how to make a good fist. She tries, and I nod. "Now use your other arm to guard."

Pretty soon she's playfully attacking, flushed and excited, her eyes sparkling. Brooke can attack all she wants—and in the meantime, I'm watching her perky little breasts bounce up and down. She wants me to show her a new move? All right then. I do, taking advantage to touch her as much as possible. She's a fast learner, but something dark and bloodthirsty is in her eyes. They glitter murder as she looks at me. I don't know what she's in a twist about, but I know that if she were mine already, I'd kiss her so hard she'd forget about everything but the way I fuck my tongue into her mouth.

She smashes her fist into my abs, and I'm so taken aback by her speed, I blink. "I'm so good," she taunts.

Fuck, that's about the hottest thing a woman's done to me. She's fucking *punching* me. I'm too distracted now. Here she is. In my ring. The first woman to ever get up here with me, and I'm sure god made her just this ballsy so she could stand up to me. I'm selfish like that. I think everything about her was made for me. I feel proprietary. Territorial. I want to make a claim. I want to take her down and strip her down and pin her under me.

She swings out with her foot and yelps when her foot strikes my sneakers. Instantly, I catch her by the arms, frowning in confusion. "What was that about?"

She scowls furiously. "You were supposed to fall."

"You're kidding me, right?"

"I've toppled men much heavier than you!"

"A fucking tree topples sooner than Remy, Brooke," Riley shouts.

"Well, I can see *that*," she grumbles, then cups her mouth and yells, "Thanks for the heads-up, Riley."

I'm so annoyed she hurt herself with *me*, I lead her, as she hops on one foot, to the corner, where I drop down on the chair and haul her on top of me so I can prod her ankle. "You fucked your ankle, didn't you?" And she says I'm reckless? That I hurt my body deliberately? Did she think she was better than my ring opponents, or what—the—*hell*?

"I just seemed to *wrongly* send all my weight to my ankle," she admits.

"Why'd you hit me? Are you pissed at me?" I demand.

She scowls. "Why would I be?"

Fuck me, I know she's angry—I'm no idiot—and I want to know what the hell I fucking did. If she doesn't like me right now, then I don't stand a chance when I get manic. Worse. When I get depressed like some loser asshole. "You tell me."

She ducks her head as she catches her breath, a sheen of perspiration on her neck.

"Hey, can we get some water over here?" I call.

Riley brings over a Gatorade and a plain bottle of water and sets them by my feet.

"We're wrapping up," he informs us, then he peers around to have a good look at her. "You all right, B?"

"Dandy. Call me tomorrow, please. I can't wait to get back in the ring with this dude."

As Riley laughs his head off, I test her ankle with my fingers, prodding into the tissue. "That hurt, Brooke?" I ask as gently as possible, and then her fingers join mine around her ankle.

"You weigh a ton," she tells me. "If you weighed a little less, I'd have toppled you. I even toppled my instructor."

"What can I say?" I peer, confused, into her face, wishing to know what she's thinking.

"You're sorry? For my pride's sake?"

I shake my head, annoyed that she try such a stunt with me—me. Bending, she grabs the Gatorade and unscrews it as she straightens, and the blood suddenly boils in my veins as she sips. Her neck, the way the sleek, long tendons work as she swallows, fuck me now. My cock thickens painfully under her bottom, and with a voice thickened with arousal, I can't help but ask, "Can I get some?"

When I set my lips on the rim, it's wet from hers, and the way she watches me drink makes my balls hurt. I want to toss this shit aside and drink directly from her mouth. Instead, I return the Gatorade and make sure I brush my fingers over hers at the exchange, because I'm a devil and I need the contact. My eyes stay locked on hers as I steal that touch that shoots like a bolt up my arm, and neither of us is laughing.

She tries standing, and I instantly take the bottle and set it down, then I wrap my arm around her waist. "I'll help you up so you can ice that."

She leans on me as I lower her from the ring and help her out of the gym, her arm coming around my waist.

"It's fine," she keeps on telling me.

"Stop arguing," I softly command.

She keeps her arm around me as we board the hotel elevator, then I lock her at my side as we ride upstairs. In profile, her nose is exquisitely dainty, and that smooth, pink mouth is perennially curved in a way that tempts me to kiss it. Her scent tickles my nostrils, and as if with a mind of its own, my nose drops as I try to find the source of that delicious smell. Holy god, I want to lick up all that sexy sweat from her neck.

One of her firm, high-perched tits softly presses into my rib cage, and I can't pull my brain out of there. I'm painfully aware of the way that sweet little tit brushes against my side as we exit the elevator.

"Hey, man, ready for the fight?" a hotel staff member asks from across the hall, and I offer him a thumbs-up as we reach her room.

"Key," I whisper to her.

She fumbles, then quietly I take it from her hand, slide it into the slot, and help her inside. The first bed has a ton of family pictures facing the nightstand. I set her down on the second one and I grab the leather bucket. "I'll get you ice."

"That's fine, Remy, I'll do it later," she protests.

I pull the lock out to stop the door and go into the hallway to fill the bucket up half with ice. When I return to the room, I add some water.

Her face is pink in embarrassment when I kneel at her feet and set the bucket on the carpet, and the black of her catsuit only heightens the peach hue of her skin. I remove her tennis shoe and her sock, then I curl my hand around her calf muscle and guide her foot into the cold.

"When we get this fixed, I'm going to show you how to knock me down," I whisper, flicking my eyes up to hers, and, god, I could eat her. Eat. Her. She's biting down on her lower lip, her eyes wide and almost vulnerable as she lets me guide her foot into what has to equal the freezing waters of Antarctica.

"Cold?" I ask.

She sounds like her lungs are closing. "Yeah."

Slowly, I sink her foot deeper, and she tenses completely, all the animation gone from her face. I'm torn between the urge to stop torturing her, and fixing her ankle. "More water?"

She shakes her head and then surprises me when she shoves her foot all the way under the water. "Oh, shit," she gasps. And I know I should hold her foot in no matter what, but my instinct to protect her is so fierce I yank her foot out, flattening her skin against my abs to suck the cold out from it with my body heat. My muscles clench in shock, and her wide, surprised gold eyes lock on my face in startlement. Every one of her tiny, cold toes burns into my flesh, and I've been so successful in teaching my body to embrace pain, I want them closer. I curve my hand around her instep and hold her flat against me.

She looks breathless. From the cold. Or from me? She also sounds breathless. "I didn't know you gave pedicures, Remy."

"It's a fetish of mine."

I smile a lazy smile, then I pull out an ice cube and stroke it gently across her ankle. I make sure that her skin doesn't burn as I circle around her, and I'm moving slowly enough that I can hear her breathing rhythm quicken. I shift my hold on her foot and rub my thumb along the arch while still caressing her with the ice cube.

Her voice trembles through me, like a feather stroking my insides. "Do you do manicures too?"

I glance up at her, on the bed, looking at me like a woman does when she wants to give herself away, and the hunter in me is so ready I let her know with my tone of voice what I'm thinking, what I truly want, when I say, "Let me do your feet first, then I'll do the rest of you."

I keep going with the ice, and when the slide of her foot across my abs feels like a caress, shocks of electricity course through me.

"Feel better?" I ask gruffly, and my head is screaming at me to kiss her. She looks like she wants it. Her pink mouth is parted. Her eyes shine with heat as she looks down on me. Her feet are on my stomach, caressing the squares of my abs—and not by accident. My hands are cupping her foot, and I crave to bend my head and lick her toes, the arch up her foot, up her leg. I want to peel that catsuit off her body, feel her skin with my lips, my fingers, my knuckles, my palms. I'm drawn to her strength and her sweetness, her bravado that makes me want to push and tease her, that draws *me* out of my own cave, my own walls, if only just to chase her and bring her back to my cave with me.

I don't know the name of this, or maybe I do.

It's the one thing in my life I don't plan on fighting.

For the first time in my life I'm thinking of things other than fucking and fighting. I want to take care of *this* girl. I'm thinking about how I want to fuck her hard and kiss her softly, hold her tight and suck her gently, when she abruptly tells me, "It feels perfect now. Thank you."

We engage in a slight tug-of-war for her foot as she tries to pull free, and I'm not too happy to let her, and then the door swings open and Diane appears. "There you are," she tells me with a big grin. "I must feed you now so you can recharge for tomorrow!"

I stare at Brooke, confused as hell, and the way she stares at me as if I'd imagined the connection puzzles the shit out of me. What the hell? Right now, I could've bet my life that she'd wanted me as much as I'd wanted her. I toss the ice into the bucket and lower her foot. "I *am* sorry, about your ankle," I tell her. She wanted my apology, and now she has it. "Don't worry if you can't make it to the fight."

"No. It wasn't your fault. I'll be fine," she hurries to say.

I'm still confused as I push to my feet. "I'll ask Pete to get you some crutches."

"I'll be fine. Serves me right for messing with trees," she calls out as I head for the door.

I stop and look at her, trying to read her, and for a moment she stares back at me, looking just as confused as I feel.

"Good luck, Remy," she says.

Pummeled by a shitload of frustration, I consider charging across the room and slamming my mouth on hers, giving her a kiss so fucking wet and deep, there will be no doubt in her mind that she is *mine*. Instead, I shove my fingers through my hair and leave, then charge straight into the suite, where I know I'll find Pete either on his laptop or on the phone.

"Get someone to look at Brooke's sprain. Get her some fucking crutches. And get two of your own cars after the fight tomorrow, I want Brooke alone." I cross the living room in search of food.

Pete dials to concierge. "Do you want the Escalade or would you like someone to drive you?" His yell reaches me in the kitchen as I scour for the food Diane prepared.

"Get me a driver, I want my hands free."

SHE FIGHTS

I'm in the zone.

Standing so I can stretch my legs and bounce in place, I curl my fingers and twist my neck to one side, then the other. Riley lifts three fingers, and I'm up in three. After a couple more jumps, I pry off my headphones, slip into my robe, and then wait until I hear it: "And noooow, ladies and gentlemen, say helloww to the one, the *only*, Remington Tate, RIPPPPPTIIIIIIDE!"

Taking off down the walkway, I follow my name, then I leap into the ring, strip off my robe, and hand it over to the guys at the corner. The noise heightens as I open my arms and turn around, taking a good look at my crowd. Hundreds of heads are turned in my direction, waving banners and shit in the air as the name *Riptide* shudders upward and across the ceiling rafters.

My arms still out, I keep turning, scanning the crowd until my eyes lock on her. Brooke Dumas. Sitting right where I want her. She's framed by the groupies Pete and Riley brought up to my room, and they have nothing on her. She wears her hair down, and her smile, fuck, her smile is just for me. I smile back at her, thinking, this is for you.

Then I focus on my opponent, wait for the bell, and take him down. Working up a sweat, I take out a second fighter, a third. On my fourth and fifth, I keep jabbing, hooking, shooting out double punches, straight power punches, countering, attacking, and defending.

On my eighth, I block a power punch from his left arm, then I bury my hook in his ribs and finish him with an uppercut to the jaw that knocks him out completely with a *thunk*. He tries to rise, but slumps back down.

The public roars as my name takes over the entire room.

"*RRRRRRIIIIIIPTIIIIIIIDE!*" The ringmaster lifts my arm, and I'm catching my breath as the announcer yells, "Our victor, ladies and gentlemen. Riptiiiide!"

The screams are almost deafening, and I turn around and look at her, the smile on her lips so perfect, I can't fucking wait to kiss it.

It takes me five minutes to shower and change at the hotel, then I cross the lobby to where Brooke waits in the back of a black Lincoln.

I slide in and shut the door behind me, and when I settle in my seat, the back of my hand rests against the back of hers. I carefully watch her for any signs of her wanting to pull away.

We head into traffic.

Brooke still hasn't protested.

So I run the pad of my thumb over the back of hers, watching her reaction.

She inhales a quick breath, and the way her tits push up against her glittery top makes me hard. I think about running my thumb up her bare arm, her slender neck, then trailing it over that plump, pink mouth I want to feel all over me.

"Did you like the fight?" My voice is low and gruff.

She stares out at the window, her thoughtful profile making me want to fucking beg for it.

"No. I didn't like it," she admits as her eyes finally come to mine. "You were amazing! I *loved* it!"

The words hit me with such joy, I laugh, and I grab her hand, lift it to my mouth, and scrape my lips across the small rises of her knuckles, looking at her.

"Good," I murmur, staring deep into her eyes. It takes all my effort to let go of her. But I want her to get used to me first. I want her to smell me, feel me right here. I want her to feel my body heat and get accustomed to me. My presence. Everything about me. When I sit next to her, this is the last time I want her shoulders to go tense and tight.

Soon, we reach the club. I help her out of the car, and when she slides her small hand deeper into mine, I feel so fucking possessive, I don't let go of her. I want every man looking in her direction to know this one's fucking *mine*. In silence, I lead her past the bouncers and to a private room in the back.

"Pete is getting a lap dance," Riley tells me at the door of the private room, and I'm disappointed when Brooke quietly pulls her hand free from mine. "You don't mind treating him to one as a birthday present?" he asks me.

We all watch as a woman in a glittering silver bikini heads for Pete, who looks goggle-eyed. Brooke squirms at my side, and Riley turns his attention to her, his eyebrows flying high. "You shy about this, Brooke?" he asks in amusement.

A soft-pink hue stains Brooke's cheeks, and a rush of possessiveness charges through me. I engulf her hand in mine again, quietly asking her, "Do you want to watch?"

She shakes her head, and I quietly tug and lead her outside, noticing how she flattens her palm against mine, her soft fingers interlaced with my bigger ones. God, she's so perfect. All my instincts are raring for me to claim her.

She lets me lead her through the throng like she knows she's mine, or like she wants to be. There's noise and a crazed crowd of dancers, and as an Usher track reverberates through the room, Brooke leaps in excitement.

"Oh, I love this song!" she tells me, squeezing my hand in a way that makes my chest hurt.

The blonde groupie spots Brooke from within the dance floor, and before I know it, she's pulling her away.

"Remy!" The redhead who'd been dancing on the table of my suite grabs me and hauls me in by their side, and I can't take my eyes off Brooke. Dark haired and sexy, she moves as gracefully as a cat as she dances. Hips swaying side to side. Long golden legs. Debbie pulls Brooke closer by the hips and they're dancing as one, the undulating movements of Brooke's small waist and narrow hips heating me up to the point of madness. She laughs and turns around, arms waving in the air, as the chorus of "Scream" begins.

She spots me. I'm not moving, even though everyone else around me is. Only my heart thunders inside me. *Mine mine mine.*

There are things you're certain about. That you'd bet your life on. Things that you just know. You know the heat of a fire will burn you. Water will quench your thirst. *She* is one of those things; the most unerring certainty of my life.

She looks into my face, the look in her eyes soft and giving, and every inch of me wants to *take* what she'll give me. I reach out, spin her around, and crush her body against mine. I dive hungrily to her lovely neck, brushing her hair to the side, and pressing into her spine, inhaling her like a madman. Her scent curls around me and I part my mouth, hungrily grazing her skin with my teeth before my tongue flashes out for a taste of her.

She moans as she reaches up behind her, locking my head to her neck as the crowd dances around us. I grab her hips and pull her harder against my cock and, holy God, I want her.

Heart pounding, I spin her once. Then, her gold eyes lock to mine, I see they're liquid with wanting. I'm shaking with need as I grab her chin in one open hand and gently nuzzle her.

"Do you know what you're asking for?" My voice is husky with arousal. "Do you, Brooke?"

She doesn't reply, so I grab her ass and haul her closer, my mouth almost on hers. I want to have her now. Tonight. I want to wrap my hands in her hair while I pound inside her, I want to smell her desire all over me and drown my tongue in her taste. She slides her fingers up my chest, into my hair.

"Yes." As she pushes up on her toes, she pulls me down by the head, and suddenly her body slams into mine. My arms fly out to steady her.

"If it isn't Riptide and his new pussy," some dipshit sneers behind her.

Over her dark head, I see the motherfucker.

Scorpion.

A human-size insect, wearing his usual shit-eating smirk, while his three goons flock his side.

The thing about fighting is you never know when to stop. They just shoved Brooke, and I want to shove each of them back to the ground, then break their arms in half. I fucking can't—and even if I could, right this moment I'd rather take her away from these motherfuckers than stay here and punch their faces in.

"What's your girlfriend's name? Whose name does she call out when you fuck her, huh?"

Gathering a piece of her top in my fist, I use it to guide her out of the dance floor, then I turn her to me and block Scorpion's view of her with my body. "Go back with Riley and ask him to take you to the hotel," I quietly tell her.

She meets my gaze. "You can't get in a fight, Remy."

"We're talking to you, douche-nozzle," I hear from over my shoulder.

"I heard you, asshole, I just don't give a fuck what you have to say," I shoot back.

I sense him move and swing around in time to see his fist coming and duck, then I shove him hard enough to slam his ass to the floor. Grabbing the other one by the shirt, I push him back a couple of steps. "Take a hike or I'll cut your fucking balls off and then feed them to your mother!" I growl as I grab the other two and shove them back, and when the first one stands and approaches me from behind, I let my elbow swing back, high.

His nose cracks under my bone, and he howls.

"Sorry, dude, my bad," I say.

Scorpion is grinning. I find myself bloodthirsty enough to grin back. *You happy I'm about to break your skull in two, motherfucker?*

Then, suddenly, Brooke materializes from out of nowhere with two bottles, and she's whipping them up in the air and crashes them over the two bastard's heads. Glass explodes and rains down on the floor, then she runs back to the bar so fucking fast she's like a little bullet.

I would be highly amused if every single protective instinct inside me hadn't shot off the charts, and if she hadn't run back with a third bottle—*a third fucking bottle!*

I grab it from her hand before she can do anything and nudge her back toward the bar, where I slam it down hard. Then I toss her over my shoulder and charge back to the private rooms. I swear if I don't get her out of here right now, I'm going to end up *killing* someone.

Brooke squirms and tries to pry herself free, slamming her fists into my back, complaining, "Remington!"

I tighten my hold on her ass to still her and see Pete chatting with a group of women. "Scorpion's out there with his fucking goons—I'm out," I growl at him, then charge outside and shove her into the back of the car.

Our driver jumps behind the wheel and quickly pulls into the traffic. I'm struggling with myself in the backseat while Brooke tries to catch her breath, and holy god, I'm trying to erase the image in my head of watching her recklessly charge two fully grown, bloodthirsty men. "What *in the hell* did you think you were doing?" I explode, shaking with rage.

For her part, Brooke doesn't look one bit concerned—she looks fucking delighted. "I just saved your ass and it felt amazing," she says breathlessly, looking like a goddamn vision in that gold little top.

God! I want to fucking shake some sense into her, and at the same time I want to push her skirt up to her hips, bend over between her legs, and sink my tongue in her until she moans my name and makes me forget everything that just happened.

I don't fucking like Scorpion looking at her.

I don't like him talking about her.

I fucking don't like him pushing her.

And I can't even put into words how I feel about her smashing the brains off his minions with a couple of fucking bottles. *Jesus.*

I scrape my hands down my face and then rub the back of my neck, all my limbs shaking. "For the love of fucking god, don't ever, *ever*, do that again. *Ever*. If one of them sets a hand on you, I'll fucking kill them and I won't give a rat's fuck who sees me!"

When she only stares at me with a defiant little gleam in her eyes, I catch her wrist and squeeze so she understands she can't fucking take on men like them, releasing her when she gasps. "I mean it. Don't fucking *ever* do that again."

"Of course I will do it again. I won't let you get into trouble," she counters.

I can only stare at her, a thousand things I've never felt in my life hitting me all at once. "Jesus, are you for real?" My chest feels like a knot as I drag a hand along my face and stare outside, trembling when I think of all the years nobody has given a shit whether I get in trouble or not. "You're a stick of dynamite, do you know that?"

Her cheeks flush a deeper red as she nods. She looks as beautiful as a fucking rainbow. I want to stop with this arguing, take her up to my room, and make love.

Going up the elevator, I stay away. I want to finish what we started at the dance floor. I want to grab her, kiss her, hold her. I want her to promise me to never do that again. Never risk herself for me, or anyone, again.

"It's okay," she says, touching my shoulder, and all I can think is, *God, Brooke. You're so sweet and so innocent. Are you going to do this when I'm black?*

I'm all knotted up inside as I see her fingers on me, and in my mind, I bend my head and lick my tongue up her fingers, all the way up her arm, her shoulders, her neck, to latch onto her mouth. Before I can, she steps back to her corner and stares at me, her eyes wide and confused.

I flex my hands and try calming down.

"I'm sorry you had to see those assholes," I say, pulling on my hair for a second. "I'm going to fucking break all Scorpion's bones and pull his goddamned eyes out when I get a chance."

She nods, and I'm calmed somewhat, but even then I'm fighting the urge to put my arms around her.

"Can I come to your room until the guys get back?" she asks.

I hesitate, then the thought of her leaving her scent all over my room makes me nod like a true masochist, and she follows me. In my suite, she settles down on the living-room couch and I flick the TV on as a distraction. "Do you want something to drink?"

"No," she says. "I never drink the day before flying or I'll get doubly dehydrated."

I bring two water bottles from the bar and sit next to her.

"Why did you get in trouble when you were pro?" she asks.

"A fight like the one you just prevented," I answer in a thick, textured voice. Then I stare off into the screen, jaw clenched as I remember. I'd awoken to find the TV ablaze with news about me. I'd been manic. I'd been provoked. I'd acted—like I always do. My life was over, just like Brooke's when she tore her ACL.

Yet she sits here, next to me, my female.

My strong, beautiful female who defended her male tonight.

The need to pull her in my arms eats me. No woman has ever made me want to cuddle and nuzzle her to me, but if I cuddle her to me, I'll kiss her pretty mouth, and if I kiss her pretty mouth, I'm not going to stop there.

I'm still jacked up, my testosterone flooding my veins, my body tight with weeks of pent-up wanting. But I need to get closer, and I find myself slowly stretching my arm out over the back of the couch. So fucking close, I feel her soft hair against my forearm.

She watches me through her lashes like she wants me to get even closer, and I realize some sort of heavy kissing is on the TV, annoying me enough to make me turn it off. I want it quiet enough that I can hear the sound of her breath, hear it quickening just for me. My hand goes to her nape, and I gently caress the soft skin at the back of her neck with my thumb. She trembles.

"Why'd you do that for me?" I ask her, my voice husky.

"Because."

She holds my gaze, her amber eyes so alive and mesmerizing, there's a fire at the pit of my gut as I squeeze her nape, insisting, "Why? Somebody tell you I can't take care of myself?"

"No."

Her mouth is more tempting to me than anything I've ever wanted and had to live without. I close my eyes and drop my forehead to hers. I'm hungry for her scent, I can't stop breathing her in. I hear her breathing me in too when a light touch of a fingertip brushes across my lips. My chest knots up with hunger and my tongue darts out. I'm anxious for a taste. For *her*. She shudders. Undone, I groan and suck her finger deeper into my mouth, my eyes shutting as I savor her.

"Remington . . ." My name on her lips makes me hot enough to blow.

"Honey, I'm home!" A slamming door and Pete's sarcastic voice stuns us. "Just wanted to make sure you guys got here okay. Scorpion sure seems to have a hard-on to get your ass back in jail."

The lights flare on, and the knowledge of what I'm doing slams into me like a sledgehammer. I drop her finger and stalk to the window, breathing hard as I struggle for control. What the hell am I doing? She has no idea about me.

"I'd better go," she says.

Pete watches her leave, then he looks at me as I stand here, feeling tortured like it's my last day. "I'll just wait for you here, Rem," Pete says calmly.

Burning inside my skin, I clamp my jaw in frustration, curl my fingers into my palms, and follow her to her room, so wound up I'm ready to burst through my jeans.

I want her so much I'm not even thinking of anything except

the way she looks, the way she smells, the way she just fucking stuck her finger into my mouth.

As she slides the key into the slot, I let myself fantasize that this is our room. Or at least that it's just hers. And she'd open up the door, and I'd follow her inside. I'd kiss her slowly. Set her down on the bed. I'd kiss her all over.

But it's not just her room. I've been booking her with Diane, so I'd stay away. But maybe I don't feel like staying the fuck away anymore!

She waits a moment and then finally turns.

"Good night," she whispers, and looks up at me.

Before I can pull myself back, I grab her face and kiss her lips. "You look beautiful." My thumb runs with desperation along her jaw. I tilt her chin and kiss her—softly, drily, quickly before I lose it. "So damn beautiful I couldn't take my eyes off you all evening."

Will You Marry Me" comes up on Pandora through the car's speakers. Pete and Riley start to hoot like a couple of dipshits.

"Coincidence or what? Or what, man?" Pete punches my arm and I punch back with the same force. "Ouch!"

Okay, maybe a little more force than he used. "Don't be a fucking pussy." I laugh.

We pull into the church's parking lot, where we spot the team's rented Escalade parked already in a spot.

"So what's this about Melanie having some fucking boyfriend," Riley says as he jumps off, lifting a box of chocolates from the back of the car and showing them to us. "The name of these is even fancier than Godiva."

"She told us the boyfriend's name's Greyson, remember? And *this* doesn't belong to you." Pete grabs the box of chocolates and puts them in the back of the car, then waits behind the wheel as the top closes.

"Sounds like some asshole. Nobody gives anybody chocolates

these days—especially not someone you're dating. Melanie's ass is fine without those, I'll tell you that."

I punch Riley's arm so he goes quiet when we walk into the church. People are finishing the touches on the floral arrangements. White. White for my bride.

Brooke.

"Still, I'll bet he's some sort of posh—"

I punch Riley lightly again. "Do you love her?" I demand.

"Hell no." He looks affronted.

"Then stop complaining and let her be happy with this dude."

"Amen," Pete says.

I pull out my phone to check the time as Riley and Pete continue discussing the love life of Brooke's best friend.

"There's my boy!" Coach slaps my back. "You ready?"

"I was born ready."

He laughs. "Season starts in two weeks, and we're going to be ready."

"I'll be ready."

Right now, I'm just ready to get fucking married to my wife.

PAST

TO MIAMI

We're in the back of the plane the next day, our iPods in hand, my eyes devouring her and her eyes brazenly devouring me back.

"Put a song on for me," I tell her.

Last night was a revelation. Maybe she's more ready for me than I'd previously thought. Fuck, I can't even think that without my hormones shooting crazy in me. As she ducks her head to choose my song, I want to brush her hair back and take her mouth, to tell her with that kiss she will be mine.

I'm playing her Survivor's "High on You" and I'm fiercely impatient to find out what she plays me now. Another girl song? One that teases me with hints that she's all right without a man?

I hand her my iPod and take hers in my hand, then I slip on my headphones and listen to her selection: Journey's "Any Way You Want It."

My lips curve in an amused smile, but holy hell, the lyrics work me up. I lift my eyes to hers, then I examine her pink marshmallow mouth. She's telling me I can get anything I want?

Including that beautiful fucking mouth?

What about those gorgeous tits? Those legs around me?

She licks her lips anxiously as she watches me listen, and the lust hits me so bad, my cock fills up and throbs until it feels like lead.

She says something, then laughs, but the music plays in my ears and I have no idea what she's talking about, or to who. I dip my head closer. I'm not used to subtlety. And I need to know if this means what I think it means. What I want it to. My will-power is shredded into pieces so tiny that I can't even believe I can sit here without dragging her into my lap, plunging my fingers in her hair, and working my tongue across hers. But what this song is saying to me just gets my lion roaring and I'm starting to wonder if I can hold him back.

"Play me another one," I command.

She hesitates, her face flushed and her eyes liquid, and I have never been more aware of my hands, the palms of my hands, my fingers, and where I want them to be. She then plays me a song by a woman who's begging to be made love to.

As the song plays to me, I make love to Brooke in my head. I move over her, inside her, in my head. She grips me with her arms, and I grip her hips and sit her down on me, and she moves with me, opening her mouth when I lick her lips, her tongue.

Now, I lean closer and dip my head to her own, and she leans back on the seat as if alarmed, her pulse fluttering in her throat. *No, little firecracker, get back here with me. Don't fizzle out now.*

Sliding my hand around her small waist, I bring her closer, then I press my lips into her ear. My cock pulses in my jeans. My heart kicks into my rib cage and it is feeding my groin. I lean back and play "Iris" to her, then I pull off both our headphones and come closer to kiss her ear again.

"Do you want me?" I ask her, my voice guttural with need.

She nods against me, and my control snaps. I clench my hands on her hips and keep her against me. God, she wants me. I knew she did. I knew it. Something in my brain snaps, and I inhale the scent at her neck, where it's always so powerfully sweet. I'm going to make her mine tonight. Suddenly, there's nothing stopping me. Nothing.

Fuck me being black.

Fuck everything but Brooke.

My hunger is a raging monster as I tug her earlobe with my teeth and lick the shell of her ear, delighting in making love to that little ear with my tongue. The blood rushes through me, hot and heady. I can't stop tasting and nuzzling her. She's fallen still in the seat, against, and almost beneath, me, and I can feel her every shudder as I work my lips on her skin. All I can think of is the songs she played me . . . how they spoke to me . . . I can get anything I want, any way I want it, and she wants me to make love to her. She's mine. I am meant to provide and to take what she gives. I won't deny her any longer. I won't deny myself.

We arrive at the hotel and I book her into the two-bedroom Presidential Suite.

"You sure about this?" Pete asks.

I nod and glance at Brooke, her eyes slightly widening when I hand her a keycard from my set.

My thumb brushes her, and her eyes clasp mine, questioning. I look back and hope she reads me, willing her to know what I want tonight. If she's not ready, I hope to hell she'll say something now.

But she doesn't. She takes the keycard and smiles, her smile radiant and shy, and she brushes back my thumb with hers. That, right there, was no fucking accident. Not the way she smiles, or touches me, or looks at me with a kind of *bring it* look that sets me on *fire*.

My brain starts running a mile a minute as we go upstairs to wait for our suitcases.

"What a pretty view," she says when we enter the living room. The door shuts behind me. We're alone. I'm suddenly doing her on the couch. The dining table. The floor. I'm tearing off her clothes. I'm sinking my cock in her and my teeth in her skin . . . my lips are on her neck and all I smell is her.

But, no, there she stands, looking outside.

Brooke Dumas.

The only woman I want.

I'm bursting the zipper of my jeans. I've had groupies in my rooms, naked, sliding their hands up my abs and my chest. Nothing hits me like seeing Brooke in my room, in her bouncy ponytail, looking excited and . . . happy.

She's happy because she's with you.

My heart kicks. I curl my hands into my palms and watch her peer nervously out the window, her teeth digging into her lower lip.

I have a fight tonight.

I can't wait for her to watch me win.

Then . . . watch me make love to her.

Heart pounding hard inside me, I walk to her, tip her head and angle it, so her ear is tilted to my mouth. I lean and lick it, earlobe up to the shell, then I dip my tongue into the crevice and tell her, "I hope you're ready for me. I sure as hell am ready for you."

❤ ❤ ❤

"COME HERE, MR. *Fucking Miami!*" A few guys swing me up on their shoulders and carry me into the Presidential Suite after the fight, and my restless eyes scan the room for my dark-haired goddess.

"Remy! Remyyyy!" they yell as they launch and catch me.

Some days, my fists just have their own will.

Today is one of those days.

Miami fucking loves me for kicking the shit out of every poor motherfucker put in my way.

Lightning courses through my veins.

Hell, if I lifted my hands and pushed out the heel of my palms, I'm sure I'd be shooting our spiderwebs.

"That's right, who's the man?" I shout, slamming my fists to my chest. I got Brooke, I'm the fucking champion! People crowd the suite, and when I finally spot my woman, my eyes lock to her. She stands there watching me, her breasts rising and falling, making me drool. Her eyes shine and her smile lights up her entire face, and the hunger rips through me like talons. Holy god, I want her. "Brooke."

I hop down and call her over with the slow crook of one finger, and she starts over. My heart pounds with each of her steps and I swear she can't reach me soon enough, so I meet her halfway, and the moment she's close enough to touch, I lift her in my arms, spin her around, and crush her lips under mine.

My blood sizzles as her small body melts into my bigger one, her mouth soft and as hungry as mine.

"Go fuck that pussy!" I hear some dipshit yell. I pull free, immediately pissed off. I don't like anyone talking about her like that. I don't like anyone even near her. I pull her closer and into her ear whisper, "You're mine tonight."

Her moan makes me close my eyes, and I cup her face and take her mouth again. I can't resist her anymore, she's got my willpower in shreds. I take it slowly, knowing we're being watched, but telling her the same thing over and over: "Tonight you're mine."

I want her now. I want everyone to leave us.

"Remy, I want you, take *me*!" someone shouts.

Brooke's eyes widen, and I want to tell her the only woman I'm taking from now on is her. Instead I stroke her face with my thumbs and kiss her again. I can't stop. She gets me high and I've been buzzed all day since I signed her into the room with me. She's warm and presses into me, her mouth hungry, killing me.

"Take her to your room, Tate!"

I hold her closer and tuck a strand of loose hair behind her, then I kiss the bare curve between her neck and collarbone, nuzzling near her ear, hearing myself murmur, "Mine. Tonight."

"So are you." With a tenderness no one ever uses on me, Brooke cups my jaw and holds my gaze, and then I'm grabbed from behind and swung in the air.

"Remy, Remy . . ." the guys chant.

When they drop me, I head to the bar to pour some tequila shots, and a woman signals for me to come get a shot glass from between her tits. I go over, but instead of complying I grab the nearest man there and ram his face into her boobs. Then burst out laughing and return to my Brooke.

Our eyes lock. I'm going crazy and hard and I'm feeling a little "speedy"—hell, I tell myself it's the buzz. I've been waiting for this, wanting this, since I saw her at the first Seattle fight, looking at me like I was some sort of god and devil at the same time.

"Come here," I whisper, and set the glass and limes down. I suck one lime edge between my lips and bend my head to pass it to her. She opens her mouth and sucks, then I draw it away and stick out my tongue. I groan with her as we linger, but eventually hand her the forgotten shot glass.

She tosses back the liquid and I hand her the lime. When

she sticks it in her mouth, I duck my head to suck the juice. She moans when I tug the lime away and replace it between her lips with my tongue.

Desire roars through me.

The empty shot glasses crash to the ground as I grab her lovely ass, lift her up, sit her down on the console, wedge between her pretty thighs, and thrust my tongue into her mouth with vengeance.

She pulls me closer as I push closer, burning inside. "You smell so good. . . ." My erection aches so bad I grind it heatedly against her so she knows what she does to me, what I'm going to give her tonight. "I want you now. I can't wait to get rid of these people. How do you like it, Brooke? Hard? Fast?"

"Any way you want it." *Shit*—I remember the song she played me on the plane, teasing me, delighting and torturing me, and my underwear is near bursting.

"Wait here, little firecracker," I say, going for more shots.

We take more shots, and I can tell she likes it. She's smiling at me, looking at me, at my mouth, as we kiss each other between rounds. Once again they grab me and shoot me up, and I laugh as they shout, *"Who's the man? Who's the man?"*

"You bet your asses it's me, motherfuckers!"

Dropping me down by the bar, they push an enormous glass of beer toward me, then yell and thump their fists on the bar top as they chant, *"Rem-ing-ton! Rem-ing-ton! Rem-ing-ton!"*

"Cool down, guys," Pete says as he approaches us.

"Who the fuck is this nerd?" one dipshit says, but I grab the dude and slam him up against the wall, scowling.

"He's my bro, you toad. Show some fucking respect," I snarl.

"Calm down, dude, I was only asking!"

Forcing my fingers to let go, I drop him to the ground and go back to the tequila, starting to get annoyed. Brooke waits for me, and these fucking people keep stopping me. By the time I head back around to where I left her, she's gone.

My stomach sinks as I scan the crowd and no dark-haired goddess is waiting for me to devour her mouth again. Glowering, I stalk to where Pete stands. "Where the fuck is Brooke?"

Puzzlement crosses his face. "What do you mean? She was just here."

Shoving the shots into his hands, I stalk down the hall and start pushing doors open. A couple is fucking on the bed of the spare bedroom. The master bedroom is empty. She's not among the crowd. I check by the elevators and then angrily push back through the entire crowd, and Brooke. Is. Gone.

I see red. A mix of pure anger shoots through me and I grab a pillow from one of the couches and tear it open. Cotton balls explode from the tear, and I do the same with the next, and the next. Because of course she's fucking gone! Fucking gone fucking gone fucking gone gone gone GONE GONE GONE *GONE*!

Soon people are screaming in panic as I grab whatever object is near me and send it crashing to the ground. "Rem! Rem!" Pete's voice pleads through the screams, but I don't listen. I want to kill something. I want to break something. I want to break my own fucking head against the wall!

I grab Pete by the jacket and he wiggles out of his sleeves to escape me, then he pulls off his tie and tosses it aside as if he thinks I'll choke him next. He slowly reapproaches me, hunching like he's approaching a rabid animal, and I hear him speaking things, but I don't hear anything except the roaring in my ears and my own yells. "What the fuck did you tell her about me? *Where the shitfuck is she?*"

I grab the closest glass bottle I can find and send it crashing into the wall. More screams. Nervous laughter.

Riley is busy ushering people out of the open suite doors when a familiar voice joins from the direction of the hall.

"Out, out, *out*!"

I swing around. *Brooke.* There she is, cheeks flushed and looking concerned. Heat and relief flash through my body and I realize I have something in my hands. I toss it behind me and hear a shattering sound, then clench my fingers as I start for her. Holy god, my Brooke. I need my hands on her, I need my body in hers, my tongue on hers.

Pete grabs my arm and pulls me back with wild, pained eyes. "See, dude? She signed a *contract*, remember? You don't need to destroy the hotel, man."

My knees feel weak from the sheer insane relief I feel.

My Brooke my Brooke my Brooke is *here*.

As I charge for her, Pete sticks me in the neck and I feel a prick and a burn of liquid pushed into my skin. The roiling energy inside me halts and dies, my feet slow, and my vision fogs and tunnels on her. Fuck! Fuck no! No no NO!

My brain sputters one last stream of panic that she, Brooke Dumas, who looks at me like I'm a god, is watching this. My head hangs and it's all black. Black like me. And now she will know. She will know. And she. Will. *Leave.*

The despair hits me so hard, I want to die right here, right now. I try to lift myself but can't, and Pete, with his diminutive power, is struggling to prop me up against the nearest wall. The frustration I feel, and the pain that comes when all my hopes shatter over Brooke and me, is indescribable. If this whole building sat on top of me it wouldn't even compare.

Pete maneuvers one of my arms around him, and Riley comes to drape my other arm around the back of his neck. My feet drag, and I'm burning with the shame and humiliation of not being able to pull free and stand upright on my own. Me. I've fought like a madman to show her I'm strong and there could be no better protector for her than me. Now I'm a pitiful mass of muscles and bones, slumping into the guys, but the last of my adrenaline, coupled with all the panic in me, still forces me to speak.

"Don't let her see."

"We won't, Rem."

I want to lift my head to try to make sure that what she's seeing is hopefully not me, but I can't move. It takes the energy it would take me to move a mountain just to strain out the rest of what I need to. "Just don't let her see."

"Yeah, man, got it," Pete assures.

They drag me into the room and start mumbling about me maybe getting strangled in my clothes and they strip me and plop me on the bed. My mind is already tormenting me. If she saw, she's going to leave. She will fucking leave. She's mine, but I can't have her. She's fucking mine and I can't tell her that she is, I can't take what I want, I can't do anything but lie here and try to stay awake, so that if she leaves, I can stop her.

"There you go, big man."

"Don't let her see," I groan.

Pete grunts and so does Riley as they try centering me on the bed. "She's all right, she won't see anything, Rem. Hang tight, we'll get someone to come and make you feel good," Riley tells me.

I bury my face in my arm and know it's not possible. I'll never feel good.

Brooke saw me. I saw her face for a moment. I saw her wide, scared eyes, *fuck me.*

I hear the door close quietly after them as the blackness claims me. It's a familiar place I've been in a thousand times. Sometimes I sink to it willingly, but today I ache in all the places inside me that Brooke Dumas touches with her smiles, and all I can think of is clawing my way out of here to stop her from leaving me.

♥ ♥ ♥

THE SOUND OF clapping wakes me. The sheets rustle at my side, and this is something I don't understand because I sure as hell am not moving. "Get your lazy asses out of bed, guys, and let's try hitting the gym," Riley says from the threshold.

Gym, I tell myself, even when today is one of the days when I don't give a shit. My body feels about as flexible as a building, but I make the effort to push up on my arms—

And stop short, squinting when I spot Brooke lying next to me.

She jumps to a sit when she sees me, and all the cobwebs in my mind clear in a fucking second as I take her in.

She's sitting like a fantasy in my bed. No. More than a fantasy. She's fucking *unreal*. Gut-wrenching, ball-twisting, chest-punching beautiful. Her dark hair tumbling down her shoulders, her lips pink, her eyelids heavy and sleepy. She's breathing fast as if she's got on her fight-or-flight from the mere sight of me, and she wears a Disneyland T-shirt that looks so fucking old it's screaming at me to tear it off her. The sun touches her skin and reveals a trio of freckles on her temple that I'd never seen before, and if I weren't so sedated, I'd be tracing them with my fingers while I latched my fucking mouth onto hers.

Struggling within myself, I watch as she takes a deep breath and eases off the bed like she can't get out of here fast enough. My heart gives a wild, helpless kick as I watch her cross the room and close the door behind her. *Fuck.*

As I stand to go after her, a wave of dizziness hits me, and I plop back down on the bed with a groan. A wave of grief hits me and I roll flat to my stomach. I slide back into bed and curl my hands into fists like I always do when I can't assimilate what I'm feeling. My muscles feel leaden and I can barely move from where I dropped. That fucking sedative Pete gives me is meant for a damn rhino and I still can't unwind my hands. I want them in her hair, at her hips, splayed over her juicy, little bottom.

I groan again. I'm naked. Hard as marble. I don't even have the energy to jack off, and my balls are in fucking misery.

Sometime later Pete comes in. "How are you doing, Rem?"

"Why was Brooke in my fucking bed?" I demand into the crook of my arm.

"He talks," Pete croons laughingly at me. "Our boy is doing well then."

"Where is she now?" I growl, twisting my head with a glare.

"I let her take the day off and relax some."

"You let her see me like this, dipshit," I growl, smashing my palm as hard as I can manage into his shoulder, which still jerks him aside.

"Ouch! Watch that, you're still you, you know! And the entire fucking city saw you like this." He sighs as he paces to the window. "She signed a contract, dude. She's not leaving you if she sees you like this or not." He spins around and levels me a somber stare. "Look, I promise you I won't let her leave until her term is over and you guys have sorted whatever it is you want to sort out between you."

The thought of her leaving fills me with anxiety. "What did she see last night?" I push up on my arms.

"She saw you in your famous Destructor mode."

God, I hate myself. Groaning, I bury my face in the pillow.

"We hired some girls for you last night, Rem," Pete tells me, like I give a shit.

I roll over to my back with a grunt, cross my arm over my face, and fold it over my eyes. The sun bothers me. Pete bothers me. My fucking life bothers me.

"But Brooke wouldn't let those hookers in," Pete adds.

It takes my sedated brain like a whole fucking minute to process what he's telling me. Then it takes another minute for me to tame the urge to chase after her.

"Ex-plain," I enunciate.

"All right. She's *into* you, Tate. She was pissed last night because I sedated you and she got all protective."

The thought of Brooke getting protective over me makes me feel *doubly* as protective of her, and half-crazed with the urge to claim her. But it has to mean something. It has to mean enough to her so that when she finds out I'm not . . . *right* . . . she'll still be with me.

"All right, Rem, recover. Text me if you need me. I'll go ahead and hang the DO NOT DISTURB, ALREADY DISTURBED HUMAN BEING INSIDE sign out the door."

"Thanks," I mumble, and roll to my stomach.

Don't want to eat.

Don't want to move.

Don't want to fucking live.

Then I notice the pillow smells of her. I sniff all of Brooke Dumas on the fabric, and my dick jerks in excitement, so I exchange my pillow for hers and fall asleep.

HOURS LATER, I hear movements out the door. *Brooke!* my brain screams. My cock jumps to attention. I groan in misery once more.

I force myself to take a shower and come back to bed. The sun is setting in the horizon, but I can't sleep. Setting my headphones on my head, I click SHUFFLE on my iPod. Song after song plays in my ears, but I don't listen. I don't feel them for shit.

I spend exactly two hours lying in bed, replaying the image of her in that Disneyland T-shirt. She was in bed with me like she belonged here, like a part of her already belongs to me.

I spend another hour on Scorpion, and how I can't lie here like a loser for long. I'm not letting him take what I want from me again, am I? He provoked me and made sure I couldn't box again—but now he's got me in his territory, and I'm marking it as mine every single season. Points-wise, I'm on top, as usual, but I can't allow myself to miss more than a couple of fights, even when the last thing I want to do is fight right now.

I. Want. *Her.*

Pushing to my feet, I ram myself into a pair of pajama bottoms, then stalk across the suite and open the door to her room. My eyes almost bug out of my head as they run over her silhouette on the bed. With a rustle of bedsheets she sits up and her startled gaze finds me at the door, watching her.

"Are you all right?" Her voice is whisper soft, and for the first time in my life I realize a woman is worried about me. Something twists hard inside my chest.

My voice comes out rougher than I intend, gruff and slightly drugged. "I want to sleep with you. Just sleep."

For a moment, nothing happens. Brooke just sits there . . . as if waiting. My pupils are adjusted to the dark, and I see every inch of her on that bed. And I want everything I see. I want it so much my frame is tight with barely checked need. Inhaling slowly, I walk over, scoop her up in my arms, and carry her to the master bedroom and to my unmade bed.

She clings to me like I was made to carry her somewhere. She weighs next to nothing, her little muscles tight and tiny compared to mine. I set her down and join her under the covers, pressing her face to my chest and my nose against the top of her head.

We stay like this; she holds me and I hold her. The drug is still in me. If she runs, I couldn't catch her. My strength is there, but not my speed. But instead of leaving, she nestles closer to me, her body instinctively seeking my heat.

"Just sleep, okay?" she then whispers, her voice thick.

"Just sleep," I murmur. "And this."

Curling my hand around her jaw, I start kissing her. Nobody ever told me I needed more than food, air, and water to live. But I do. Holy god, I do. I need this sweet mouth now, just as much. A soft moan escapes her as she sifts her fingers through my hair and arches, and I feel the push of her firm, little tits against my chest. My testosterone shoots through the roof. I want to pull off her T-shirt and tear off whatever she wears underneath until all I can see are her gold eyes, her pink nipples, and her sweet pussy. I want to suck her clit into my mouth and slide my fingers into her sex, one, then two, then three, until she's soaked and stretched and my little firecracker is coming for me.

I'm swollen to the max and I'm so fucking ready to make her mine I can't breathe right, but I'm greedy when it comes to her, and making her come is not all I want. It's only a part of it.

So I brush my tongue to hers and feel her small body tremble. *When I take you, baby, I'm taking it all. I'm taking every fucking breath, every inch of your skin. Every. Beat. Of your heart.*

Her taste drugs me all over again—her wetness, her heat, the way our mouths move. It's not enough. Soon I'm fucking her mouth and sucking and tasting her harder. She's so hot and hungry. She runs her hands over me, like she wants all of me. Those sounds she makes deep in the back of her throat, the ones that almost sound as if I'm hurting her, send all my instincts into a frenzy, first the mating ones and then the protective ones. I want to fuck her and make her yell louder and I want to cradle her against me and protect her from everything—especially from me.

She eases back to look at me, and her lips are stained with my blood. Moaning softly when she realizes the cut of my lip opened, she comes and licks me, making me groan as I grab her closer. I want every bit of her skin on mine. She's burning and I know she's strong as fuck, but I've never wanted to hold something so gently. We kiss some more, deep and hungry, I push her face back to my neck and nestle her to me, my chest heaving as fast as hers. I think I fall asleep, but when she squirms against me in the middle of the night, I stir awake to the strange sensation of sleeping with something warm and soft against me.

She awakes too and peers up at me in the dark as if she's never awakened with someone in bed before either. I never sleep with the women I fuck. I like my space, but I like it when Brooke is in it. I know men laugh about this. About being pussy-whipped. About panting like a dog after a girl. About wanting a woman more than you want to want her. I don't fucking care. They can keep their sarcasm. I'll take the girl.

Holding her curious gaze in the dark, I duck my head and I lick her mouth so she knows I want her sleeping here, then I cuddle her close and lock my arms so she won't leave me.

DENVER

I'm not happy with the way the guys are looking at Brooke.

I'm not happy, period.

I've told them to back off helping her with her luggage, and she gave me this amused little smile. As if I'm some sort of jealous dickhead.

Maybe I am.

But I'm still not letting Riley carry her goddamned luggage.

Now she's in the front of the plane, talking to them on our flight to Denver, and I've got the perfect view of her ass.

The ass that has been sleeping with me. In my bed. I think of her mouth. I've kissed her for four days. I won't do anything else until she's ready for me to. God, sometimes I think she's already there. I think of how her little tongue comes to play with mine. It's wet and playful and also anxious. Her hands rub my shoulders as she rubs it to me. She undulates her body against mine. Her legs part beneath me. I try to ignore all the green lights, the delicious press of her tits against me, and instead I focus on her mouth. I slide my hand up her throat and stroke my thumb along her jaw. She breathes as fast as me. She moans. She responds to me so hard, I have to stop and take cold showers when I'm a second away from exploding on her.

She waits for me in bed, her eyes on the door.

The instant I'm back she's spreading out her arms and opening her mouth to me. The scent of her arousal hits me as I tell her she's so fucking pretty and smells so good. She moans softly and tells me my name, in both ways. *Remington . . . Remy . . .*

She jacks me up and I taste her throat, her collarbone, keeping my hands where my mouth is—if I touch her breasts, I'm going to lose it. Even the feel of her legs parted under me and the way she shifts to nestle my erection drives me crazy.

I taste her ear. I fuck it. I pretend every part of her body can feel my tongue. She shivers and the sounds drive me crazy as an animal. She lets me work her up so much her teeth chatter until I cover our bodies with the sheet and use my body heat to heat her up.

When her breaths are jerking out of her and she sounds too worked up, I ease back and play her some music. She likes it when I play her songs. And when I turn on the TV to help cool myself down, she leans her head against my shoulder and watches it, the gesture making me tip her head up to me and take her mouth once more until we can't stand it.

My cock is in constant strain. The instant she looks at me, I'm hard. She looks at my mouth, smiles at me . . . everything she does runs straight to my dick.

She turns to me now, and I smile at her as she comes straight back to sit at my side, her legs and ass in those tight, pink jeans that beg to be peeled off her. I pull off my headphones and lean over to place my ear in her mouth, so she tells me what all the fuss is about with the team.

"They're worried about you."

"Me or my money?" I quietly ask. Another day I might not ask this. But I know they're worried about my stupid bet. One black fucking night, I bet all my cash and savings on my win this year. Pete and Riley are worrying about it, especially Pete, who's in charge of the finances.

"You. And your money."

I smile at her. "I'm going to win. I always do."

Her lips form a small smile too, and my mouth is drawn to that mouth of hers that tastes like peaches dipped in sugar. My blood heats when I notice how swollen and red her lips are from all our kissing, and the need to take that mouth in mine runs through me when she shudders.

So, she knows what I'm thinking about?

I swear I don't even want to be here today. Only because of her did I manage to get out of my suite today and into this plane. But I don't feel like doing anything except *her*.

"Do you want to run today? To get ready for tomorrow?" she asks.

I shake my head no.

"You're tired?" she prods.

Nodding, I whisper, "So fucking tired I could barely pull myself out of bed."

When she nods that dark, little head of hers in understanding, all the heaviness in my chest lifts for a moment, and she's like a little sun in all my gray.

She leans back on the seat, her shoulder up against mine, and she looks so badly slept because of me, I slide myself lower on the seat so my shoulder is close to where her head is. And she can rest it on me.

She does.

Quietly, I pass her my iPod so she can hear Norah Jones's "Come Away with Me."

She listens while lazily leaning her head on me, and I duck my head to try to listen with her.

Jerking as if she's just thought of something, she grabs her iPod, finds a song, and passes it to me. Then the Gym Class Heroes' song "The Fighter" begins.

Her eyes are glued to my profile as I listen, and if I've kissed her for four fucking days straight and she's playing me a song about fighting, I'm fucking not doing something right. "You play me a song about a fighter?" I ask her in disbelief and annoyance at myself.

She nods.

I toss her iPod aside with a scowl and then grab her by the hips and lift her onto my lap, hearing her breath catch when my erection bites into her juicy, little bottom. Bending my head down, I place my lips close to her ear. "Give me another one," I demand.

She shudders, and suddenly she starts shaking her head. "We can't keep doing what we're doing, Remy. You need your sleep."

I whisper. "Give me another song, Brooke."

My heart kicks when she obeys me and reaches for her iPod, and I feel like I'm finally getting a bone today. Taking it from her, I click PLAY and listen intently when the familiar song of "Iris" begins.

God, this woman kills me.

I lift my head to meet her gaze while my heart beats fast and hard in my lap and in my chest. "Ditto," I say.

"To what?"

The team up in the seating area is quiet, but they're not looking at her and me. I slide my fingers in her hair and draw her head down so I can hungrily drag my lips along the seam of her lips. "To every lyric."

She pulls back from me with a shudder that clearly tells me she doesn't want to. "Remy . . . I've never had an affair before. I just won't share you. You can't be with anyone else while you're with me."

God, I'm so wild about her, I can't even think of anything else anymore. Dragging my thumb along the lower lip I just licked, I look into those golden eyes that seem both pleading and demanding of me and tell her, "We won't be having an affair."

She doesn't react for a moment.

I'm so hungry for more of our kissing sessions that I crush her against me and trace my nose with the shell of her ear.

"When I take you, you'll be mine," I promise her, trailing my thumb along her jaw as I gently kiss her earlobe. "You need to be certain." Her gaze latches onto mine as I warn her, "I want you to know me first, and then, I want you to let me know if you still want me to take you."

"But I already know I want you," she protests.

I watch her mouth as it moves, telling me she wants me, and the thought of her not knowing what she's talking about feels like a wrench in my chest. Slowly, I stroke my hand down her bare arm, my voice thick and tormented. "Brooke, I need you to know who I am. What I am."

"You've had tons of women without this requisite," she says pleadingly.

I engulf her ass in my hands and drag her deeper into my lap, memorizing the way she looks right now as I look into her eyes and will her to understand me.

"This is my requisite with *you*."

Her eyes darken with pain, and she leans close to me and whispers, "We still can't keep this up, Remy. Not when your championship is on the line. So you either come get me tonight to make love to me, or you leave me alone so we can both rest."

For a moment I'm not sure I heard right.

She's telling me I can't kiss my mouth . . . my woman . . .

She's telling me I either fuck her and take her all, or I take nothing.

If she were any other woman in the world, I'd have fucked her the night I met her. Maybe I'd have fucked her another time. Then I'd have forgotten her. But she is Brooke Dumas and I am not messing it up with her if it kills me.

"All right," I say, smiling like I don't feel as if I'd just swallowed down my own cock.

Suddenly, I can't have her on my lap. Her bottom lush and juicy and mine—but unavailable. Fuck me. Setting her aside, I reach for my iPod and look for something. Metallica. Marilyn Manson. Something crazy that will shut the fuck up all the protests sputtering in my head and the sensation in my chest of having lost some unknown battle before I even fought it.

LOS ANGELES

I booked a suite for Brooke and Diane, and one of the ladies doesn't like it.

My lady, to be exact.

I was caked with sweat and still panting from my workout when she massaged the back of my neck, leaning close enough to whisper in my ear, "Mind telling me why Diane and I are together in a suite, Remy?"

She turned my neck to one side, then the other, her fingers light on my jaw, but I still refused to answer.

"You can't do this, Remington."

Biting back a laugh, I turned and touched two fingers to her lips, holding her gaze for a long heartbeat. "Stop me. I dare you," I told her, then I grabbed my towel and walked away to my suite to drown all my frustrations in a cold shower.

Now I'm in the LA Underground locker rooms, sitting on a bench at the end while Coach wraps my hands, some song in my ears, when I see Pete in my peripherals wave someone over.

I see Brooke heading over to me, at Pete's insistence, and I immediately hook my finger on my headphone cord and pull them down.

Brooke holds my gaze as she quietly leans over and pauses my iPod, then she walks behind me to seize my shoulders and starts working on my knots.

The instant I feel her fingers on my bare flesh, I groan and feel my body both tense with arousal and relax from the knowledge she's with me.

I haven't kissed her in what feels like a year.

I miss her in my bed.

I miss the way she moans and the way her soft, silky mouth swells under mine.

I miss her touch; I want it badly.

"Deeper," I command her, and she goes in deeper with her fingers, using her thumb to roll over one of the larger knots. Relaxing my neck, I let my head hang and drag in a deep breath as she presses down until the knot disintegrates, and I groan from the pleasure of feeling the heat spread into my tissue.

"Good luck," she whispers into my ear before she draws back, and my skin feels taut as a drum cover.

I stand and look at her, and I don't know why she's so determined to make me fuck her that she keeps her kisses away from me until I do, but I'm going to make her cave in to me before I cave in to her.

I'm not fucking her yet, no matter how ready I am to kill for it.

I'm not touching that sweet pussy until it's ready to be taken home—permanently.

Behind me, Riley comes with my robe, and I spread out my arms and ram them into the sleeves while I keep my eyes on her.

"Riptide!" I hear the call, and I bounce in place for a second, then trot out into the arena.

I take my ring like I always do, but tonight's not a normal one. Tonight, I fight—

"Benny, the Black Scooooooorpion!"

I see him charge out of the walkway on the other side. That ugly black tat on his face, he storms out to the general booing of the crowd, but grins nevertheless.

Remembering the club incident, where he dared speak of my girl's pussy, I remind myself I owe him a beating. The moment he takes the ring, he comes up to center, and so do I, fixing my gaze on his yellow eyes.

His rage and my rage combine to create a powerful effect on the air.

"Fucking pussy needs a woman to defend him now?" he says, spitting on the mat.

I laugh softly. "The bad news is, not even a woman can defend *you* from *me* now."

We tap knuckles, and the fighting bell rings.

We wait it out, both of us inspecting the other, and I want my little firecracker to see this.

I want her to see me beat the living daylights out of this dipshit.

Flicking my eyes to the side, I notice Brooke's chair is empty.

Scowling, I scan the arena and duck when Scorpion swings, then I come back and punch him, fast and hard, on the jaw.

Then I see her.

She's calling out to a girl heading to the exit with one of Scorpion's minions, while another of those motherfuckers holds her—Brooke—by the arms.

My blood runs cold, then hot in fury. I slam my fist into Scorpion's jaw, shove him aside, grab the nearest rope and leap out of the ring onto the cement floor, leaving Scorpion spitting blood on the mat. The arena erupts with shouts and screams and the announcer yells through the speakers, "The victor, Scorpion! Scooooooorpiooooooon! Remington Tate has been disqualified from this round! *Dis-qualified!*"

I reach Brooke as she struggles to break free, and she looks tiny and feisty in that motherfucker's grip, making me livid. I grab the hands on her arms and thrust them back, delivering him a look that promises he will *die* because of me, then I yank her into my arms and forget about everything but that she's safely nestled against me.

Still, she fights me.

"No. No! Remy, let me go, I need to follow her." She twists in my grip and lightly hits my pecs, her expression twisting in pain. "Let go, Remy, let go, *please.*"

I clench her tighter against me and walk her to the exit, because I don't think she realizes what's going on. "Not now, Little Firecracker," I softly warn her. She stops squirming and peeks over my arm at the angry faces of some of Riptide's fans, and I use my shoulders to shove through the crowd as they start getting vicious.

"Bitch. It's your fault, you stupid bitch!"

Her eyes widen in horror as the crowd starts clawing angrily into the air, then she curls into me and lets me guide her out to the car.

"Fucking shit!" Coach thunders as the limo pulls into traffic.

"You're down to third. Third. Possibly fourth," Pete glumly tells me, handing me the T-shirt and sweatpants I wear after matches.

"You had this one down, Rem. You were training so fucking well you would have had his ass on a stick, man."

"I've got it, Coach, just relax." I shove into my casual clothes as quickly as I can, then I reach out and pin Brooke to my side, my blood still pumping hot as lava.

Rubbing my hand down her arm, I notice she won't take her eyes off the window as if searching for that woman.

"You're in the worst placement you've been in years, man, your concentration is shit!"

"Pete, I've fucking got it—I'm not screwing this up," I assure him, rubbing Brooke's arm faster so she knows it will be all right.

"I think Brooke should stay in the hotel next fight," Riley mutters.

I burst out laughing. "Brooke comes with *me*," I snap, shaking my head in disbelief at them.

"Rem . . ." Pete tries to reason.

I clench my jaw and shoot him a warning glare, not in the mood for this bullshit. We ride the elevator in tense silence, and I'm getting worked up by Brooke's unease. The need to protect her from whatever it is that's made her this uneasy is eating at my gut.

The doors roll open on her floor, and she gets out like a whirlwind I'm determined to calm the fuck down. The guys yell back at me and demand we have some words, making me snap, "Pete, we're talking about this later, just cool your nuts, all three of you."

"Get back here, Rem, we need to talk to you!"

"Talk to the wall!"

The door to her room is about to slam shut when I reach it and push it open to follow her inside. "You all right?" I demand.

The door shuts behind me, and she faces me with bewildered gold eyes and the face of my fucking dreams, and suddenly I feel as impotent and useful as a damn table, standing here while whatever it is tears my woman apart.

I'm not going to fucking let it.

Life can throw the curveballs at me, but not at her. I'll catch them for her and I'll throw them back. She'll be untouchable if

I can help it. She'll be untouchable to everything and everyone but *me*.

She has to stop fucking risking herself!

As she eyes me, I hear her sharp inhale as she signals at the door behind me. "Go talk to them, Remy."

My voice is rougher than usual, even to me. "I want to talk to you first."

I start pacing for a moment, dragging my hand through my hair all the way down to the back of my neck. Then I drop my arm with a sigh because I'm at a loss for words here. "Brooke, I can't fight and keep an eye out for you."

"Remy, I had it *covered*," she cries.

"My fucking ass, you had it covered!"

She jerks in surprise, and my fingers curl into fists as the need to drive my hands into that dark hair and crush her against me starts to slowly and painfully consume me. Suddenly, her eyes flash in fury. "Why is everyone looking at me like it's my fault? You're supposed to be fighting *Scorpion*!"

A dark scowl settles on my face. "And you're supposed to be in your goddamned seat on the front fucking row to my left!"

"What difference does it make? You've been fighting for years without having me in the audience! What does it even matter where I'm at?" She glares at me and dares me to tell her all the shit I feel for her, and the lack of words in me only frustrates the hell out of me. "I'm not even a fling, Remington! I'm your *employee*. And in less than two months, I won't even be that, I'll be *nothing* to you. Nothing."

God, is that what she thinks?

Does she think I haven't taken her because . . . what? She's a toy to me? I'm fucked-up and imperfect, but I'm human and I want things. And what I. Want. Is. *Her*.

I want her too much to fuck it up.

I exhale through my nose and ask, "Who was that girl you were chasing?"

She drops her voice to a whisper. "My sister."

A silence stretches between us as I register that her sister apparently is *friends with* Scorpion's crew. "What's your sister doing with Scorpion's goonie?"

"Maybe she's wondering the same about me," she says with a bitter laugh.

I laugh right along with her, my laugh a thousand times more bitter than hers. "Don't mistake me for a fuckup like him. I may be fucked-up but that guy eats virgins and spits them out like vomit."

Brooke starts pacing, her face scrunched up in worry for a moment, then she closes her eyes sadly. "Oh, god. She looked awful. *Awful*," she whispers.

That's it.

That's fucking it.

Brooke won't be suffering like this over anyone.

Not in front of me.

I'm not a person who can stand and talk about stuff when there's something to be done.

Quietly, I open the door, but before I leave, I look at her pretty face, all its color lost, and I have to say something. I'm no good at this, but I make an effort and gruffly tell her, "You're not nothing. To me."

Shutting the door behind me, I head straight for the elevator.

It's not difficult to find a man who tattoos a fucking insect on his face.

Plus the fighters always stay in one of the hotels close to the Underground location.

Feeling bloodthirsty, I curl my hands into fists as I cross the lobby and head out into the night. A huge crowd litters the hotel driveway.

"Riptide!" they scream.

Camera flashes explode all over the place.

"Ohmigod!" A woman starts crying while members of the hotel staff struggle to keep the crowd at bay.

I've successfully shoved through one side of the crowd while a good dozen hands rub my ass and my chest muscles when I hear, "That's her. Her fault he was disqualified tonight!"

Turning in confusion, I see something white flying in the air and smashing straight on Brooke.

Another white ball follows the first.

Simmering with rage, I clamp my jaw and stomp my way back to her as the fucking crazy people keep throwing shit at her.

Brooke has ducked and run to one of the parking valets, who sees me come up and says something to her.

Another egg crashes into her shoulder as I reach her, and I swear I feel like the fucking Hulk. I'm so damn mad, I feel fucking green!

"Whore!" they shout. *"Bitch!"*

Using my back as a shield, I catch an egg on my trapezius as I lift her up in my arms and swing around to face these fucking lunatics.

"It's because of this woman I'm still fighting!" I shout at them, feeling angry, feeling betrayed by them.

A sudden silence falls across the crowd, and I'm not done yet—motherfuckers!

"Next time I'm in the ring, I'm going to fucking *win* for her, and I want all of you who hurt her tonight to bring her a red rose as an apology and tell her it's from me!" I demand.

After a second, they get it.

They fucking get it. . . .

And they start screaming and clapping as I take her back inside.

Breathing through my nose, I'm trying to calm down when Brooke starts laughing in my arms, her eyes shining in disbelief as she looks up at me.

I frown in confusion and press the elevator button a dozen consecutive times.

"And they say Justin Bieber's fans are crazy," she gasps.

My voice is raspy and rough as I brush off some eggshells from her shoulder. "I apologize on their behalf. I disappointed them today."

Her laughter fades, and she links her fingers at the back of my neck and stares up at me as I carry her into the elevator. A couple decided not to join us and remained outside the doors.

"You coming?" I snap as I cradle her against me.

They both step back and say, "No."

So we ride upstairs alone, and Brooke presses the tip of her pretty little nose into my neck. "Thank you," she breathes.

I tighten my hold. She feels so right and perfect in my arms, I never want to let her go. I don't care if we smell like sulfur; I've been hungry to have my arms around her and her arms around me, and right now I can't think of anything else that I'd rather be doing or anywhere else I'd rather be than here.

After sliding the key into the slot of my suite, I carry Brooke inside. "What the fuck is going on, Rem?" Pete demands as he and Riley charge over.

"Just get the hell out, guys." I hold the door open for them with one arm and cradle Brooke to my chest with the other. They stare at Brooke as if she can solve some unnamed mystery for them, so I snap at them, "I do what I want, you hear me?"

That reminds them I'm here—glaring—and they turn their

attention to me. "We hear you, Rem," Riley answers as he follows Pete out to the hall.

"Then don't fucking forget it." I slam the door shut and bolt it so no dipshit can come here to interrupt my time with her, then I take us into the bath of the master bedroom. She tightens her hold when I pull open the shower door, and I'm so fucking happy that she wants to stay with me, I keep her in my arm as I turn on the shower.

The water falls, and I quickly kick off my shoes, take off hers, and then step into the shower stall with her in my arms.

"Let's get this shit off you." She slides down to her feet as I run my hands over her wet hair, the water falling on her face as I pull her dress over her head. I toss it aside and soap up my hands, then watch her face as I run them up her body.

She bites her lower lip as I touch her, spreading her arms up and sliding soap into her armpits, down her abdomen, between her legs, up her neck. My T-shirt is plastered wet to my chest, and I grab it in one hand and jerk it off me, quickly running the soap over me.

"I can't believe your groupies called me a whore," she says as she watches me.

Quickly, I lather my hair. "You're going to survive."

"Do I have to?"

"Yeah, you do."

Then I lather Brooke's hair, my fingers digging down to her scalp. "They hate me," she tells me miserably. "I won't be able to go to your fights now without fear of getting lynched."

Taking the showerhead, I turn it so the water slides over Brooke's head, and her eyes drift shut as the soap slides down her body.

Holy god. Holy god.

Her nipples poke into her bra, soft peach and puckered. And

the cotton of her white panties clings to her pussy lips. Fucking bare as the rest of her. My eyes jerk up to hers before her eyelashes flutter open, and she looks at me. Her oval face, pink lips, dark, wet hair, those eyelashes glistening wet, and those gold eyes, looking at me like they do. Like there is nothing on this earth she would rather see but me. My throat feels thick as I brush a strand of damp hair behind her forehead, my heart beating as fast as it has ever beaten for anything in my life.

She's so beautiful and so perfect, my lungs hurt. Lifting my arms, I frame her face as gently as I can in my palms and stare at her, then I use one finger to touch her mouth. She's kept this mouth from me, and I want it back. I want it back because it's mine. It's fucking mine and she's killing me right now, looking at me with those eyes, her body wet and shivering against me.

"That's never going to happen," I tell her gruffly, because I'd have to be dead first before anyone harmed her, fans or otherwise.

The sleek tendons of her throat work as she swallows. "You shouldn't have . . . said that about me, Remy. They're going to think you and I . . . that you and I . . ." She shakes her head, and looks at me, out of breath.

"That you're mine?" I prod softly.

She blinks for a moment, then laughs.

"What's so funny?" I ask her.

I shove open the glass shower door, then I wrap a towel around my hips and get rid of my sweatpants. She's still laughing as I come back to get her, engulfing her with a towel as I scoop her up and carry her to the bed.

I set her down on the center, and I'm not sure if her laughter amuses me or not. "Is the thought of being mine funny?" I tease her.

Reaching under the towel, I tug off her panties and pry off

her bra, then I rub the towel over her body and hair with brisk, sure moves.

"Is the idea of being mine funny?" I insist, running the towel over her bare little tits as I watch her. "Is it funny, Brooke?" I repeat, looking deep into her eyes.

"No!" she gasps, her laughter completely gone as she tilts her hips to help me dry her. I dry her legs, and when I reach her knee with the small scar, my movements slow down as I survey it. I've never wanted to kiss anything other than lips and pussy, but I'm fighting the urge to kiss her bad knee.

A small hand trembles against my hair, and I hear her whisper, "Have you ever been anyone's?"

My eyes flick up to hers, her pupils dark as night as she watches me. A consuming jealousy rips through me as I think of someone else having her before me. Feeling a roiling in my chest, I cup her cheek in my palm and look at her. "No. And you?"

She tucks her cheek into my hand and whispers, "I've never wanted to be."

"Neither have I."

We stare, and the air crackles between us. She needs me. And I fucking need *her*.

I trace her jaw with my thumb, searching for words to tell her. "Until I saw this lovely girl in Seattle, with big gold eyes, and pink, full lips . . . and I wondered if she could understand me . . ."

Her chest heaves, and I bend closer and scent her, pulling the towel up to cover her body before I break down and take this little body of my dreams, and fuck this woman of my life, and let her shatter me when she realizes who I am, what I am, and what is completely fucked-up about me.

My voice roughens at the thought. "I want to say so many things, Brooke, and I just can't find the words to tell them to you."

Resting my forehead on hers, I inhale deeply as I run my nose along the length of hers.

"You tie me up in knots." My lips find hers for a moment, briefly kissing before I withdraw and look into her eyes. "I want to play you a thousand different songs so you get a clue of what . . . I feel inside me. . . ."

A shiver runs through her as I caress my index finger along the bow of her top lip, then her bottom one. She whimpers softly, and I hold her face between my hands and set my mouth on hers, pulling her tongue into my mouth so I can suck her.

She moans and sinks her nails into my shoulders, gasping, "Why won't you take me, Remington?"

Groaning at that, I pull her closer to me. "Because I want you too much."

Pushing my tongue harder against hers, I lean over her and feel her body pressing into mine, her tits, her abs, her legs tangling between my thighs.

She gasps when I pull her closer and keep devouring her mouth.

"But I want you *so* much, and I'm protected," she pleads to me. "I know you're clean. You get tested all the time and I . . ."

The tips of her nipples brush against my ribs, and she shudders and tilts her hips upward, silently begging me to slide in there and take what I want. What I fucking crave. Fuck me.

"I want you in my bed again. I want to kiss you, hold you," I tell her roughly.

She grips my shoulders harder and whispers against my lips, "I can't do this anymore, please just make love with me. . . ."

I silence her with my mouth and fuck my tongue into her as I shift my frame, which makes my cock hit her hip bone . . . and my thigh feels her pussy.

She's wet.

Wet as fuck.

I'm so hot for her, I can't stop nibbling her lips, biting softly, fisting my hands in her wet hair as she rakes her hands down my arms and rubs herself against my thigh. She whimpers softly, and my gut coils with need as she rocks her hips against me and kisses me back.

Two . . . three rocks . . . and she starts shuddering uncontrollably against me.

I stop kissing her for a moment—then I realize what's happening. My cock starts dripping semen as I feel her come, and I spread my hand on her back and push up my leg, forcing her to ride me harder, making sure her clit gets a nice little rub as I take her mouth with mine and force her to take my tongue as she comes for me.

The noises she makes . . . the way her body goes slack against mine . . .

My chest feels heavy with tenderness as I brush her hair back and look down at her flushed face and glazed eyes. "Did that feel even half as good as it looked?" I ask, trailing my finger along her cheek.

She pulls the towel around her and angrily avoids looking at me. "I assure you that's not happening again," she whispers.

God, I love her. I love her sass and her spunk, and I love how she gets shy with me. Amused by her shyness when she just came for me in a way no other woman has ever come before, I bend closer to kiss her ear, my voice husky. "I'm going to make sure that it *does*."

"Don't count on it. If I wanted to have an orgasm all alone, I could have taken care of myself without giving *anyone* a show." She keeps the towel to her chest as she sits up and asks, "Can I borrow a damn shirt?"

She's so cute angry, I smile as I head over to the closet and grab one of my usual black T's.

Her dark scowl is still in place when I come back. "This okay?" I ask, feeling possessive as fuck when she takes it and slips it on.

She still looks shy and embarrassed about it all, which I don't want her to be.

"Come eat something with me," I say, and I'm happy when she slides off the bed and follows me to the kitchen.

"Let's see what Diane left you," she mumbles as she pulls out the contents from a hot drawer and uncovers a plate, her smile mischievous. "Eggs. They must've been on sale tonight."

My smile flashes, and I look at her lips, and I want them more than the eggs and more than anything in this kitchen. Watching her so she doesn't leave, I pull out two forks from a drawer and approach her. "Come share." Because I want to fucking *feed* her.

"Oh, no," she quickly says, palms up in the air. "No more eggs for me tonight. You enjoy."

I set the fork down and follow her to the door, catching her wrist before she leaves and telling her, "Stay."

She holds her breath and her eyes fly up to mine.

"I'll stay," she firmly whispers, "when you make love to me."

She stares at me and I stare back, battling within myself. I want her. Fuck, I want her more than anything. She has to know that. I can't fuck it up because I'm hornier than a goddamned devil.

I won't fuck it up because of my cock.

Sighing drearily, I hold the door open for her and place myself so that she has to brush past me to leave. Every muscle in my body contracts as she brushes past . . . and I watch her as she heads down the hall, a vision in my fucking T-shirt, giving me the bluest balls of my life.

After dinner I have to take another shower, this one cold, and when I set up our clothes to dry, I find myself sniffing her wet dress, her wet bra, and her wet, fucking, cute white panties.

For hours, I imagine charging into her room and forcing her back here with me.

I imagine stripping her, fucking her, then kissing and petting her all night until the sun appears.

And then I imagine the look on her face when I tell her I'm bipolar.

AUSTIN

I feel like murdering something today.

Something curly haired and brown eyed. In a black fucking suit I paid for. In a tie I paid for. Wearing a fucking smile *he* is going to pay for.

Pete and Riley are my brothers.

I'd kill for them.

But Brooke is holding back from me, and I can't stand watching her smile at them the way I want her to smile at *me*.

I hear them joke around. Laugh during breakfast, lunch. Dinner.

Now I slam the speedball, straight in the belly, while my gut hardens with anger as Pete walks with Brooke out of the house—out of my house—and they come toward me. Austin is a test to my stability. I can feel every moment of my life here choking around me, setting the wheels in my head spinning with memories that are too vague to recall clearly, but too painful to forget. This house I bought to get close to the same parents who abandoned me as a youngster. They wanted nothing of me, but like some hungry dog, it took me a while to get it in my head that they weren't going to throw me a bone. And I kept coming and coming, somehow expecting I was going to get it.

I feel just as starved for a bone as I see Brooke coming my way with Pete.

No. I feel *more* starved. I feel rabid with pent-up longing for her, and my temper is in shreds. So when Pete grabs her elbows and whispers something to her, and she whispers something back, my gut roils as my jealousy corrodes me.

Oh, yeah, I feel like murdering something.

"Hey, B, you might try stretching him, his form's not ideal. Coach thinks it's a lower-back knot," Riley calls out from the door of the barn.

She starts heading over, and I scowl and pound the speed bag as fast as I can. *Whackwhackwhack* . . .

"Coach isn't happy with your form and Riley thinks I can help," she tells me, watching me hit.

And I keep hitting because I'm fucking mad at her.

She belongs with *me*.

I want to make out with her and make her as addicted to me as anyone can be addicted to anything, and maybe when she knows the truth about me, she won't leave.

"Remy?" she prods.

I shift my body so she doesn't keep distracting me and keep my eyes on the ball, making it fly as I hit it madly.

"Will you let me stretch you?"

Shifting even more, I keep slamming both my fists into the belly of the bag and notice she drops an elastic band to the ground before she reaches out to me.

"Are you going to answer me, Remy?"

Her hand makes contact with my back, and a jolt runs through me. Stiffening, I drop my head and angrily wonder if

Pete feels a jolt when she touches him too, then I whip around and toss my boxing gloves to the ground.

"Do you like him?" I demand.

She just looks at me blankly, so I reach out and put my taped hand on the exact spot Pete touched on her arm. "Do you like it when he touches you?"

Please say no to me.

Please say no.

There's no word for the way she's tormenting me. I'm trying to protect her from me. I'm trying to protect myself . . . from what could be the biggest disaster of my life.

"You have no right to me," she says in breathless anger.

My hold tightens on her, and I growl under my breath, "You gave me rights when you came on my thigh."

"I'm still not yours," she shoots back at me, her cheeks red. "Maybe you're afraid I'm too much of a woman for you?"

"I asked you a question, and I want an answer. Do you fucking like it when other men touch you?" I demand, my temper rising.

"*No*, you jerkwad, I like it when *you* touch me!" she cries.

This appeases me.

It appeases me so much, the ice in my gut immediately morphs into lava. Dipping my thumb into the crease of her elbow, I gruffly ask, "How much do you like my touch?"

"More than I want to."

She's furious, but I know why she is.

Because we're fucking killing each other being apart, and I want to end it. "Do you like it enough to let me feel you in bed tonight?" I prod.

"I like it enough to let you make love to me."

"No. Not make love." Fuck, she not only makes my cock hard, she makes life hard, period. "Just touching. In bed. Tonight. You and me. I want to make you come again."

She surveys me in silence, and for a moment I feel her consider my proposal.

I have never before in my life seen a woman come like she comes for me.

Because she's mine—and she's as stubborn as they come. *Fuck!*

"Look, I don't know what you're waiting for, but I won't be your plaything," she says as she starts to pull herself free of me.

Grabbing her close, my voice is thick with frustration. "You're not a game. But I need to do this my way. *My* way." Before I can help myself, I bury my nose in her neck and scent her, my tongue sliding out to lick a wet path to her ear. A low groan rumbles up my chest before I seize her chin and force her to meet my gaze, silently willing her to understand. "I'm taking it slow for you. Not me."

She shakes her head as if she doesn't believe me. "This is growing old. Let's just stretch you." She walks to my back, and right now all her touch does is remind me what I want and she won't fucking give me.

I jerk free and glower. "Don't fucking bother. Go stretch Pete." I wipe the sweat off my chest with a nearby towel, then ignore my boxing gloves and take up hitting the speed bag with my knuckles.

Whack, whack, whack.

"He doesn't want me," I hear her tell Riley as she stomps away.

I clamp my jaw and hit the bag harder.

❤ ❤ ❤

THE AUSTIN CROWD loves me a thousand times more than my parents ever did. It's my city. Where I should've been raised. Where I hear people yelling my name, telling me they love me.

But it doesn't feel real. It doesn't feel like home. Not even the ring feels like home anymore. I feel fucking homeless lately. I walk around with a hole in my chest, and no matter how hard I punch, how much I train, it won't go away.

Banners wave all over the arena. Women scream my name. Yet all I want is for Brooke Dumas to scream it. But she never does.

I take down my last opponent with a solid KO, and the screaming that follows is deafening.

"Our victor of the night, Remingtooooooooon Tate, your RIP-TIDE!" the announcer yells.

Sweat drips down my chest, my body hot with exertion. My arm raised in victory, I glance at her to see if she's watching. She is.

My lips curl into a smile as I point a finger at her, and I watch as a line of people start heading in her direction. Holding her gaze with an even wider smile, I point at a girl coming toward her with my red rose. Brooke's gold eyes widen in disbelief, and my chest swells with happiness as she's soon crowded by my fans, handing her roses.

She looks stunned, grasping each rose with an expression of consternation.

On our way back to the house, she's trembling in her seat. I'm wound up too. There's no way in hell she'll be able to deny my kisses tonight.

"You were awesome, Rem!" Pete bursts out inside the car. "Man, what a great night."

"Great fight, son," Coach adds, his voice deep with pride. "Never broke form. Never dropped guard. Even Brooke felt the love tonight, huh, Brooke?"

Silence.

Brooke is completely silent, not looking at me, her lap filled with roses. My roses. And yet she won't look at me.

"You totally killed it," Riley continues.

I've stopped listening to the guys. The only thing I hear now is the silence coming from where Brooke sits, tense across the seat from me, with an armful of roses and completely fucking *ignoring* me. Frustration eats at me. Don't all women like roses? She's clenching her jaw and won't even look at me, and I'm so fucking confused I want to pull my hair out.

My blood boils in my veins as I stalk into my room and step into the shower, open the cold water, and stand there, closing my eyes and reliving the way she stood there, watching the roses come at her. She'd looked surprised. But had she looked excited? Had she looked happy? This just isn't playing out the way I'd planned. I'd planned to have her in my fucking bed tonight. Where I wanted to watch her look at me the way she does while I rammed into her panties and made her come a couple of times and gasp, *Remington* . . .

I'm still simmering in frustration and have just stepped out of the shower and grabbed a towel when I hear the door of my bedroom slam shut.

Suddenly my senses heighten. Every pore in my body buzzes with the knowledge she's near.

And there she is. *Brooke fucking Dumas.*

I drop the towel.

She's standing inside my bedroom and looking straight at me—even after the cold shower, my cock jumps to attention.

Her gaze drops, and her face flushes red as she stomps forward with gold eyes that flash with anger and hurt. She strikes my chest repeatedly, and the pain in her voice reaches into even deeper, more vulnerable places inside me.

"Why haven't you touched me? Why don't you fucking take me? Am I too fat? Too plain? Do you just delight in fucking torturing me senseless or are you just plain damn *mean*? For your information, I've wanted to have *sex* with you since the day I went into your stupid hotel room and got hired instead!"

I react instinctively and yank her up against me while pinning her arms down. "Why'd you want to have sex with me?" I angrily demand. "To have a fucking adventure? What was I supposed to be? Your one-night fucking stand? I'm every woman's adventure, damn you, and I don't want to be *yours*. I want to be your fucking *real*. You get that? If I fuck you, I want you to belong to me. To be mine. I want you to give yourself to *me*—not fucking Riptide!"

"I won't ever be yours if you don't take me," she shoots back at me. "*Take me!* You son of a bitch, can't you see how much I want you?"

"You don't know me. You don't know the first thing about me."

"Then tell me! You think I'll leave if you tell me whatever it is you don't want me to know?"

"I don't think it, I know it." I grab her face, my insides roiling painfully as I look into her hungry, frustrated gold eyes. "You'll leave me the second it gets too steep, and you'll leave me with nothing—when I want you like I've never wanted anything in my life. You're all I think about, dream about. I get high and low and it's all about you now, it's not even about me anymore. I can't sleep, can't think, can't concentrate worth shit anymore, and it's all because I want to be the fucking 'one' for you, and as soon as you realize what I am, all I'll be is a fucking mistake!"

"How can you be a mistake? Have you seen you? Have you seen what you do to me? You had me at hello, you fucking asshole! You make me want you until it hurts and then you won't do shit!"

"Because I'm fucking *bipolar*! Manic. Violent. Depressive. I'm a fucking, ticking time bomb, and if one of my staff messes up when I get another episode, the next person I hurt can be *you*. I was trying to break this to you as slowly as possible so I could at least stand a chance with you. This shit has taken everything from me. Everything. My career. My family. My fucking friends. If it takes this chance with you, I don't fucking even know what I'm going to do, but the depression will hit me so deep, I'll probably end up killing myself!"

When I notice the shock on her face, I force myself to release her.

Holy god, why'd I just do that? Why'd I say it like that? I sound like a fuckup. I thought she would one day stomp away and slam the door? Hell, all I have to do now is count the seconds. My nerves are run ragged like wires. I haven't slept, and everything I've told her is not even half of the truth. My chest is a mass of tangles as I go grab a pair of pajama bottoms, then I grab a T-shirt from the closet.

I can see her struggling with the word. *Bipolar.*

Manic-depressive.

Crazy fucking loon.

I give her time to process and clench my hands, the T-shirt still at my side, and I feel like a grenade is about to explode inside my chest as I watch her struggle. I've just shot my plan of taking it slow and proving myself to her all to fucking hell. I'd been postponing. Biding my time. Maybe I didn't want her to know. I wanted to pretend she'd never have to know. And I could be just this normal guy with her. I've tried all my life not to let it define me, even when for years that was the only thing I was.

Nobody told me I was a fighter, or that I could be a friend, a son, or a companion. All the medics told me was I was bipolar.

And now she knows. She knows this is me—and I've lost her. Before I had her.

I'm still adjusting to the fact that she will want nothing to do with me when, one by one, she slowly flicks open the top buttons of her top. At first I'm sure my brain is fucking with me. One button pops open, then the next, revealing sweet, tanned skin, more and more skin. My pulse jumps and my throat starts closing from the force of my need. Somewhere in the room, someone speaks, and it's probably me. I'm in denial. I can't believe it. I won't believe it and she better get out of here before I do. "I'm take as-is," I warn her. "I'm not medicating. It makes me feel dead and I intend to live my life alive."

She nods.

I clench inside, right there, where my fucking heart is, as her fingers keep moving over her buttons.

"Take your clothes off, Remy."

She flicks open her last button and parts her shirt through the middle, and my fingers spasm so hard at my side that the T-shirt I hold falls to the floor.

She's so beautiful my eyes devour the parting of her shirt and the smooth skin she just revealed, and I still can't believe something so beautiful and perfect would want to be with me. "You have no idea what you're asking for," I rasp, and I don't know who I'm angry with. I'm just angry that I'm bipolar, and right now nothing can convince me that I'll ever be good enough for her.

"I'm asking for you," she counters.

"I won't let you fucking leave me."

She holds my gaze steadily, and my heart pounds so fast in my temples, I can barely hear her. "Maybe I won't want to."

My heart whams hard in hope, and I feel like it's about to break all the ribs around it. "Give me a goddamned guarantee. I won't let you fucking leave me, and you're going to want to try. I'm going to be difficult and I'm going to be an ass, and sooner or later, you're going to have fucking *enough* of me."

She tosses her shirt to the floor and then pushes her skirt down her hips. She stands in a cotton bra and panties, her chest heaving, her eyes so deep and endless I feel sucked down to the pit of me. "I'll never have enough of you, never," she breathes.

I swear, in my life, nothing can come close to this. To the way I need her. Want her. Fucking love her. I'm being devoured on the inside with my feelings, tons of stuff I've never felt in my life, and a low, hungry sound rips unbidden up my throat.

She stops breathing, while I'm breathing so hard I can hear myself in the room, and I need to grab her to me so bad, I curl my fingers into fists at my sides as I speak roughly to her. "Come here then."

She looks at me helplessly, and I wait, my heart crashing into my rib cage as I take her in, in that underwear. She's the sexiest, hottest thing I've ever seen, every little muscle in her body sleek and compact, while her hips are curved like a soda bottle, her little nipples poking into her bra. When she takes the first step forward, my entire body tightens. Her pulse flutters, and my mouth waters with the need to taste her, suck her.

She stops a foot away, and I reach out and instantly tangle my hands in her hair and yank her head back, burying my nose into her neck. Her feminine scent makes me growl, and as she shudders and scents me back, I lick a wet path up her neck and engulf her in my arms. *"Mine."*

"Yes, yes, yes, Remington, *yes*." She fists her hands in my hair and I inhale her like a madman, then I grab her face and drag my tongue up her neck, her jaw, and lick the entry of her lips.

Hungrily, I part her open and nibble the soft flesh, making her whimper as I thrust inside. Our tongues tangle, and holy god, I swear I can feel her melt for me while I burn for her. I burn so fiercely my nerves crackle like fireworks inside me as I strip off my bottoms and her bra. I fill my hand with the flesh of one full breast and lift a puckered nipple to my mouth. I wet it with my tongue while I sift my fingers under her panties . . . and then she's in my hand. Hot and slick. *Mine.*

"Tell me this is for me," I gutturally command, teasing the tip of a finger inside her.

"It's for you," she gasps, then she kisses my temple and jaw as I tear off her panties with one quick yank.

Her eyes widen in pure female excitement as I lift her and swing around, slamming her back against the wall, her legs coming around me. I settle the length of my cock at her entrance and yank her arms up above her head.

"Are you mine?" I demand, sliding a hand between us and easing my middle finger inside.

"I'm yours."

The words ripple through me as I scrape my middle finger deep inside her channel. "Do you want me inside you?" I huskily demand.

Her eyes are glazed with desire, her lips reddened and wet by me. "I want you everywhere. All over me. Inside me."

I struggle to stay in control when I start penetrating her, slow and easy. Slow enough not to hurt her. Only to pleasure her. She whimpers as I stretch her, and as I start to pull out, she holds on to me and drops herself lower—taking all of me inside. Pleasure rips through me as her heat envelops me.

Crazed with desire, I grab her breasts and push my tongue inside her mouth, and she sucks me, drinks me. I feast on her jaw, her chin, her tasty little neck, then I duck my head and suckle one of her pretty nipples into my mouth.

"Remy," she moans, and tightens her arms around my neck. Her strong, lithe, little thighs clench around my hips, and a bolt of pleasure shoots through my body, making me tremble as I hold still.

"Remy . . ." she pleads, rocking her hips. "Please, please . . . *move*."

I groan and try not to think about how good she feels so that I can make it last, but she wants it . . . fuck, I want it more than I want to live. Slowly, I withdraw from all that wet, delicious heat, then thrust back in. A sound of pleasure tears from both of us. Her pussy ripples around me, and my cock is so ready to jet off, it takes everything in me to pull out of her snug warmth and thrust back in, and when I do, I growl and drop my forehead to hers, kissing her without control. I rasp her own name into her mouth and clench her hips as I pull out and ram back in, deep enough that every part of my cock is embedded inside her. I'm so worked up with this new rhythm, I go off violently inside her. She comes with me, and we shake and clutch each other. She twirls her little tongue up my throat as our bodies contract and unwind as we press together, and when I finally relax, I growl softly.

I'm still hard as rock and she's still wet as fuck, so I grab her ass and keep her legs around me, carrying her to the bed. Still inside her, I set her down gently, prop a pillow under her head, and I start moving again.

Testing her first, doing it slowly, I'm wordlessly asking, *You want more?*

She responds with a sexy little mew as she rakes her nails down my back, and she's stunning beneath me. A fucking wet dream looking up at me. Swollen lips. Glazed gold eyes. Flushed cheeks. Dark hair. She pants for air as I bend to force my tongue into her mouth.

"You wanted me," I rasp, and, god, I can see that she does as she stops gasping to suck on my tongue. "Here I am."

I claim her harder this time, plowing her so that every cell in her body is jarred by my fucking thrusts and so she knows I'm her fucking man now. She takes it so well and looks so hot as she comes, I pull out and rub my wet cock over her thighs, her abdomen, squeezing her lovely breasts in my hands and tasting her neck as I get her all sticky and wet with me.

"I've wanted to touch you for so long, Little Firecracker."

I love how she likes when I play with her nipples. I love how hard and tiny they are, and how pink and responsive. Tweaking them until they look red and happy from my pinching, I grab her hips and take her again. Deep. Hard. My fingers dig into her hips, and she's so hungry and tight, she moans my name, *"Remington."*

I'm claiming her—and she's giving it up to me with no protest. She wants to be claimed. She wants to be mine.

She *is*. Mine. Now.

She gasps . . . *"Please, oh, god, you're so hard, you feel so good."*

And I tell her she's "so sweet and wet" as she grabs my buttocks and pulls me closer as she twists underneath me, and I can't resist the way her pussy starts milking me. Her orgasm tears out a soft cry from her lips, and I release a low, ragged moan, my body clenching and releasing with her.

We collapse on the bed, and she draws my arm around her body and cuddles closer, kissing my nipple. I shift her so I lie on my back and she lies straight over me, her tight tummy against mine.

I feel like a goddamn king. I'll never get enough of you, never. . . .

She's the first woman I've ever come inside of. She fucking let me. To me, that's code for *You're definitely my man*.

Yeah, I feel fucking fantastic and I still want to bathe her in me so every inch of her beautiful skin smells of Remington Fucking Tate tonight, her man.

Shifting her, I spread her small, loose body over mine, stomach to stomach, and nuzzle her ear as I run my hands down her sweet curves. "You smell of me." I fucking like it so much, I start sniffing her neck.

"Hmmm" comes her lazy answer.

My nose brushes against her temple as I clench her juicy ass. She sounds sleepy, but I'm too wired now to rest. "What does *hmmm* mean?"

"You said it first," she saucily counters, and I can hear the smile in her voice.

My gaze trails down the curve of her jaw in the darkness as I gently tell her, "It means I want to eat you. Your little biceps. Your little triceps." I nudge her nose with mine so she tips her head back, then I kiss her sweet mouth. "Now you."

Easing sideways, she takes my hand and spreads it over her abdomen, where I left a damp trail on her skin. "It means I'm going French this week and not showering so I can smell you on me."

God, I swear only my woman would say that. Groaning, I shift us sideways so that we face each other, then I reach between her legs and slide my semen up the inside of her thigh, into her pussy. "Sticky?" I croon as I bend my head and tongue her shoulder, meanwhile penetrating my wet finger back inside her. "Do you want to wash me off you?" I gently prod.

Brooke wiggles almost unnoticeably, but not so unnoticeably that I don't see she wants to get closer to me, my lips, my body, and my fingers. I fucking love it. "No," she breathes, parting her legs just a little bit for me. "I want you to give me more."

What I want is for her to taste us, so I rub my wet finger across her lips and push it into her mouth.

"I wanted you since the first night I saw you," I gruffly murmur to her, watching her suck on it.

"So did I."

Her admission tangles all over my gut, and I shove a second damp finger into her mouth, watching her soft, gold eyes drift shut as she licks up our taste like it's a banquet. When she moans, I'm swelling back up again.

"Do you like my taste?" I prod.

"Hmm. That's all I want from now on." She lightly bites my fingertips, and my cock jumps to full length as her teeth sink into my flesh. "I'll always want my Remy fix after dinner," she continues. I'm getting painfully hard and the teasing glimmer in her eyes is driving me insane with lust. "And maybe before breakfast. And after lunch. And at teatime."

I groan, I can't take it. A man with a purpose, I slide down her parted legs and my tongue lashes out to taste her sex. She archs up in offering, and I grab her buttocks to lift her higher to my mouth, her taste intoxicating. Sweet, with a little kick that lands straight in my fucking balls. I'm so fucking horny and thirsty for her, I can only speak in between licks. "I . . . want to . . . come . . . on every part of your body." I suck her taste in, pinching my eyes shut as I savor, then I rise to stroke my erection along her entry once more.

She grabs my head and rocks in a silent plea as she takes my lips with hers. "Come wherever you want, inside me, outside me, in my hand, in my mouth."

Her fingers curl around my cock, and the touch is so unexpected, so sweet and so bold as she gently strokes me, my cock jerks and I start coming, splashing semen all over her arm, her wrist. She rolls me onto my back and jumps on me, impaling herself on my shaft, and I bark out in pleasure and thrust my head back as I grip her hips and pull her up, then ram her back down, still jetting off inside her.

Later, she shudders with a soft scream, tossing her head back as she explodes with me, then she falls, limp and unresponsive, on my chest. I spread her over me and leave my cock inside her, panting, sliding my hands down her back, tracing her ass, the dents of her spine.

We lay for hours, petting. She's weak, but I'm still hyped up from being with her. I can't stop stroking my hands down her curves. I touch her knee, her bottom, her hair. "The night they sedated you . . ." she asks me groggily, hours later, "that was an episode?"

She caresses my abs, but not even her touch keeps me from tensing up at the topic.

"Can we even talk about it?" she asks.

I close my eyes as she continues caressing. I haven't been given caresses that aren't foreplay before. I don't allow these when we're done, I'm done. Like a fight. But she's touching me and I like it so much, I press her down to my neck so she doesn't put any distance from me. "You can talk to Pete about it," I whisper.

"Why don't *you* talk to me about it, Remington?"

Ah, *fuck*. I sit up and twist my feet off the bed, then drag my hands down my face. "Because a lot of episodes I don't remember what I do."

I start pacing. I hate talking about it. The topic distresses me. It's something I can't remember and usually have no clear control over. What does she want me to say? I do shit, and then I'm not sure I did it? I seem to lose control, and when I come to my senses, I usually find out from someone else what a major dick I seem to have been?

"All right, I'll talk to Pete about it, but come back to bed," she blurts out, but she ceded too easily. I'm no moron and I know she wants to know. Hell, she deserves to know.

"I remember you," I tell her, just to be clear about that. "In my last episode. The tequila shots. The way you looked. The little top you were wearing. The nights you slept in my bed."

She seems to absorb that for a moment and then whispers, her voice holding the most tenderness I've ever heard anyone address me with, "I wanted us to happen so bad."

My chest tangles with emotion, and I swing around. The depth of her eyes is endless. The way they stare right into me. I feel seen. Without reproach, disgust. I feel hungered for. Wanted in a way I have never, ever, been wanted.

"You think I didn't?" I whisper in disbelief. "I've wanted us to happen since . . ." Heading back to bed, I can't resist kissing her. "Every second I want us to happen."

Three fingers touch my jaw, her gaze curious on my face. "Have you ever hurt someone?"

God damn I hate having to tell her this. I want to tell her I'm strong, fast, the strongest and the fastest. I don't want to tell her I'm a fuckup. Dangerous. Volatile. Yeah, I'm a mess. But I've never been a liar. "I hurt everything I touch. I destroy things! That's the only thing I'm good at. I've found whores in my bed I can't remember bringing back with me and I've tossed them naked out of my hotel room, pissed like hell because I don't remember what I did. I've stolen shit, vandalized shit, woken up in places I don't even remember getting there. . . ." I drag a breath, then sigh. "Look, since Pete and Riley alternate days off, there's always someone to knock me out for a day or two when I get out of hand. I hit a low, and then I'm back. Nobody gets hurt."

"But you. Nobody gets hurt but *you*." With a worried crease in her forehead, she takes my hand in hers, and I can't believe how something smaller than you can give you such a great sense of well-being. "Remy, do they have to knock you out like that?" She laces her fingers through mine, and I glance down and stare at her. At that crease on her forehead. Those gold, gold eyes, worried for me in a way that's so new to me, it's almost amusing. But it's not. I want her to know I've got this. She's holding my hand, and I grip her tighter so that I'm the one holding her. I will always hold us both.

"Yes," I say emphatically. I don't care what Pete has to do, but I need to be kept in line, now more than ever. "Especially if I want . . . this . . ." Using my hand, I signal to her, then at myself.

"I want this. Very badly." Then I nuzzle her. "I'm trying not to fuck it up, all right?"

"All right."

I kiss the back of her hand. "All right."

❤ ❤ ❤

BROOKE WAS MISSING her friend, so I decided to bring her up from Seattle. With some reluctance, I agreed she could go with Pete to pick up Melanie at the airport.

"Remy, you're so good," Brooke said, sloppy kisses all over my jaw, making me laugh. Yesterday I caught her and her best friend laughing, and Brooke made love to me all night. I've never been so connected to anyone in my life.

When I handed her one of the sedatives Pete and Riley use—because I want her to know how to put me down if she needs to—she wouldn't so much as look at it.

"No, Remy, don't ask this of me."

"It's just to make sure I don't hurt you."

"You'd never hurt me."

I get hot just thinking about the ways she keeps on trying to protect me. I'm fucking sure she knows I'm her mate. If we were in other times, and I couldn't hunt for a day, I know damn well she could hunt for both of us.

Coach yells from the corner, "Too slow, Riptide, too damn slow. Hit it!"

I glance at the hard bag and punch. *Whack. Whack.* Concentrating on hitting. It comes from your core, and as long as you direct it properly, there's no fucking way there won't be power in that punch. I work my core more than anything. Everything I do works it, even jump rope.

I spend all day at the gym, and when I get to my sparring

partner, I see Brooke and Melanie at the door. My chest swells with happiness and proprietariness. She signals that they're leaving, and I pull off my headgear and smile.

I get a rush making her happy. I turn back to my partner and focus. My life had never felt so right. So good. I've never felt so accepted or so fucking understood.

That night, Pete summons me to discuss my finances. Brooke is having dinner with Melanie. I glance at my phone but get no text from her.

We're at the hotel bar.

A woman walks up. "You have amazing eyes."

I ignore her and turn back to Pete, drilling him: "At what time did she say she'd be back? . . . You sure Riley's getting her? . . . Why the fuck are they taking so long?"

"Riley texted they're on their way back," Pete tells me after like the tenth question, and he sends me up to my room.

I'm withdrawing into myself. I'm restless. My gut feels tight and I don't trust when I feel this. I grab my headphones and sit down, tapping my foot. I listen to Chevelle's "The Red."

When she finally comes in, my chest tightens. Her cheeks are pale, but her eyes well with emotion when she sees me. I don't know why my gut tightens.

She jumps on my lap, pries off my headphones, and slips them over her head. She frowns at the song. Yeah, she hates those rock songs, and I need to kiss away that frown. I kiss her nose, cradle her jaw, and rub her lips with my thumb. She jumps, drops the headphones onto the desk, and runs to the bedroom.

My gut tightens again, and I sit there, turning off my headphones, restless. I can feel the darkness teasing into me. I'm trying to calm myself. She's here. She's back. She's all right.

I watch her return. Something in her eyes that I can't pinpoint is feeding my monster ten times over.

"Remy, would you hold me for a bit?"

I study her, confused about what I feel. Then I realize she looks anxious and in need. "Come here." I shove my chair back and extend my arm, and she wiggles against me as I engulf her. I chuckle softly, instantly calmed in a way that only happens when I touch her.

"You missed me?" I cup her smooth cheeks and tip her head to me.

"Yes," she gasps.

I gather her to me and set my smile to hers. We stop smiling as the heat crashes through me.

My fingers outline her breasts, my mouth on her jaw, then I'm at the back of her ear, inhaling her, growling softly when her scent fills me. Winding me up and relaxing me. "Remy . . ." I hear the need in my name as she pushes my T-shirt up my shoulders.

I grab it in my fist and toss it aside, then strip her down to her skin, then yank her down to me again, my covered erection grinding in between her thighs. She strokes my chest and kisses every part she can.

"I missed you so much," she says, running her lips over my jaw, grabbing my hair as she presses close to me.

I engulf her in my arms and stroke her back, then seize her face. "I missed you too." I set a kiss on her sweet lips, and her nose, and her forehead.

She trembles, pressing so close. I want to open up and let her in any way I can. "But I missed your voice. Your hands. Your mouth . . . being with you . . . watching you . . . touching you . . . smelling you . . ." She takes my lips more desperately.

I try to slow down, but her mouth tastes amazing, and I need to remind myself that she is mine, mine, so I unbutton her and strip her bare as quickly as I can.

I draw her back to my lap when she's naked.

My whole body clenches when I feel her pussy nestling my erection. She seems undone.

She slides between my thighs and I yank my sweatpants partway down my hips until my hardness pops free, and her fingers are all over me, rubbing, squeezing, caressing.

"I want to kiss you here. . . ." Brooke's voice shakes with desire as she looks into my lust-tightened face, into eyes that I can barely keep open from the want. "I want to drown in you, Remington. I want your taste . . . in me. . . ."

She takes me in her mouth. Ecstasy burns through me as a sound rumbles up my throat. I need this so bad I rock my hips, slowly, up to her mouth, giving her what she wants and taking what I need. Her tongue runs all over me and her eyes are halfway down as she watches me, and I watch her back, amazed, undone . . . losing myself in her, praying she can rescue me from the dark already starting within me, the high of being manic.

❤ ❤ ❤

I FEEL LIKE a million fucking bucks.

Who the hell wants to sleep? I feel like climbing a mountain with Brooke on my back, taking her to the top, then flying down on a damn fucking parachute.

I prowl the kitchen and peer into the cupboards. I not only feel like a million bucks, my body feels like a million bucks. My fucking cock feels like a million fucking bucks and I want to give them all to Brooke Dumas.

I stick a granola into my mouth, orange juice, a spoonful of peanut butter. I pound in some more so Brooke can rest, but I am so fucking wired and so fucking hard just knowing she's in my bed. . . .

I want to feed her and then fuck her and then feed her and

then fuck her again and make her feel like a million bucks too, all in that order.

I start with the food and bring a huge bowl of cherries and granola to our room.

She's there, lying in bed with the sheets at her waist, her tits pressed into the mattress. Fuck I want those tits squished against *me*.

Setting the food aside, I jump on the bed, and as I run my hands all over her satin skin, I growl, "You look especially good, Brooke Dumas. Good, and warm, and wet, and I wouldn't mind having you on my breakfast platter."

Nudging my face in between the mattress and her chest, I drag my tongue up between her breasts, then lick her collarbone, and her sweet taste seeps into me and drives me wild. "All that's missing is a cherry on top, but I'm sure we have some."

I grab a cherry and rub it against her clit.

Groaning with a half smile, she rolls to her back, her legs spread open, her pussy all wet and mine, her eyes all melted for me.

"Who's your man?" I kiss her, rubbing the cherry around her clit. "Who's your man, baby?"

"You," she moans.

"Who do you love?" I prod as I roll her clit under the pad of my thumb and ease my middle finger into her pussy. She stares up at me with half-mast gold eyes, liquid with wanting.

"You drive me crazy, Remy," she whispers as she wraps her fingers around my cock and pulls me closer.

"If that's a lie, I'm going to make it true," I think it fair to warn her.

I grab her hips and shove myself in between her thighs to rub my cock against her sex. I bend down the length of her body because I want to eat her. Lick up from her tiny toes, up the arch of her foot, her delicious calf, her precious knee—where I will linger and give it some love—then up her lean, toned thigh, up to her sweet pussy—which I hope will be soaked like a raining heaven by the time I get there.

Getting down to business, I go forward and nibble my way up the inside of her thigh. She starts laughing and kicks me on the shoulder, but I catch her leg to still it.

"Remy! That tickles." She's laughing, trying to pry her leg off my grip.

I cock a brow and run my finger up the arch of her foot, then up the inside of her leg. "This?"

She laughs and kicks again, twisting to get free.

So I swiftly change plans, grasping her wrists and pinning them above her head as I spread my big body over hers. I know she loves it when I hold her down. She can't move unless I let her, and her eyes are darkening and she's panting softly beneath me.

"Remy . . ." she says, sobering, her gold eyes both playful and caring as she looks up at me. "Are you speedy?"

I smile wickedly and drag a finger along the inside of her arm. "What do you think, little girl?"

"I think you're very speedy." She tugs free and runs her fingers over my hair as she looks into my eyes. My, probably, black eyes.

I bite her thumb gently and then lick it before I let it go. "So what are you going to do about it? Do you want me to lift the bed with you on it? Or do you want me to take you on it?"

She laughs and rolls over, flinging a pillow in my direction. I shove it aside and I grab her by the ankle, pulling her back easily to me. "Get over here."

She laughs and fights to get free and I watch as she edges to the side of the bed, a peek of her pink pussy teasing me, driving me insane with want. I'm crackling with energy. I think I can fly her out of here if she wants me to.

She drives me so crazy, my every muscle is clenched and

poised for me to make her mine. My blood storms through my body like fire rushing through my veins. Right now I want nothing more than to take her to heaven. I feel all-powerful, all-feared. I am Remington Tate "Riptide" and this girl is *Mine*.

I reach over the bed and she squeals and tries to stay free, attempting to crawl off the bed. I laugh when I catch her ankle and drag her back to me. "Where do you think you're going? You're mine. You get over here and let yourself be taken."

"No, I need to pee!" she cries, flinging the other pillow at me, then she hurries to the bathroom and closes the door.

"Gah. Come the fuck here," I growl, knocking on the door. She's started brushing her teeth, from the sounds of it. Finally, the water stops and I hear her unlock the door. I open it and find her toweling off her hands. I go to her, scoop her up, and she nuzzles my neck as I carry her to the bed.

She sighs. Because she knows I want her. She's being playful, making me chase.

"What am I going to do with you?" she groans tenderly, her fingers linked on my nape. She's smiling up at me like I'm some long-lost prince. And what she doesn't know is that this long-lost prince is going to fuck her into oblivion.

I fling her to the bed, and she squeals delightedly. I drop down on her and ram her legs apart.

I kiss one naked thigh first, then the other, then I kiss her pussy. "This is mine." I lick it.

Her head falls back and she moans as my thumb steals between the swollen sex lips and dips inside her. My mouth waters and I growl softly as I use my thumb to enter her while I rub my tongue across her clit.

She parts her thighs and releases a mew that drives the hunter in me wild with the need to conquer. She starts thrashing and I grab her and hold her still. "Give me what I want, Brooke."

Tossing her head side to side in pleasure, she whimpers and bites her lips and pumps her hips up to my face. "I'm all yours."

"That's right." I tenderly urge her thighs apart as I come to my knees. "That's right. Now open up. Let me in." She does, and I sink between her legs, grip her hips, and my body tightens as I enter. "Yeah," I say when she moans, tossing her head back. "Who do you love?" I drop my voice, undone by her, and then crush her mouth when she can't answer me. "Who do you love?"

She moans and buries her lips in my neck, biting me. She murmurs something into my skin, clawing my back.

I moan back and hiss out, "Say my name, Brooke."

"Remington." She kisses my ear and tugs on my earlobe with her lips, breathing in my ear, excited. She's gasping my name in lust, but I pretend she's answering my question.

She's wet and hot, and she loves me, and she's all I've ever wanted. Stronger than I imagined, more female than I ever imagined. Funny and nurturing, vulnerable and sassy.

I love her so much my chest hurts as I watch her arch her spine and take me inside. I groan and duck my head as she clutches me to her. I clutch her back and try to slow down, and she rubs my skin with her fingers. She knows I need it and she gives it up to me with no protest. When she's tired, asleep. When she's busy, when she's sweaty, when she's hungry. She gives it up to me whenever I want, whenever I ask for it, because I'm speedy. Because I'm me. Because I know, deep in my gut, where it sometimes hurts to look at her, Brooke Dumas loves me.

❤ ❤ ❤

I'VE BEEN AWAKE for eighteen hours and twenty-eight minutes. My heart is pounding thirty-nine beats a minute. Brooke has been in my arms for exactly nine hours and twenty-eight, now twenty-nine, minutes. I'm jacked up and I can't sleep.

She's cuddled like a little kitten against me; I want to pet and lick from the top of her head to the soles of her little feet.

I've cataloged the room in my head. I know where everything is. I could run in it in the darkness without bumping into anything. I could carry her in my arms without danger. Everything's in my head—perfectly visualized.

But nothing as perfectly as her face.

Her lips are parted and they shudder on each breath. Shaped like a heart, the bottom one just as juicy as the top. Her cheekbones are high and her eyelashes rest over them, soft-tipped crescents.

I just want to lie here in this bed in this darkened hotel room and drink her in all over again until I'm drunk and high on her.

I am a fucking pendulum.

Any disturbance to my balance, and I swing.

The doctors taught me this.

Once I swing high, nothing on earth will stop me from crashing back down. I fall by gravity. Natural urge of the body to restore balance.

But that's the thing. A pendulum always seeks its balance.

She's my balance. I need her more than air.

Ducking my head to her neck, I breathe her in and growl.

❤ ❤ ❤

AND IT'S A fucking crappy week.

I don't like the way Brooke looks at Pete and Riley with a smile and talks to them. We're flying to New York and I can't help thinking how much I don't fucking like that Coach treats me like I'm a goddamn pussy and need to fucking rest, and that Diane is giving me the same fucking food, over and over. But Brooke. I'm onto Pete and Riley, by god, I am. If they so much as give one look at her—they are done with.

I glare at them from the bench. They tried to help her with her suitcase; the dickwads think I don't know they're crushing on her?

I pull her closer to me and set a kiss on her forehead.

"Who are all these people here for?" she asks. A huge crowd is at the FBO where my jet parks when we arrive at New York, and security has cords holding them back. She's so puzzled, it's adorable.

"For me, who else," I tell her.

Pete laughs. "Get off it, Remy."

I swear they are all staring at her. I pull her to me. "Come here, baby. I want these good folks to know you're with me." I squeeze her ass to mark my property.

"Remington!"

I usher her into the limo before the rest come in, then I grab her to me and kiss her. I'm so fucking starved for her, I need to feel her heat, her warmth, her tongue.

My hunger is wild and unleashed, completely crazy. "I want to take you somewhere tonight," I rasp into her mouth. "Let's go to Paris."

"Why Paris?"

"Why the fuck not?"

"Because you have a fight in three days!" She laughs delightedly, and I want to take her to Paris, I don't care about the rest, but she whispers, "Let's go anywhere with a bed."

I immediately fuck her in my mind on a bed, and then I imagine— "Let's do it on a swing."

"Remington!"

"Let's do it in an elevator," I propose. I am fucking her in an elevator, standing, my tongue hot and hard and pushing into her while I plunge my cock inside her, over and over.

Laughing, she shakes her finger at me, and I grin. "I'm never, ever, doing it in an elevator so you're going to have to find someone else."

"I want *you*. In an elevator." Standing in that elevator, my tongue in her.

"And I want you. In a bed. Like normal people."

My eyes dip to her cleavage, then down her body, to her pussy tightly hugged in the most delicious pants I have ever seen. I want to write a fucking letter to the makers and praise them for a job well done. Thanks to their jeans I have a good view of my woman all the time. "I want you in those pants you're wearing."

She nods and grins, then twines her fingers through mine and lifts my hand to kiss my knuckles.

I'm curious to see what she's doing because I don't remember her kissing my knuckles like this. She crawls closer and cups my jaw, sets a kiss on my cheek, and runs her hands through my hair, and my entire body homes in on her touch and the tenderness in her eyes as she looks at me.

Car doors open.

Coach rides up front with the driver, and everyone else slides onto the bench across from us. Brooke tries wiggling free but I tighten her fingers in mine and make her stay put. I don't want her to stop touching me, all my body craves it. My mind is not thinking any shit anymore. Who cares what Coach does, Riley . . . I just look at her. And feel . . . good. Calm. Calmer. I want to rest my head on her and I slide down—fuck me for being so large— then I pull her closer and set my head on her chest. I can hear her heart pounding under my ear. She went very still, and I want her to relax. I pull her closer and shift so she's comfortable, and I feel her melt with me.

I close my eyes and my mind feels quiet. It is quiet. I like it. I'm not thinking of anything except the pounding of her heart under my ear. Then I feel her fingernail along my earlobe and I tighten my hold to keep her locked to me. Tenderness oozes out of her like a blanket. I shouldn't want it this much, but I do. Nobody can take this from me.

"You guys want a time-out when we get to the hotel?" Pete asks us in a voice that I can barely recognize as Pete's.

She's moving her fingers in my hair, and when she doesn't speak, I move my head yes, not lifting it so that she won't take her hands away. I crave her hands. It's not the contact as much as the tenderness in her touch. The way her fingers respect my muscles, push just enough, support and help them let go. It happens inside me. I don't believe in words, but I believe in this.

She strokes me all over with both hands, softly, and I hear her chatting with Diane about a recipe for me while we ride to the hotel, and her heart is steady and strong under my ear, and she's small and fragile and smells like she does, and I am never letting her go.

I will. Kill myself. Before letting her go.

When we get to the suite, I'm anxious again. She's getting her cosmetics out of her suitcase, and I watch her hands move on her bag and pull out her toothbrush, and then she brushes her teeth. And I do nothing but crave crave crave. Inside me in the very pit of my being.

I want to break that fucking toothbrush and anything that takes her from me.

She rinses and towels her hands as I approach. She looks at me questioningly and I can't explain what I need, but I am in a tangle and roiling and I need her like my next breath, and if I had to choose, I would choose her over oxygen.

I lift her in my arms and carry her to the bed, and she cuddles into my neck and breathes me as I lower her.

I pull off her small shoes and toss them aside, then take off mine and speak gruffly. "I want your hands on my head."

She edges back on the bed. "Does it calm your racing thoughts?"

I take her hand and spread it over my chest. "It calms me here."

Just feeling her fingers spread over me, I can breathe better, I stop thinking. I stare back into her eyes and slide next to her, then I drop my head to her chest and smell her neck. I'm so fucking in love with her I don't think anybody could ever hurt me like this girl could. Not Scorpion, not my parents. Because I don't care about them. Now all I care about is her.

I feel her softly kiss the top of my head as she runs her fingertips through my scalp.

This is the way I want to die one day.

With her at my side, our bodies touching. I won't need to say anything, and she won't need to hear it, because she gets me. She gets that words are sometimes bullshit and people don't mean what they say and through it all it's only actions that matter. And all I care is that she gets me. We are yin and yang or whatever that shit is called; she is my female and I need her. I knew it from the instant I saw her, and she knew it too, and that's why she ran. She wanted me to chase and I did. I will chase her every time she wants to see if I want her and need her enough.

Quietly, she caresses me. I lie completely still and soak up her caresses, taking what she gives me, because she makes me realize I am so starved for it that I would kill for this, and for her.

And my brain goes quiet and my heart is calm and my life is at a standstill, and the pendulum that I am, all the swinging to and fro, finally stops and I feel like I finally found my center.

❤ ❤ ❤

I THINK I fall asleep. I dream of elevators, pink pants, swings, and Paris. I dream of her laughing in a Hummer limo and cupping my jaw and touching my hair and looking at me like I am the only man alive and like she loves me.

I wake up and she's holding me in her arms and I don't know what time it is, but I see she's still in those pants. She tells me to take them off her, and I do, and I make love to her, and to my disbelief I fall asleep again.

My stomach wakes me. It is empty and grumbling. There's warmth all around me, and Brooke's hair. And I absorb it. I'd stay here all day if my stomach weren't so vicious and my muscles so demanding.

I grumble at her, "Hungry," and grab some sweatpants and stalk out to the kitchen. I grab some celery and peanut butter and start wolfing down to calm the hunger, a bit, then immediately start thinking about what else I can shove down my throat.

She appears and starts exploring what food is in the hot drawer. When I see her, I'm scooping up peanut butter on a celery stick and munching and almost swallow my tongue.

My eyes widen, and I drop the celery and cross my arms, staring while I feel a whole lot of good things rise up in my chest.

"Look at you," I growl.

Clad in my RIPTIDE robe, she brings over some plates and I am delighted that her scent will get all over my robe and then on me when I wear it.

"I'll return it when we get back to bed," she tells me.

I shake my head and pat my lap. "If it's mine, it's yours."

She sets down the food and I cup her hips and set her down on my lap as I stare down at the plates with a watering mouth.

"I'm so fucking starved." I grab a red potato and chomp on it.

"You would love my mom's red potatoes. She adds cayenne

pepper and gives them just a little kick," Brooke tells me as she forks one up and munches.

"Do you miss home?"

I chomp on another potato while Brooke looks at me for a moment. She has an *expression* and sets down her fork and fully faces me, then strokes the scruff of my jaw with her fingertips. "When I'm not with you, I do miss home. But when I'm with you, I don't miss anything."

I smile because I'm relieved. She brushes a dimple with her lips, and I growl and rub my nose against her little one. "I'll tuck you close so you don't miss it," I promise her.

"Please do. In fact I'm sure there's enough space right here." She wiggles on me and I nip her little earlobe and squish her easily, saying, "That's right!"

We laugh, and I take her fork and grab a potato and feed it to her. She takes the fork back and feeds me too. I eat, but I like feeding her more. All my instincts home in on her mouth's opening for me and on her eyes watching me as I come feed her.

The way her eyes shine on me make me feel like I am a god.

I slide my hand under her arm and caress her while I fork up a bite for myself, then I cut some for her.

She watches me as I cut, and I watch her as she bites and savors it and gets all my blood pumping so fucking hot, I'm burning all the way down into my soul.

"Who do you belong to?" I ask her, stroking my fingers up and down the divots of her spine. But suddenly food isn't what I want. I set down the fork and slide my hand through the parted fabric of my RIPTIDE robe, curving it around her waist. I set a kiss on her ear, rasping, "Me."

"Entirely yours." My heart tangles at her admission as she maneuvers so she's straddling me, and she buries her nose in my neck and slides her arms around my waist. "I'm getting so nervous about the big fight. Are you?"

I chuckle and peer down at her. "Why would I be?" I tip her head back, and she looks worried, frowning. "Brooke, I'm going to break him."

I want her to know there is no doubt in my mind I am going to break that motherfucker. I don't hate him, I don't give a shit about him, but he's not taking what's mine. I've worked all. Fucking years. For this. My whole life. I fight to live, and I live to win.

"Remy, I love the way you fight," Brooke whispers, searching my face, "but you have no idea how nerve-racking it is for me."

"Why, Brooke?"

"Because. You're . . . important to me. I wish nothing touched you, and every few nights, you're just . . . out there. Even knowing that you will win, it does a number on me."

My chest tangles again at the thought of her leaving me, getting sick of me. "But you're happy, Brooke? With me?"

I wait for her to answer. I don't know if she understands that I don't ask a lot of things I want to, I am not used to asking. I am asking her if she loves me. If she wants to be with me. If she will stay with me. If I make her as happy as she makes me.

She looks at me and I see the concern and tenderness in her gaze, and the knot inside me starts loosening before she even speaks, for I know the answer.

"Deliriously." She slips her arm around my neck and presses close like I like her, whispering, "You make me happy. You make me deliriously happy and delirious, period. I don't want to be without you for a second. I don't even want all those women to look at you and shout at you the things they do."

Her possessiveness gets to me. It speaks to me so deeply that I instantly feel possessive of her—I want to physically show her she has all my devotion, so my voice comes out rough. "I'm yours. You're the one I bring home with me."

I go to her neck and drag her soft scent into my lungs until I'm relaxed and satisfied, then I buzz the back of her ear and tell her, "You're my mate, and I've claimed you."

I can tell by her soft smile that she likes it. That she likes that I've claimed her. I start feeding her again, and it gets all my instincts up and running in the satisfaction of being able to provide and feed her, protect and love her.

We fall into an easy rhythm and she starts telling me about Melanie, Riley, and how those two have become friends, and I tell her, "Tell me more."

"My sister, Nora, used to fall in love with anything. She used to make fun of me and tell me I didn't like men."

I scrape my hand down her spine, smiling. "Did you tell her you were waiting for me?"

She laughs and pokes a finger into one of my dimples. "I'll gladly tell her that now." She smiles and pokes both my dimples now. We keep eating, and I feel immense satisfaction that she's never given her heart away. It is mine. She is mine.

"Do you remember anything nice about your parents?" she asks when we get back into the bedroom.

"My mother used to cross me every night." I lock the door, and briefly I remember my mother. "She crossed me on my forehead, over my mouth, and over my heart." I don't mention that she also mumbled and prayed words all day that had nothing to do with the rest of the things she did to me.

"She was religious?"

It comes easily to block out the memory as I pull out my iPod and my headphones and shrug, bring my stuff to the nightstand. I won't be sleeping for shit tonight. My head is already starting to buzz with things to do, punching bags to hit.

"Do you miss your family?" she asks softly.

I get into bed with her and I tell her the truth. "You can't miss anything you've never had." I grew up with my music, and that will always be with me. I would miss that like crazy and couldn't live without it. Frustrated with my robe, I pull it off her and ease the satin off her shoulders. She knows I need her naked and pulls her arms loose for me, then cuddles her small, lean body against my bare chest.

She feels so good, I feel her breasts rising with her breaths, my nose in her neck, her scent calming my thoughts. I might be okay for a while, but I know it won't last and I'll be needing to do something in a moment.

I think she notices my feet are restless. Fucking feet fucking feet fucking fuck it *fuck*!

"If I told you something," she whispers with a twinkle in her eye as she slides one leg between my thighs, our bodies tangled and close, "would you remember tomorrow?"

I pull the covers over us. "I hope I do." Fuck me, I hate myself sometimes.

I'm trying to calm down the buzzing inside me when she strokes my head, and my leg stops. I bite back a growl and close my eyes and suck in her touch, then she reaches over me to the nightstand. I see she grabs my iPod and headphones.

"Put these on," she says. She looks so excited, I grin. I fucking love my music, and a song becomes doubly important when she shares it with me. I straighten up against the headboard, drag her with me, put on my headphones, and drag her to my lap, where she crawls on and selects a song.

It starts, and I don't think I've heard it, but I have tons of shit in there.

Then I start hearing a woman singing and she sounds up-beat and hopeful. The way Brooke looks at me, smiling, watching me with brilliant gold eyes, makes my gut clench, and I hear the words and what she's telling me and my body tightens as I hear the chorus come: *You're so beautiful, but that's not why I love you. . . .*

I scan her face because a part of me just won't take this as the truth. I look at her eyes, her nose, her cheekbones. She's killing me, and I need to know she's not messing with me, but she isn't. She almost wears the expression of being the one who is softly singing it to me.

My body seizes and tightens in excitement. I feel made love to mentally, in my head.

"Play it again," I tell her roughly. She bites her lower lip and clicks the button to replay it, and I can't take listening to it one more time or my chest will explode into a million pieces—I will be all in fractions from now on.

I roll her over and set her on her back and place my headphones on her little head, brushing her hair behind her ears so it doesn't get caught. Her eyes widen as the lyrics start playing to her, and I can see the way her irises flare and her lips part in surprise. Then she closes her eyes so tight, I see the crinkles at the corners, and I watch her listen.

I kiss her, slowly parting her lips with mine, so that it's not the lyrics that tell her I love her, not a voice, not a word, but me.

SEATTLE

Will you still love me if I marry you in a dress Racer just baptized with a little bit of sweet baby vomit?

I stare down at Brooke's text, and quickly type back, Yes.
I wait for her to reply, but getting nothing for a moment, I write, I fucking love you. Don't let me stand here like some moron today.

Never! Not even if I had to walk naked up to you.

Don't fucking do that.

I'd kill someone for sure.

All right. Plus you know our son pukes roses so . . . it's okay!

Right.

I chuckle as I tuck away my phone and watch the church fill up with people. Including Melanie's new boyfriend.

"That's him," Pete tells Riley. "Melanie showed me a picture on her phone the other day."

Riley is speechless for a moment. "You're shitting me."

"What? Nothing else to say?" Pete baits. "He's almost as good-looking as Remington."

"I'll bet he's got a choad for a dick."

"And . . . he's also got manners. He's waiting for her by the door," Pete baits.

"Well, I could do that, but we're kind of busy up here with Rem," Riley grumbles.

"Will you both excuse me for a second? I believe *that*, over there, is mine," Pete says, pointing at Brooke's sister.

NEW YORK

We're at the hotel dining room, the entire team sitting down at two separate tables, one for the ladies, one for the men, when I get an e-mail from an unknown source, with the heading *Thought you might like to see this.*

I open the attachment, and I see Scorpion, and a woman in familiar clothes, and familiar hair . . .

Brooke.

My.

Brooke.

On tiptoes. Mouth puckered. Kissing Scorpion. My blood drains, then shoots back through me with desperate anger. I don't know what happened. Why I'm looking at this. But I shoot to my feet and send the table crashing to the ground. Coach ends up on the floor as I throw my cell phone and it crashes into the wall. Then I start for her.

"No, Pete, no!" she bursts out, panicked from her seat.

My blood boils as she calls out to her precious Pete, my body suddenly trembling as betrayal and hurt flood me. God, I want to shake her. I want to do more than shake her. I stop before her, breathing and trying to calm myself, squeezing my fists together with the urge to pound them on something. Brooke's eyes are bright with worry, and the truth in them makes my gut sink.

"Do you want to talk to me, Remington?" she asks me, in deceptive calm.

My god, *the gall* of this woman. I'm shaking so bad my arms tremble beside me. My throat feels so raw, I can barely talk. I can barely even breathe. I've never given myself to anyone, and yet I've fallen like some fucking imbecile for *her*. I have never shared my music with anyone. I have never, ever, believed anyone could love me until I looked into her eyes and I thought I was her *god*. . . .

But I'm nobody's god.

I'm just a fucking sick fool.

The pain is excruciating. I want to do some damage, but I just don't want to damage *her*. My voice is grim with rage, and it's a miracle I can even speak as I fight to stay in place, to keep my hands down, to try to control myself. "I want to do *more* than talk to you," I rigidly tell her.

My nostrils flare, and I don't want her to look at me in fear, but all I can see is her mouth.

Her beautiful mouth.

On that motherfucker's face!

"All right, let's talk. Excuse me, Diane." She surprises me by saying it almost as calmly as if I've just proposed a fucking picnic to her! She pushes her chair back and makes a whole circus about folding back her napkin.

The anger builds inside me and I keep seeing, in my mind's eye, her mouth puckered and kissing the very man whose fault it is I'm no longer a boxer. I want to grab her. I want to crush her to me and shake her. I flex my hands at my sides to keep them from doing that and more, and I can't breathe right, I can't think right. I want to kill Scorpion and carve his motherfucking skin off!

I want to throw something. I want to yell. I want to take her clothes off and fuck her and show her She. IS. MINE! Mine to touch, to hold, to protect.

"I just went to see my sister," she breathes.

My gut coils in rage that she would not trust me to get her sister back to her like I'd promised.

I reach out, and my hand trembles as I touch her mouth, then I duck and angrily bite it. She gasps at the feel of my teeth, and it gives me pleasure, perverse pleasure, that she is reminded that that mouth is for *me*.

"You go negotiate with scum like him? Without me knowing?" I scrape my thumb across. I want to drag her up to my room and wash her mouth with soap. I want to lick it clean and then make her tell me that picture does not really *exist*!

"I went to see my sister, Remy. I couldn't care less about the scum," she softly tells me.

I touch her hair, trying to be slow while my insides roil and pull and twist, and I keep rubbing her lips. These are lips I love, lips that move me, that kiss me, the only lips I have ever thought loved me. "Yet you kiss that fucking *asshole* with the same mouth you kiss me?" I growl.

"Please just count to ten." She touches my sleeve, and the anger rises in me even more. She thinks that I can count to a fucking million and forget this?

"One-two-three-four-five-six-seven-eight-nine-*ten*," I angrily rush out, then I grab her collar and pull her to me, leaning over her with narrowed eyes. "You kiss that *motherfucker* with the same mouth I would kill for?"

"My lips hardly touched the tattoo," she whispers pleadingly.

"I did just what you do when you let them get a hit and give them false confidence so I could see my sis."

I slam my chest. "You're *my* fucking girl! You don't get to give anyone false confidence!"

"Sir, we need you to leave the premises now."

I swing around to watch some idiot coming over. Pete and Riley stop him and start telling him I'm going to pay for all the shit I do, and, hell, the man has no idea I have done nothing yet. He can stay and watch me break everything in this stinking place, and then I'll gladly invite him to come over and watch me crack Scorpion's skull in two.

Shooting him a warning glare, I turn back to Brooke and slide a finger down her pretty jaw, watching the way her breasts rise and fall with her panting breaths. "I'm going to go break that fucker's face," I whisper to her, then I lean over and push my tongue into her cruel, delicious little mouth, "and then I'm going to break *you* into submission."

"Remy, calm down," Riley begs me.

"That's all right, Riley, I don't break that easy, and he's sure welcome to try," Brooke snaps, scowling at me.

Scowling back, I fist her hair in my hand and crush her mouth with mine, giving her a hard, angry kiss meant to punish her. "When I get you in bed, I'm going to scrub you raw with my fucking tongue until there's nothing anywhere on you from him. Only me. Only *me*."

She seemed to like my punishing kiss—goddamn her—now I'm so fucking hard I want to take her right here, right now.

Her pupils are dilated, and her body seems to lean on mine as she breathes, "All right, take me there."

I want to. Fuck, I almost do. Fuck everything else but me and her.

Jerking back, I look at her narrowly. "I don't have fucking time to take care of you," I snap before I head to the door.

"Remy, come back. Don't get in trouble!" she calls out.

I stop, then I drag a bunch of air into my burning lungs, but it's impossible to calm down, the anger and the possessiveness, the fucking jealousy in me is so great, greater than me.

I whirl around, then I jab the air with one finger so she fucking understands the situation and where we fucking stand. "Protecting you is my *privilege*. I will protect you and anything that *you* value as if it were *mine*."

She stares breathlessly at me, and I don't think she gets it. She loves her sister, but she needs to know that I am her man and she is untouchable by anyone but me. Anyone. But *me*.

"That sick asshole has just begged me to end his miserable life, and I'm happy to oblige," I angrily inform her, running my eyes meaningfully over her body, every inch of which belongs to me as completely as mine belongs to her. "He's just taken something sacred from me and pissed on it!" I storm back at her and push a finger between her breasts. "Understand me. You. Are. *Mine!*"

"Remington, she's my sister," she pleads.

"And the Scorpion will never let go of her. He keeps his women drugged and dependent, their minds in pieces so tiny they can't even think. He'll never give her up unless he wants something even more than her. Is it you? Does he want you, Brooke? He could have drugged you. Stripped you. Fucked you—goddamn my life, he could have *fucked you!*"

"No!"

"Did he touch you?"

"He didn't! They're doing this to provoke you, don't let them! Save it for the ring tomorrow. Please. I want to be with you tonight."

"I was with her the whole time, buddy, nothing happened," Riley suddenly intercedes, calmly patting my arm.

When I realize what he's telling me, I swing around to grab his shirt in my fist, the fury skyrocketing inside me. "You let my girl get in that scumbag's face, you little shit?" I lift him off the ground.

"Remy, no!" Brooke comes to my side and futilely tugs on my arm.

I shake Riley. "You let her kiss that filthy scum's ink?"

Pete taps my shoulder. "All right, buddy, let's put Destroyer to bed now, huh?"

There's a prick on my neck, and my adrenaline kicks in with a vengeance. Motherfucking shit, I can't fucking black out now. I drop Riley and yank out the syringe and toss it aside. I go grab Brooke and stare at her. I want to tell her never to doubt me again, never to go behind my back again, and never—ever—believe I won't protect her and what is hers, but I open my mouth and she looks so scared and so beautiful, panting and worried, that instead I make a low, gruff sound and crush her mouth, punishing myself with her taste, the sweet, wet taste of her, so pure and good, and how I hate that she put her beautiful mouth on that motherfucker because of her love for her sister. I tear free and release her before charging off.

My heart kicks wildly in my chest, fighting the sedative. All I can think of is introducing my knuckles into Scorpion's face. I'm going to make him eat my fist, and then I'm going to make him go pick up his teeth from where they fall.

I know where he's staying. We all know where each other is staying, if only to avoid each other. There are usually several hotels close to the designated Underground location, and Pete always finds out where Scorpion is so the only place we meet is in the ring.

He's four blocks away, in a cheap five-story building littered with groupies at the lobby. When they see me, I hear a collective gasp, and all I have to do is growl, "Scorpion," and two of them begin moaning excitedly and rubbing up against my sides, sandwiching me as we take the elevator. When we reach Scorpion's floor, I get them to lead me to his door before I halt their roaming hands and squeeze their wrists so they stand still.

"Get them to open up," I growl.

One of them rubs my chest while the other knocks. "Willie! Hey, Willie, it's Trish," she calls out.

The door opens and I immediately swing out my arm, my fist connecting with Willie's face. He falls splat on the floor. Two other assholes sit on a flowery sofa watching TV, and they leap to their feet.

I go straight for the nearest one and grab him by the shirt. "Hello, motherfucker," I tell him as I swing my fist. Bones crack. Blood sputters as I toss him down and grab the next, smashing my knuckles so his nose cracks just as hard. When I let him drop to his knees, I see him—Scorpion—at the door to a bedroom, his eyes slightly wide and as yellow as dog piss.

Clamping my jaw, I angrily stalk over as he lifts his palms up to ward me off. "Now, now, Riptide, you don't want to do this here."

"Yes, I do." I grab his shirt and pound my fist three consecutive times into his face.

He tries to hit me back but I'm pounding him too fast. I shove him down to the ground and spot a girl there, crying, watching us from a chair by the bed. She looks nothing like Brooke. Her stare is empty, her hair is atrocious, and then I see a pencil at the nightstand as Scorpion tries standing. I grab it, and before he can stand, I ram it into the black tattoo he made Brooke kiss, tearing it downward. Blood spurts, and he releases a low, bloodcurdling scream as he tries to pull the pencil out.

As he winces and yanks it off, bloodied and broken, I pull him up by the T-shirt and force him to look at me.

"STAY. AWAY. FROM MY GIRL," I spit into his face. "You MOTHERFUCKER. Stay away from my property. I'll KILL you next time."

I swing out, and the girl cries, "No!" and when I turn, his fist slams into my face.

I stumble back, then scowl, roar, and lunge at him. As we swing hard and fast, the only sounds in the room are the weeping of that girl and our hard, fast punches.

The thing about Scorpion is he's not me. He's not as fast, he's not as strong—he will never win, unless he provokes the shit out of me and I fuck up like I did with my boxing career.

Like I'm doing now.

And I don't care. Right now nothing will feel as good as breaking every one of his bones. Roaring, I deliver a killer right hook that drops him to his knees, and he raises his arms to stop me.

"Halt! I say, *halt*, Riptide!" My swing halfway there, I halt and glower down at him as he signals at her. "Do you want her?"

Blood dripping down my eyebrow, I wipe it off and look at her, as Scorpion grits out, "I'll give her to you. I'll let you take her if you let me win tomorrow."

"I kill you now," I growl, hauling him up by the shirt and forcing him to his feet with an angry shake of my fist. "And I take her."

He shakes his head and pulls his shirt free. "Kill me and my three boys will tear her apart while you do."

The soft weeping continues from the corner, and she's whispering, "Please stop, stop."

I scan the minions approaching her. I can take them all, but I don't fucking want to do it in front of her. Clamping my teeth, I shove Scorpion away and approach her. I'm no fucking murderer even if the desire to kill is swimming in my veins, making me tremble. "You're Brooke's sister?"

She nods.

I take her by the arm and lift her to her feet. "You come with me."

"Not so fast, Riptide," Scorpion calls. "You want her, then one of your guys and mine stay with her in lockdown until you deliver the championship tomorrow."

My laugh is dripping in sarcasm. "Ahh, asshole, when are you going to realize? I can give the championship away tomorrow, that won't mean I won't take it back. And when I do, everyone's going to watch me break you." I grab my phone and call Pete.

"Where the fuck are you—" he starts as soon as he answers.

"Get your ass over here. I need you to do something for me." I tell him where I'm at and hang up.

Five minutes later, when Pete arrives, he sees my eyebrow is bleeding into my eye, that my fists are cracked and my knuckles bruised. He stares at Scorpion, his mouth hanging open. "Rem, what have you done," he gasps.

"No one's talking," I stress out to placate him, and when he keeps gaping, I snap my fingers before his eyes. "Hey, hey, man, focus! You're to secure Brooke's sister until I tell you and they release her to me. Do you hear me?"

He blinks. "Dude, you need stitches."

"I'll get some fucking stitches," I growl. "Just take her away from that asshole."

I turn to look at Scorpion. Holy god, I still want to kill him. He's slumped and bruised, and bleeding, but he has a gleam of victory in his eyes.

"I can't wait to break you up on that ring," he tells me as I walk out.

And it doesn't matter.

❤ ❤ ❤

"AND NOWWWW, LADIES and gentlemen, the moment we've all been waiting for. Our reigning champion, the defender, the one and only, Remington RIPTIDE Tate!"

I am zoned off from the crowd and even of the way my body is primed and pumped to fight. I trot out to the ring and all I can see is Brooke draped in this same fabric around her skin. It brushes against me. I feel calm. I am reminded that she's the reason why tonight I'm going to be hitting the canvas.

I can feel her gaze on me as I hop into the ring and let Riley pull off my robe.

This is the moment I always look at her.

My stomach is burning with determination. If I look at her, she'll be wearing that worried look on her face. She'll weaken me. She'll make me want to fight. *Fuck.*

The crowd yells my name in a chant, and I hate that she's going to have to watch this. But she wants her sister back. I won't let her be with Scorpion.

The announcer then calls, "And nooow, ladies and gentlemen, the nightmare you've all been dreading to come alive is here. Watch out for Benny the Blaaaaaack Scorpion!"

And here he comes, the motherfucker. Walking slow as poe to test my fucking patience, with both his middle fingers stretched out to me and the public.

He feels badass tonight 'cause he knows I won't be having any game tonight.

I wait for him to get up here, reliving the way I stuck a pencil into his fucking tattoo. I think of Brooke kissing him and my blood boils again.

He hops onto the ring and his black cape is removed, and I'm glad to see the motherfucker looks like shit. He's been stitched up where I carved the tattoo off his fucking skin, and his yellow eyes land on me, and I can see the joy he feels that he'll get to publicly kick the crap out of me.

Ting ting.

For a blind second, instinctively, I feel my body start to bounce into place: guard up, feet apart, going toe to toe with him, but I catch myself before I swing and let him have it. He punches me in the ribs, then my jaw, double. I shake myself to recover, then go back toe to toe.

I'm so wired up, it even feels good.

Scorpion hits me right in the gut, then goes for an uppercut, and I straighten my head. I'm not going to be knocked down by those sissy swings. If I land on the canvas, I fucking land on it because I can't stand.

I take three punches in the body again, chest, and rib cage, and my body, my muscle memory, is at war with my brain. I'm going against every single instinct inside me. But I tell myself I might not have the championship, but I will have *her*.

I can see myself and the way she will look at me when I bring her sister. She will have that young girl back and she will know, once and for all, that I will fucking do anything for her.

Scorpion goes for my jaw, then goes straight and knocks me to my knees. The public doesn't like it. I stand up, a little dizzy.

"Boooo! Booo!"

"Kill the bastard, Riptide! KILL HIM!"

We keep going. Punch after punch, I concentrate on not protecting, on not punching back.

We're going round after round, and I'm just taking it. I feel my systems shutting down somehow. My muscles throbbing, my skin bruised, my bones tender. My brain slowing, my lungs straining to oxygenate every bruised part of me. I don't even know where it hurts, my body is producing tons of numbing shit, and I am grateful for it.

I wipe my forehead and keep breathing, my arm ends stained in blood from my eyebrows, my lips, my temple. I slam onto the ground again, and I hate that this motherfucker can't knock me down unconscious even when I want him to. I jump back up and spit at him, angering the motherfucker so he will *give it to me good*.

"Remy, fight him!" I hear Brooke's unmistakable voice, and it freezes me. "REMY, FIGHT HIM! FOR ME! FOR *ME*!"

I hear it. Holy god, she has never screamed for me like this. It breaks me, and for the briefest second, I want to knock Scorpion with whatever force I have left. I am the strongest, the fastest, so she knows I *don't go down*. I am her mate and I want her to be proud of me. The jabs come, and all I can hear is her begging me to fight. For her. And for the first time in my life, I feel completely humiliated. Can't she see I'm allowing this?

This one's for you, little firecracker—ooof.

My breath goes, my body contracts to hold the pain. My thoughts scatter and my head spins.

He goes for my head now, and my brain spins in my cranium like jelly. I can hear his fist connecting with my jaw until my head swings on the last *crack!*

Keeping balance is impossible.

I slam to the floor.

I feel it under me. I almost like it. The only solid thing as my world spins. Something about knowing I can fall and the motherfucking floor is there for me is comforting.

A wet puddle of blood is beneath me. My eyes are nearly shut and swollen. And my ribs feel like they've been punched into my lungs. I plant a hand on the canvas, and then the other, and I hear counting. I try pushing up, and for a moment there I don't know if I can.

I hate him. I hate him with a passion. All I can think about is me standing here, seeing those yellow eyes and that face, and busting it open the next time I face him.

I push up and spit blood, and as soon as I am up, I catch a left hook on my side that swings me around.

I stumble and almost fall again, need to shake my head. The room is spinning. And all I can think of are Brooke's arms, and how good they will feel when she holds me tonight. I'm going to cuddle her to me and let her put ice on me and work her magic, and she's going to love me for giving her back her sister because I thought I wanted the championship, but not now.

Now all I want is the woman I love. To love me. Like nobody in my life has loved me before. And I'll fight harder for her than for anyone.

I hear Riley and Coach yelling at me over and over, "Your fucking guard! What the fuck is wrong with you?"

People yell all over the arena. They're getting thirstier and thirstier for blood, but today I can only give them mine.

"KILL HIM, RIPTIDE! KILL HIM!"

The next hit sends blood splattering across the canvas, and the people shout even louder. *"REM-ING-TON! REM-ING-TON!"*

My heart has never pumped so hard. No part of my body understands why I'm not using it. My fight tonight is with myself, with every fucking instinct inside me, my muscles, which want to work, my nerves, which jump reflexively to protect. But I can't move my right arm anymore. It hangs limp at my side, and it doesn't even hurt.

"Remy, Remy, REMY!" people continue yelling.

Scorpion growls in rage. I know for a fact there has never been a moment in his life when anyone rooted for him.

I spit in his face. "Next time I see you, you're going to eat my fist," I tell him.

He swings his arm back with a roar and I wait for the slam. It comes and I'm down. My vision tunnels and goes black.

❤ ❤ ❤

I HEAR MUSIC in the dark. I hear the songs Brooke has played me, songs I have played her. My body aches and I try to move but can't pull out of the dark. I feel hands on my jaw, and I hear sounds close to my ear. Sobbing little sounds. I feel her kisses on my temple, her fingers on top of my hair. I hear the music and lose it . . . lose her . . . No, I'm never going to lose her. I'd do everything for her. She has to know I'd do everything for her.

Light burns into my retinas. My body is leaden and numb. My chest hurts. I peel open my eyes wider and assess my surroundings.

Hospital. Riley.

And Brooke?

Panic seizes me. I try to talk and something is stuck in my throat, so I groan.

Riley's head shoots up from where he sits in the chair. "You're up, thank god!" He comes to me. "Holy god, Remington, I'm fucking glad you made it so I can kill you myself. You had us all—"

I grab his arm and squeeze so tight, he halts, and a noise emerges from my throat, through the stupid breathing tube I've got jammed in there.

"You want to know where Brooke is?" Riley asks when he looks into my eyes.

I nod and groan again. The panic claws through me. She saw the debacle in the ring, and I need to see that she's all right.

When Riley goes to get her, I count the seconds with my heartbeat.

She comes in and stops when we see each other. I've never before felt what I feel now. Every cell in my body leaps, but at the same time I'm immobilized in this bed, trembling with the sight of her. She's there, looking at me, in clothes that are wrinkled and her hair a mess, her face pale, and she has never looked so good to me. My body tenses with the urges burning through me. I want to tell her, *I love you, Little Firecracker. I fucking love you so bad. . . .*

I want her to bring me my iPod so I can play a song to her. "I Love You" again. Or another one. Shit, nothing can capture the feeling of loving her.

She starts trembling on her feet, and my eyes start burning when I hear the sobs that start wracking her. They tear from somewhere so deep, her voice sounds completely unfamiliar, and it makes me hurt in places I didn't even know I had.

"How d-dare you make m-me watch t-that . . . how could you stand there and make me watch h-him destroy you! Your bones! Your face! Y-you . . . were . . . mine! Mine . . . to . . . to . . . hold. . . . How d-dare you break you! How dare you break me!"

My eyes are on fucking fire and I can't fucking move, all I can do is lie here as her pain and mine tear through me.

"A-all I wanted was to help my sister and not g-g-get you in trouble. I also wanted to protect *you*, to take care of you, to be with you. I wanted to *ss-stay* with you until you were sick of me and didn't need me. I wanted you to *love me* because I . . . I . . . Oh, god, but you . . . I . . . can't. I can't anymore. It's hard to watch you fight, but to watch you murder yourself is . . . I won't do it, Remington!"

I make noise and try to move even when an arm is in a cast, hating how heavy my body feels. My fast, trained body fails me, and it is as broken as I suddenly feel.

Tears trickle down her cheeks, and suddenly she comes to me and she touches my free hand and bends to my chest as she kisses my knuckles, her tears falling on my scars.

I want to touch her so bad I force my cast to move so I can place my hand on the back of her head, stroking her hair.

She wipes her cheeks and looks through tear-filled eyes at me, and I silently will her to understand that I can take this, that I can take a beating.

But suddenly she stands to go.

I grab her hand and clutch it as tight as I can without breaking her little bones. She pulls it free and grabs my face and sets a kiss on my forehead. I feel all her pain explode inside me, and she's fucking killing me. A sound tears from my throat as I grab the tube and try pulling it out, and the machine goes crazy and so does Brooke.

"Remy, don't, don't!" she pleads, but I won't fucking have it, I need to take this fucking shit off. I've never been a man of words, but I won't have shit in my throat when I have something to say to her, but Brooke panics and yells for a nurse. "Nurse! Please!"

A nurse rushes into the room, and something shoots through the IV to my veins, and I am instantly as heavy as a bull and my head is closing in on me. Brooke looks at me with a face I will never forget. I think I broke her. She's strong, she's my mate, and she is naturally strong enough to take me—no.

Nobody can take me.

I see the look in her eyes, the same look I imagine everyone gets when they realize I'm hopeless. I'm a fucking mess. But then she smiles at me, and it's a smile that brands itself in my head. I cling to it as I start sinking, trying to think of what song I will play her when I wake. . . .

♥ ♥ ♥

Dear Remington,

The very first moment I laid eyes on you, I think you had me. And I think you knew. How could you possibly not know? That the floor was shaking under my feet. It was. You made it move. You colored my life again. And when you came after me and kissed me, I just knew somewhere deep inside me, my life would forever be touched and changed by you. It has been. I have had the most amazing, incredible, beautiful moments of my life with you. You and your team became my new family, and never for one second did I really plan to leave. Not them, but most of all, not you. Every day I spent with you only makes me crave more of you. All I wanted for days was to be closer. It hurts to be close and not to touch you, and I wanted to spend every waking moment with you and every sleeping moment in your arms. So many times now, I wanted to tell you all the ways you make me feel, but I wanted to hear you say it first. My pride is gone now. I have no room for it, and I don't want to regret not telling you: I love you, Remy. With all my heart. You are the most beautifully complicated, gentle fighter I've ever known. You have made me deliriously happy. You challenge and delight me and make me feel like a kid inside, with all the amazing things to look forward to, just because I was looking at the future and thinking of sharing it all with you. I've never felt so safe as when I am with you, and I want you to know I am completely in love with every part of you, even the one that just broke my heart.

But I can't stay anymore, Remy. I can't watch you hurt yourself, because when you do, you're hurting me in ways I never thought anybody ever could, and I'm afraid of breaking and never being right again. Please never, ever, let anyone hurt you like this. You are the fighter everyone wants to be, and this is why everyone in the world loves you. Even when you screw up, you get back up fighting again. Thank you, Remy, for opening your world to me. For sharing yourself with me. For my job. And for every time you smiled at me. I want to tell you to get well soon, but I know that you will. I know you will be blue-eyed and cocky and fighting again, and I'll be in your past, like all the things you've overcome before me. Just please know that I will never hear "Iris" again without thinking of you.

Yours always,
Brooke

I've read this letter over and over today. I've read it in disbelief, in anger, in self-loathing, in loneliness, in desperation, but never in detachment. And now, I read it another time, and it's finally sinking in that she—my girl—has left me. My body implodes and I groan and drop my head with the sort of intense pain they don't make painkillers for. My eyes blurring, I scrape my thumbs over the *I love you, Remy* over and over while I hear Pete out in the living room, talking as if it's a normal day.

Another fucking day of the life of Riptide.

Before he ever met . . . her.

"Fifteen hundred shares of that one. Sell. . . . Yes." There's a silence that makes me figure out he hung up, and I watch the doorknob turn as he peers into the bedroom. The curtains are open, and he starts when he sees me. "Your eyes are blue."

I rub my face and try to piece the past weeks together in my head, but all I can think of is bits of this letter. *I love you, Remy. . . . You have made me deliriously happy. . . .*

Pete steps into the room and strides over. "You've been out for almost three weeks. Do you remember?"

Silent, I just look at him, holding the letter in my hand.

"Remington, do you realize what you did? You lost the fucking championship. You threw. The fight! You gave up everything you've worked for. Every last penny of your liquid cash is gone. Years of endorsements and work. The championship . . . *gone*." His voice breaks, and he looks at me. "Do you remember that?"

"I know what I did, Pete. Nothing I gave up is something I can't get back."

"You, you moron. You could have fucking died! Remington, who fucking does that? You *willingly* let him beat you unconscious."

Twisting around, I sit on the side of the bed and rub my neck with one hand as I stare down at the letter and impulsively smell it. Fuck, it smells like her. Even the sight of her handwriting gets me.

Riley comes in.

"He's blue," Pete instantly informs him.

"Hell, that's fucking great! Hey, Rem."

I look at them, and they're my brothers. My brothers I care about. "You're disappointed," I tell them.

"We're not disappointed, dude, we worry about you. No woman is worth that," Pete says.

"She is." But I'm so fucking pissed at her for leaving me, I crumple the letter in my fist and stand. "I'm sorry about the fight. I'll make it up to the team."

"We're not sorry for us," Pete repeats.

I stretch one biceps, then the other, testing my body while I ask, "Scorpion?"

"Somewhere in the Bahamas or some shit. Having fun spending your money," Pete says, still sounding glum.

"Put the Austin home up for sale," I mumble. "That should get us through this season."

He nods. "We've also got some endorsement interest. You've been doing great—"

"What about her? Is she all right?"

They blink.

"Brooke."

"Dude, why are you asking?" Pete looks at me in alarm, then at Riley, then at me. "You're getting over her, Rem. You've had like dozens of ladies over! They're wild for some Riptide, just like old times!"

"Yeah, Rem, the kinds of ass you get," Riley says. "Jesus!"

An image flashes in my head of gold eyes, brimming with tears, in a hospital room. I stare down at the letter and uncrumple it from my fist, aware of Pete and Riley watching me, and then watching each other.

"Dude, hand that over, I can put that away from you." Pete comes over for the letter.

I instantly fist my hand around it. "You touch it, you die."

He drops his arm and sighs, and I look at both of them. "Where's her sister?"

"Not out of rehab yet. Another week."

I keep testing my body. Coach must be using the TENS machine on me to maintain muscle mass. I fold my muscles, they're hard as ever. All electronically manipulated to make them believe I trained—when I did not.

"Coach has been shocking every inch," Riley says, confirming my thoughts. "You're filled up with glutamine and all kinds of supplements."

I drop to the floor and do a push-up. Nice. It flows. My back isn't fucked from lying in bed. I jump up and twist my neck, then I open my suitcase and spot my boxing robe. And I know, with every inch of me, if I grab it, it's going to smell like her. In that moment the urge to expend all my rapidly building energy becomes acute. "Call Coach, let's hit it hard."

"You're seriously going to train? You've been in the hospital for over two weeks and getting shocks in the head! That's the only way we could pull you out of your depression."

"But I'm good now." I take her letter and my training gear into the bathroom, then I open the letter and read it again: *I love you, Remy.*

I close my eyes and throw it away.

Then I go get it, read it, and trace her letters. Damn you, Brooke. You should've told me to stay away. That you hated me. That you can't live with someone like me. Instead you tell me my team is your family. That you're happy. That you think about me when you hear my songs. You tell me that you fucking *love me.* Now, Brooke, I'm coming after you.

❤ ❤ ❤

EVERYONE, EXCEPT DIANE, rides in the Escalade. We're only blocks away from the building and there's a war zone in my chest. I drum my fingers on my thighs while the knot in my gut tightens as we get nearer. Brooke needs to be set fucking straight, and I'm sure when she sees the little package we've brought, there won't be much explaining to do.

I rub the back of my neck and then ram my hand into my jeans and grab the letter. The letter burns me. I've read it until my eyes cross and they burn from my rage. She held me like I was golden. She said she'd never leave and every inch of me believed her. I want to know what I said. I want to know what I fucking did. I want to know if she meant what she said in her fucking letter or if it's all a load of fucking bullshit.

"Oh, there's Brooke, and Melanie," Pete says from the back.

My head snaps toward the two figures trotting down the sidewalk as the car heads farther down the block to stop before her apartment. *Holy god, it's her.*

My heart starts pumping, the arteries in my heart widening to feed my muscles. I curl my fingers and yank open the door, but Pete and Riley descend from the car first. I step out on the sidewalk after them, and I see her. And she sees me. And we stare, neither of us moving. My eyes have been so starved, they hurt when I take her in—ponytail, running shoes, exercise gear, the oval face I dream of and those marshmallow lips of my fantasies and those gold eyes shining as they look back at me.

God, I love you.

With every bit of my fucking being, and every inch is buzzing at the sight of her. She wears tight running gear and sweat glistens on her forehead and throat, her hair held back in a cute ponytail, and she's frozen on the spot as she looks at me. I don't know if she's going to launch herself at me when she starts to move; all I know is, if she does, I'm so fucking ready to catch her. I'm going to catch her and never set her down on the ground.

Jesus, she looks so right and so glad to see me, I get all knotted up as they start heading for the three of us.

"Miss Dumas?" Pete asks her as she and her friend keep heading over. "We believe this belongs to you?"

He signals past me, and from our Escalade Nora emerges.

Brooke looks at me first, then blinks. "Nora?"

"Nora?" her friend Melanie repeats.

"We just wanted to make sure she got home safe," Pete says.

"Nora?" Brooke can't take her eyes off her sister, and my chest swells at the joyous disbelief on my little firecracker's face.

"It's me!" Her sister runs over for a hug, and I've never been jealous of a woman before, but I want Brooke's arms around me, her scent in my nostrils, in my lungs, caressing my soul. "It's me, big sis! I'm back! I've done work in rehab. Pete helped me. And I got the tattoo off." She points to the place where Scorpion's fucking ink used to mark her face. "I felt so little when you looked at me that day, Brooke. I felt so little and so . . . dirty."

"No! No, never!" Brooke hugs her again, and my gut clenches in jealousy and my arms feel leaden with the want to go around her.

"Nora! Nora Camora Lalora Crazyora!" Brooke's crazy, funny friend dives for Nora and swings her around, and Brooke turns to stare at the group of us, my heart kicking in anticipation.

But she looks at Pete, only making the knot in me tighten even more. "Pete, what's going on?"

"Surprise." He signals happily at her sister. "She's done great. She's such a sweet girl."

Then he nods in my direction, and Brooke's gold eyes return to me, but I can't take standing here, like she's not mine, and I'm not hers. I ram my hands into my jeans pocket and can't stop checking her out, the way her curves fill out, her sweat clings to her pretty skin.

"The night Remy went to fight with Scorpion, Scorpion offered your sister to him instead of the championship. And Remy agreed," Pete explains.

I watch her, and her eyes meet mine in utter confusion, and I wait for her to say something.

"You mean he agreed to . . . lose?"

My body tightens at the disbelief there, at the pain. She thought I did it because I'm a fucking BP, and I know it.

She starts shaking her head, clinging to my eyes with hers. I see her pulse pounding, her face changing in color, her eyes darkening in pain.

"You did this for . . . Nora?" she breathlessly asks me.

She's so exquisite, she's my girl, my little firecracker, and when her eyes flood with tears, I want them to fall only so I can lick them away.

Pete grabs a green duffel bag from the back of the Escalade and heads inside with Nora. "Let me take this in for you, Nora."

Riley stands by me, and the girls are looking back at us. No. Melanie is looking at Riley. But Brooke can't take her eyes off me. I push my hands deeper into my pockets. I could grab her to me. Crush her to me. Give her a punishing kiss for leaving me, and then a loving kiss because I'm fucking insane about her.

She wraps her arms around herself and drops her head. "Why didn't you tell me? That you threw the fight for . . . her?"

She looks forlorn, and, god, I wanted her to feel protected by me. Not ashamed of what I will do for her. "You mean for *you*," I softly tell her.

"I didn't know either, Brooke," Riley says. "Or Coach. Only Pete knew. He's the one who found him that night, and he helped secure your sister while Remington delivered the win."

Her eyes briefly meet Riley's, then they come back to roam all over me. I can feel her touch. Her want. It's in her eyes, trembling in her voice. I want to reach it, touch it, see it, feel it closer.

"How are you? Are you all right?" she asks me, and her sweet concern makes it impossible to think straight. I only nod. *I'm not all right, little firecracker, not even near all right.*

"What does this loss mean for you now?" she asks. She wants to talk, but I don't want to talk about the Underground. I lost something far more important that day and I want it back.

"Other than we're poor?" Riley answers for me. He chuckles too hard. "He has a couple million to get him through the year.

We're making a comeback when the new season starts. Remy's fans demand retribution."

"You do have loyal fans, don't you?" Brooke asks, those gold eyes softly massacring me.

I want to tell her that for a month I have not been aware of everything I have, only what I don't.

"Well, time to go." Riley slaps my back. "Actually, Brooke, we're also here because we're looking for a sports rehab specialist for the upcoming new season. Good to get a head start on training." Riley gives her the card with the details. "In case you're interested, Mr. Tate's number, if you consider, is on the back. There's the hotel where we're staying too. We leave in three days."

Riley climbs into the car, and so does Pete, but I wait for her reaction.

She looks at me, and I stare directly back at her.

My pulse is wild as I want to say a thousand things, play her a thousand songs, and nothing comes out. Out of the mess inside me, the roil and tangle of emotions, I can't say a single word. Not even *Why? Why did you leave me. Why did you say you loved me and leave me.*

"You're looking good, Remy," Melanie says happily.

I smile briefly because I like the way she makes Brooke laugh. I like that Melanie gave me the phone number that started all of this.

She skips away and Brooke remains watching me, and I don't even know where to begin. In my life, nobody has ever told me what she told me in that letter. I'm used to being dropped. I'm conditioned to expect it. But when she said she'd never tire of me, I believed her. When she played me a song about loving me, I fucking *believed* her. And I need her to come back to me on the same two long, sleek legs she used to leave me.

"You know where to find me," I murmur, then I get in the car with the guys and we ride off.

I grab her letter and squeeze it, and for a moment I'm angry again. At myself. At her. At my fucked-up body. I could go back and carry her up to her own fucking apartment, fuck her brains off, and remind her who she cries for, who her man is, perfect or not.

But my pride is so battered, I feel like that stupid boy left at a mental institute, who kept waiting for somebody to come and get him out.

❤   ❤   ❤

I RUN AND run until I am dripping, and even then, every inch of me is tense and waiting. Tomorrow we're scheduled to leave. And I know I can't leave without her. I know me, and I'm going to come back and take her if she doesn't come.

Still, I want for once in my life for someone to come to me because they feel I'm worth it. No, not *someone. Her.* I want the woman I love to come to me because at last someone in this world understands me. How the fuck am I supposed to leave, to live, without her?

I go back to the suite and slam the door—

And like a vision, I see her, sitting in the living room with Pete and Riley.

She leaps to her feet and an awareness of every stitch of clothing she wears and every detail of her seizes me. I feel the calm I feel for a fraction of a second before a fight, and then the fight is inside me. A thousand emotions racing one after the other. The air buzzes with tension. I can feel arcs of lust leap between us, pulling at my gut. My chest heaves, and I am stunned, and still angry, and then I'm just desperate to bury all of this turmoil I feel inside her and remind her that she's fucking *mine.*

"I'd like to talk to you, Remington, if you have a moment," she thickly whispers.

"Yes, Brooke, I want to talk to you too."

I start walking and let her follow, hating how her voice gets me. The scent of her reaches me, and as I lead her into the master and close the door, my instincts betray me, and I curl a hot hand around her neck and bend to drag a deep inhale of her into my lungs.

She grabs my T-shirt in her fists and buries her face in me. "Don't let me go please," she begs. Renewed anger makes me wrench free, and I hate my weakness.

"If you want me so much, then why'd you leave?" I demand. She sits at the foot of the bed, on a bench, and I am so vividly pained I cross my arms, blocking myself. "Did I say anything when I was manic?"

She looks at me with emotion and her voice carries it. "You wanted to take me to Paris."

"That's a bad thing?"

"And make love to me in an elevator."

"Did I?"

"And to have me in my pink pants," she admits, and blushes all the way up her throat to her cheeks.

I keep waiting for her to tell me the rest, and when she doesn't, I remind her. Because it's something I have played in my head this past month—every part of that moment.

"You forgot the part where we played each other a song," I murmur, and I can't keep looking at her when every ounce in me demands I make a connection.

I take her hand and hear her breath catch softly as I lift her fingers to my lips. My pulse starts getting faster as I turn her hand, spot the flatness of her palm, and drag my tongue over it.

"That picture made me very angry, Brooke," I tell her into

her skin as I drag my tongue all over, tasting her. "When you belong to someone . . . you don't kiss anyone else. You don't kiss his enemy. You don't lie to him. Betray him."

I add my teeth, and it affects her, and her voice trembles through her lips. "I'm sorry. I wanted to protect you, like you protect me. I won't ever go behind your back again, Remy. I didn't leave because you were manic, I just didn't want you to get manic or low because of me."

I nod in agreement, my eyes running over her in confusion. "There's something I might have missed then. Because I still can't understand why, the fuck, you would leave me when I fucking *needed* you!"

Her eyes glisten. "Remy, I'm sorry!" she cries.

I groan in pain and go get the letter from the pocket of my jeans on the chair. I have read it until my eyes can barely stay open. I have held it at night, in my fist, when I was black and depressed and kept telling myself that I was worth something to her. "Did you mean what you wrote to me?" I demand.

"Which part?"

I yank the letter open and point at the words I have clung to, like a sick man, words nobody has ever said to me before. Words I want to hear from her, feel from her:

I love you, Remy.

I want so much to hear it, it infuriates me, makes me crumple the paper again and look at her, burning with need, anger, and despair. Did she mean it? She stares at me and suddenly she begins to nod, and my body tightens with want to hear it. My senses scream. My heart hurts.

"Say it," I whisper.

"Why?"

"I need to hear it."

"Why do you need to hear it?"

"Is that the reason you left after the fight?"

Her eyes well with tears, and they tear at me, but I can't stop pushing, I need to know with every part of me, I'm so fucking hurt.

"Is it, Brooke? Why you left? Or because you're ready to quit on me? I thought you had more mettle, Little Firecracker, I really did."

I scan her features, one by one, and suddenly feel her little finger connecting with a scar on my eyebrow, arrowing pure heat and emotion to my core.

She bursts out saying, "I love you. I *love* you." My breath seizes as she painfully rushes the words out. "More than I've ever thought it possible to love any other human being. I left because you broke my heart, again and again that night, with every one of your bones. I left because I couldn't take it anymore!"

I close my eyes. *I love you* making my breath rattle, leaving me shaken, tormented.

She drops her hand and sounds pained and afflicted. "I don't want you to ever let anyone hurt you deliberately again. Ever. Not even for me, Remy. Never. You are worth. Too. Much! Do you *hear* me?"

I grab her face between my open palms, and I feel the shudder that runs through her body as she absorbs my touch. I look into her eyes and I am not ashamed. I am proud. I am letting her know, quietly, before I tell her in words, what she means to me.

"I'd do it a thousand times for you." I scent her, and I want to growl when I hear her scenting me. "A thousand. A million. I don't care if I'm humiliated. I don't care about anything. All I knew was you were willing to kiss that motherfucker's ink for your sister, and I had to give her back to you."

"Oh, Remy, you didn't have to do anything."

"I did. And I will. And I'd do it all over again. I'm only sorry that only Pete could know. He stayed in a hotel room with her and one of Benny's thugs, then helped transfer her when I delivered the championship. I just couldn't let you stop me, Brooke."

"But you wouldn't even look at me. . . ." She squeezes her pretty eyes shut. "That was as painful as the rest of what happened."

"If I'd looked at you, I wouldn't have been able to go through with it."

She covers her face, and I can see her suffering. I can feel it inside me.

I release her, a painful sound wrenching out of me.

I stand and pace, simmering with frustration and helplessness. "I knew this would happen." My scowl bites into my face and my fucking helplessness eats at me. "That's why I didn't want to touch you. I knew I'd go crazy if I touched you, and now, it tears me open to ask you to *be* with me when I know I'm just going to do something to fucking hurt you again!"

"Yes! Yes, you probably are, you idiot! And it's going to be a damned skydive for me, and I'm going to hang on tight and just jump with you because that's what you do to me. I'm crazy about you. My life now *sucks* without you. I'm not here for the job. Although I love it, but it's *you* I want. It's you I came for that first night. It's always been about you. I want to be with you, but I won't do it only on my side. I want you to love me back, Remy. You've never told me how you feel about me!"

I look at her questioningly, surprised at first, and then dead serious. "Brooke, you honestly don't know?"

She stares, and I kneel before her and hold her face between my hands.

"Jesus, when I saw you that first night in Seattle, I felt like I'd just gotten plugged into a socket. I got high just with the way you smiled at me, Brooke. The way you looked at me with an expression of pain and awe drove me crazy. You turned away to leave, and you wore these really nice pants. Your butt was just up there as you walked away, all perky and round. And I just wanted to finish the damn fight so I could go after you. The former fight I swear I just fought for you to watch me. So you'd see me. See that I'm strong and could fight for you, *protect you*. I daydreamed of kissing you, of making love to you. I was planning it in my head even when I jumped out of that ring and went after you. When your friend gave me your number, I got to the hotel to find a roomful of girls, the kind Pete always has for me, and I couldn't look at any of them. I wanted to look into your eyes and make you smile at me."

I tell her how I googled her. How I immediately told Pete to send her these tickets. How I saw those videos on YouTube. How I decided to *hire* her.

She looks flabbergasted for a moment, her face going pale, her eyes going even wider.

"I tried taking it easy with you. I wanted to know you, and for you to know me, and every day I wanted you more, Brooke. So much. I couldn't touch you and risk messing it up until you knew about me. I wanted you to care for me. I wanted to see if you could understand me. . . . I tortured myself every night, thinking of you in your room, while I was in mine.

"The night we went to the club, and you danced with me, I just couldn't stop myself. I'd been so wound up. And when you knocked down two guys for me, I went crazy protective. I wanted to tuck you into bed and go back and do some serious damage to all four of them. But you stayed with me, and I forgot about fighting, and all I wanted was to have my mouth all over you. I tried to control myself, but on the plane, you killed me with those songs about making love to me. I just had to have you. The thought of having you had me so damned high, I was already drugged with it, and by the end of that fight, I was manic and high on you before I could even get you into my bed.

"And then you woke with me, and I saw that you'd cuddled with me, Brooke. Soft and sweet. The next time I was lying alone in bed, I wanted to cut open my fucking veins wanting you next to me, so I went back for you. That was all that got me through the day, those days. Thinking of getting you in my bed and kissing you breathless. I kept looking through my playlist just trying to find one song that could tell you how you made me feel. Inside. I'm not good at saying this, but I wanted you to know you were special to me, you're unlike any other woman in my life.

"You wanted me to make love to you and you don't know how many times I almost broke down. When I showered you, I swear to god, I was breaking inside. But I couldn't do it, not without telling you there's something deeply wrong with me, and I'm such a coward, Brooke. I couldn't even find the courage to say the word 'bipolar' to you. So, I prolonged my time with you. Because I'm selfish, and I wanted you to care before you knew. Thinking it would make a difference and you'd stay. Not even my own folks could do me long term. But something about you made me think you'd *know* me, *understand* me on a level no one else does."

"Remy," she whispers.

"I was right, Brooke," I add, looking firmly into her eyes. "When I told you about me, you still wanted me. And I've been in love with you for I don't know how long. Ever since you tried to knock me down in the ring, and I ended up putting your little feet against my stomach to warm them. Jesus, when I saw that photograph of you and Scorpion, I wanted to *kill him*. I wanted to give you whatever it was that had made you go to that fucking asshole and kiss his fucking face! I wanted to give that to you, so you would kiss mine instead."

I explain to her what went down in the hotel room with Scorpion, her eyes going soft and teary as she listens to me tell her everything, and that it's the first time I did something right when I was black.

I edge closer and nuzzle her temple, and she shudders against me when I whisper near her ear, "I'm sorry I couldn't tell you, but it had to happen like this. When I told you I wouldn't let you leave me the night I made love to you, I meant it. I want you, Brooke, for me. I can hurt you, I can do stupid shit, but I . . ." I draw back to look at her. "I'm so fucking in love with you I don't even know what to do with myself anymore."

She nods and wipes her tears, and I can see the way she's struggling with her feelings like I am.

"You're going to want to leave me again," I whisper, cupping her jaw. "You can't, Brooke, you can't leave so easy."

I stroke another hand down her hair, and she curls into it, like a kitten seeking my petting.

"You've claimed me, Little Firecracker. You kicked a pair of two-hundred-pound men's asses. I will never get over that. You kicked my whores out. Pete told me. You staked your claim on me, even before you realized I'd staked mine already." I grab her hair in one fist and pull her close. "I'm yours now, and you can't ditch me like you just did. Even if I screw this up, I'll still be *your* screwup."

She presses her body to mine and hooks her slim arms around my neck, her shirt getting soaked with my sweat. "Not my screwup. My Real."

I groan and lick her cheek, and she sinks into my arms as I take my mouth lower. I lick her jaw, her chin, and then her lips. Holy god, I think I won't ever lift my head from these soft, pink, edible lips. I feel her shudder against my diaphragm, and I slip my arms around her back and draw her closer. I lick my way into her mouth, probing her entry, until she opens and gasps and lets me.

"Don't fucking leave me ever again," I murmur, my tongue tracing her lips, top and bottom, then delving deep inside as I open my hands on her ass and give it a squeeze.

She makes me high, rubbing her nipples on my chest, making me throb in every part of me.

"I've got about a thousand songs in a new playlist that says 'Brooke'—all about me missing you, loving you, hating and adoring you," I rasp as I reach under her dress to pull at her panties.

I love that she wore a dress, that she looks sexy, female. Mine.

I want to peel it off with my fucking teeth and try not to get rough as I pull her panties off her legs as she confesses, "I've got some too, I want to spend all day playing them to you."

When I've got her naked, I haul her back on my lap, and she's got me in tangles, my cock pulsing against her through my shorts.

She straddles me and rubs my hard-on, and she's trembling with need. "I love you," she breathes, and I take it from there.

HOURS LATER, SHE'S spent in my bed.

Brooke Sexy-as-Fuck Dumas.

I could lie here with her all night.

Her shiny mahogany hair is spread all over my chest and falling down my right shoulder.

Her warm breath coasts over my pecs while her long, slim, little fingers are sweetly delineating the squares of my abs.

My hands run up and down her back.

I don't know what to touch, where to lick, bite, suck, I just want to do it all at once.

I take a loose strand of hair to rub it between two fingers, then I bend my head and inhale. My head buzzes as her scent fills my lungs. I can never get over the way that feminine scent gets into my gut, tangles me like a knot. It's a sweet fragrance unique to her, and the first time I caught a whiff, I knew she was mine.

All mine.

I'm not letting anyone take her.

I'm not letting her go.

I'm her Real.

She's Mine.

I can barely fit inside my skin. I feel like a fucking king who's just inherited a kingdom named Brooke Little Firecracker Dumas.

I open a hand to cup the back of her head and place a kiss on her forehead. She moans softly and turns her head to kiss my chest. I peer down at her pretty face and trace my thumb along her lower lip. I'm wild about this mouth. The things it says to me. The things it does to me. The way it feels, the way it tastes, the way it looks.

I drag my lips along her forehead, the shell of her ear, inhaling her and feeling every inch of her small, lean body against mine. She's sweaty and sticky with me and she's warm as a little sun. I nuzzle her earlobe and then I lick her, pushing my tongue gently into the crevice.

I feel her shudder as I pet my other hand down her head and then down her smooth back while I have my way with her ear, slowly letting my tongue make love to it, and I can't get enough.

I pull her over me and swipe her hair to the side, then I bury my face in her neck so her nose is tucked into my throat and I'm tucked in hers. "Brooke Dumas," I murmur huskily into her ear. "I love you, my little firecracker."

She sighs into my neck and slides her hands into my hair and sifts her fingers through my scalp. "I'm so happy," she says. She eases back and looks at me, her eyes shining in the darkness.

She meets my gaze with a smile, and I know I'm smiling back at her, and she's naked like I like her and suddenly my eyes rake her up and down. I've been starved for the sight of her, and now I'm going to look my fill until my eyes burst. Her breasts, her abs, her toned little arms, her slim throat, her lovely chin, her high cheekbones, her smart, proud little forehead.

"Remy . . ." she whispers.

She reaches out with one hand, and she starts caressing my jaw so tenderly it's like she can't believe she's in my arms.

I cup her little face in my big hand and stroke my thumb across her lips because I can't believe it too.

"Come here." I sit up and cup the back of her head and pull her to me. I bury her face in my neck and squeeze her closer. She straddles me and wraps her arms around my neck. She kisses my neck and I rub my hands all over her body.

"You won't leave me again," I growl softly into her hair, and she kisses the tendons of my neck, then grasps my jaw in her small hands and kisses my nose, my forehead.

"I love you. I'm going to say it until you're so sick and tired of hearing it, you'll kiss me to shut me up," she tells me.

I laugh. "That'll never happen." I clutch her tight and pull her face back. "I'll kiss you anyway."

I buzz her lips and she licks me softly, like I lick her, and I growl and suckle her tongue. I love her so much. She's given me love in ways no one in my life ever has. I had never known someone could love me until she loved me. So alien it is to me, I wasn't even sure why she spent nights stroking my head and I'd wake up to find her sleepy but still running her little hands all over me. I know how she defends me when I can't. I know how strong she is. As strong as I need her to be.

"I'm going to rain kisses all over you," she whispers.

I growl softly and nod. When she speaks, I listen because her words are my sweetest music. When she tells me her stories, about her friends. Her words have always done stuff to me—and her touch . . .

The knots inside me tighten as she drags her teeth up my jaw, up to my temple, and I squeeze my eyes shut and inhale heavily through my nostrils while my body responds fiercely to her caresses.

My muscles tense; my heart picks up, and I want to sink inside her and feel her warmth and her love, her understanding and her acceptance. Making love to her makes me feel whole and perfect, like I was made to provide and protect and mate with this woman. *My* woman.

She just came back to me.

I've been hurting like a motherfucker for over a month, wanting nothing but my Brooke.

I want her to know that she's mine. That I'm going to protect her and that I'm going to be there for her. That I love her. That it doesn't matter to me anything except she's here and she's not leaving me again because I won't allow it. Not a single part of me will allow it.

No. I'm the one who wants to feel that she's mine.

That she'll never leave me.

That she will love me and touch my face and my hair in the way she touches me and everything inside me goes still and focuses on that single tender touch, the point of contact of my body with hers.

I rub my thumb over her tears and lick them one by one as they keep coming, my brain shooting a thousand words in my head. *Female. Beautiful. Mine.* I want to say it all but instead I don't say anything and roll her over and cover her. I tug on her earlobe, and her sobs have turned to whimpers as I ease inside her. She slides her arms up my chest and curls her fingers on my shoulders, and I grab her breasts and squeeze them gently like she likes, then I kiss each tip with only my lips.

She arches her spine and mews when I add my teeth on the tips, and a shudder rocks her body when I swipe the little, hard points with my tongue.

She twists her neck aside when I twirl my tongue up her skin, and she opens her throat to me. I bite close to her pulse point, and she gasps and grabs my hair to lock me in place. She moves her body under mine, keeping my face to her neck. My every muscle is coiled for release. My body is used to pain, I've trained it to embrace it, but this is soul deep and I hurt with it.

I lick the spot on her neck where I just bit, and she claws her nails along the bunched up muscles on my back. *"Remington . . ."*

A desperate plea is in her voice. I grasp her hips and thrust harder as I sink my teeth into her and suck her skin.

Mine.

If I'd even known she existed before, I would have hunted her. I would have caught and conquered her.

Mine mine *mine.*

I scrape her gently with my teeth and then suck again. A bubbling sound leaves her and she tightens her hold on my head. I smooth my tongue out to caress the spot in case it stings, and then I take it up again, sucking so it leaves a mark, so that she will feel it, feel me on her skin tomorrow. She shudders. I delve my hand to rub her beautiful little clit as I mark her.

I'm going to mark her in every way I can. I want her to wear the clothes I give her, the food I get her, I want her to wear my ring, my body on hers, I want her to wear my name.

Mine.

She's going to be mine.

In every way possible.

PRESENT

SEATTLE

The church is small, hot, and, now, packed with attendees.

Up front, flowers line up against the wall beneath a massive cross that seems to watch over the churchgoers.

The last time I'd looked at a cross, it had been held over my head while I was tied and furious in my bed. Not for a moment had I stopped squirming. I was bleeding from the binds they'd used to strap me in various places. I don't remember that directly. But I do remember waking up from a hypnosis session to be told exactly what I described, and what I said. Did it matter? No. Do I wonder about it? No. It's as inconsequential as a dream.

Her family is here. Her friends.

A cross. The circle.

Never cared much for praying, but for my son and my wife's safety, I pray.

From the door of the church behind me, I hear "Gah!" and I twist around and see him. Racer.

He obviously saw me, and his two chubby arms are flailing in the air and his dimple is aimed my way. Josephine shows him a toy, and he is immediately attracted to its bright red color. He grabs it and sticks it in his mouth. And my heart starts whacking when I see the closed doors behind them.

After all we've been through, my wife is finally here to marry me.

"Dude, I'm going to get sentimental."

"Shut it," I whisper.

Murmurs surround us as the choir sets up. We discussed this for weeks. We didn't want a wedding march.

But, at the end of the day, Brooke actually did. She'd frowned as we stepped out of the shower and used her towel to dry her hair first, "Now that I think about it, it's the only time in our lives we'll hear that song. I'm only ever marrying *you*."

I dragged my towel over my chest, then I hooked it around her waist, using it to pull her against me. "What do you want? Tell me what you want so I can give it to you?"

She flattened her breasts to my diaphragm as I spread the towel to engulf us both. "I want a tiny little church where it's almost just us," she whispered, kissing my Adam's apple and then reaching up to caress my dimples. "And I want the march, the white dress, white roses, and you. Every second after our vows, I want to be with you."

I seized her chin and tipped her head back farther, my lips curling. "Then your wish," I whispered, kissing her lips, "is mine to grant."

PHOENIX

We're hopping from location to location for the new season, and while Pete and I check us into our Phoenix hotel, something makes my hackles rise. I turn around to spot Brooke across the lobby, heatedly arguing with Riley, who's heatedly arguing back.

"Hey." I reach them in five steps and immediately grab Riley by the collar. "What the fuck are you doing?" I demand.

Scowling, he pulls free and signals at Brooke, who's scowling back at him. "I was trying to explain to Brooke, here, that things weren't as happy when she was away."

I don't know what Riley's arguing about, but I do know this: I don't like the look on Brooke's face. I don't like the way her lips look downturned at the corners, and I let the asshole know it. "It's done with. You got that?" I angrily push my finger into his sternum until he stumbles back. "You *got* that?" I demand.

"Yeah, I got that," he grumbles.

Good. I curl my fingers around the back of Brooke's neck and I guide her into the elevator and then into our suite.

We head inside and she goes straight to the window, and I survey her round little ass. That ass is mine. "You like the room, little firecracker?" I wrap her in my arms I press into her body. "Want to hit the running trail when it gets dark?"

I play with her neck with my lips, when she turns around.

"Did you fuck other women?"

She looks at me with a new somber gleam in her eyes, and I stare back like a fucking idiot, not understanding what the fuck is going on.

"I realize I have no right to ask you." She surveys me, and I survey her. "We broke up, right? It was the end of it. But . . . *did you*?"

It dawns on me that she's jealous.

My little firecracker. Jealous.

Of me.

"It matters to you?" I ask her, smirking as my chest crams with all the shit only she makes me feel. "If I slept with anyone?"

She grabs a couch pillow and hurtles it into my chest, eyes flashing. "What do you think, you fucking jerk?"

Grabbing the pillow, I toss it aside, smiling in amusement. "Tell me how much it matters," I croon, dodging another pillow and loving her cheeks this pink and pretty.

"Tell me!" she screams.

"Why?" I demand. She's backing away, but I'm coming right after her. "You left me, little firecracker. You left me with a sweet letter telling me, very nicely, to go fuck myself and to have a nice life."

"No! I left you with a letter that told you *I loved you*! Something you hadn't told me until I came back to you and *begged you* to tell me."

"You're so fucking cute like this. Come here." I pull her into my arms but she struggles to pull free.

"Remington. You're laughing at me!" she cries wretchedly.

"I said come here," I say, gathering her closer, and I'm fucking dying to kiss her senseless.

"Remy, tell me! Please tell me, what did you do?" she jealously begs, squirming to get free as she looks up at me. I swear I could look into her eyes all day, look into her face all day.

Using my body to flatten her against the wall, I place my forehead against hers and look into her eyes. "I like that you're jealous. Is it because you love me? Do you feel proprietary of me?"

"Let go," she angrily breathes, squirming between me and the wall.

God, she's so lovely. I cup her cheek and softly tell her, "I do. I feel completely proprietary of you. You're mine. I'm not letting you go."

"You said *no* to me," she angrily grits out, her eyes burning with fury. "For months and months. I was dying for you. I was going crazy. I . . . came . . . like a fucking idiot! On your fucking leg! You withheld yourself from me until I was . . . dying a little inside with wanting you. You've got more willpower than Zeus! But the first women they bring to your door . . . the moment I'm gone, the first whores they happened to bring you . . ."

"What would you have done if you were here? Stopped it?" My dare comes out as a whisper, and I'm struggling not to re-member how I felt when I realized she fucking LEFT ME!

"Yes!" she cries.

"But where were you?" I demand, my blood starting to simmer.

"Where were you, Brooke?" I demand. I curl my hand around her throat and caress the pulse point with my thumb, searching her eyes.

"I was broken," she whispers. "You broke me."

"No. You. Your letter. Broke me." Watching her, I trail my thumb along her throat and jaw, and then I watch as I trace her pink mouth, the only mouth I want. "What does it matter if I had to kiss a thousand lips to forget these?"

We hear a knock. I don't move.

My body is tight and ready to claim hers. She's my mate, and I want her to fucking tell me she's jealous because I'm hers, and she's mine, and that's the end of it.

Then I want her to take me inside, I want to pound her hard and fill her with me.

But she doesn't speak. My stubborn little minx doesn't speak.

Letting her cool down, I open the door, tip the bellman, and pull in the suitcases on my own as fast as I can, one of my arms shooting out to stop her when she walks past me. "Come here, settle down now," I command.

But she pushes my hand away, then steps out and says to the bellman, "Thank you. Would you send this duffel with that other suitcase to the other room?" she says, pointing at her suitcase.

Nodding, the guy pushes the cart back toward the elevators.

"Where are you going?" I ask.

She turns around and looks at me, breathing slowly, looking at me with wide, pained eyes. "I want to sleep with Diane tonight. I don't feel so well and I'd rather we talk about it when I . . . when I . . . am *settled down*."

I burst out laughing. "You can't be serious."

My laughter dies when she boards the elevator.

I stand there. My heart pounding for me to chase. But I'm too disbelieving to move.

The elevator closes.

And yes.

My woman. Just fucking boarded. That shit elevator. And left me here!

I grab my suitcase and toss it across the room with a yell, then I slam the door behind me and go kick the shit out of it.

"FUUCK!" Then I kick the pillow that is still on the floor, clamp my jaw and call Pete so he can give me Diane's fucking room number.

When he answers, and I speak, I sound murderous. "Diane's fucking room number."

"Wh-whaaat? Shit, Rem, Riley told me about the argument . . . please just count to fucking a hundred before you do anything," Pete says.

"The room. Now."

"Two–four–three–eight."

I slam the phone down and silently does as he says and count to a hundred.

I've got the phone in my hand by number 98, and by 99, I got my fucking finger on the numbers. I finally pound the keys, and when Diane's voice answers I very softly, and very angrily growl, "I'm going down there for Brooke, so you can either open the door for me, or I can break it down. Your choice."

I slam the phone and stop at the door, telling myself to breathe.

But I can barely pull the air into my lungs I'm so agitated at the thought of not sleeping with her. I'm agitated remembering she *left me*. She could leave me. Any. Fucking. Day. Again. *Until* I win this championship and make her *marry me*.

I'm so ready to make her my wife, my body preps me as if for a physical fight, and I'm ready to hunt and capture her. I squeeze my knuckles and focus on my breath as I head two floors down, and the instant I reach the door, Diane opens it.

Shit, but I think *I wanted to break that fucking door!*

"Diane," I greet her, then I head straight for Brooke. She's curled in a fucking ball, crying on that bed, and all my anger and frustration arrows to stiffen my cock up instantly.

Because more than jealous, more than possessive, she's hurt.

And my body seems to think the way to make it better is to turn those sobs into moans.

God, I need to fuck her and get fucking close to her. I need to kiss her and pet her.

I need her. In. My. Room. My Bed. And my body in *her*.

"You," I quietly tell her, opening my hand. "Come with me."

"I don't want to." She wipes a tear.

Breathing through my nose, I try to stay calm, telling her, "You're mine and you need me, and I want you to please come the fuck upstairs with me."

She sniffles.

"All right, come here." Grabbing her by the hips, I swing her up in my arms. "Good night, Diane."

She kicks and struggles, but I clench my hold on her to still her, bending to whisper to her, "Kick and claw all you like. Scream. Hit me. Curse the fuck out of me. You won't sleep anywhere but with me tonight."

She's silently angry as I head to our room, but I'm fucking angrier that she had the fucking balls to try and leave me if only for half a moment. I don't even know why we're fighting about this. I was amused by her jealousy, but I'm not amused anymore. I need to be inside her, and I need it now. One touch and she'll fucking *know* she's every woman to me.

Inside our room, I toss her on the bed and jerk off my T-shirt, then I reach out to get rid of her clothes. She flails and kicks at me, her face still streaked with tears as she edges back. "You asshole, don't touch me!"

"Hey, hey, listen to me." I trap her in my arms and hold her gaze with mine, my heart pounding as my hunter instincts kick in full gear in preparation to make her mine again. "I am insane about you. I've been in hell without you. In hell. Stop being ridiculous," I tell her, meaningfully squeezing her face. "I love you. I love *you*. Come here."

I haul her onto my lap, and she quietly starts crying. Every soft sob rips me in two. I remember it all. I may not remember what I did when she was gone, but I remember the emptiness of her like a curse on me. Maybe I fucked up, but all I probably did was try to fill the void she left in me which nobody can ever fucking fill but her.

"How well did you think I'd cope when you left?" I ask her, hurting like a son of a bitch at the reminder. "Did you think it would be easy on me? That I wouldn't feel alone? Betrayed? Fucking lied to? Used? Discarded? Worthless? Dead? Did you think there wouldn't be days where I loathed you more than I loved you for tearing me apart? Did you?"

"I've left everything for you." She looks straight at me, hurt as if I did her bodily harm. "Since I met you, *all I wanted* was to be yours. You said you were mine. That you were my . . . my . . . *Real.*"

A pained groan leaves me as I squish her to me, quietly rasping, "I'm the realest fucking thing you're ever going to have."

She still looks up, and those hurt, tear-filled eyes of hers claw me like talons. "It should've been me all those times," she says tearfully. "It should've been just me, only me."

"Then don't fucking tell me you love me and leave me. Don't fucking beg me to make you mine and then run the first chance I'm not fucking looking. I couldn't even come catch you. Is that fair to me? Is it? I couldn't even get up on my own fucking legs and come stop you."

She sobs harder, and my chest fucking hurts for the both of us.

"I woke up to read your letter instead of getting to see you. You were all I wanted to see. All. I wanted. To see," I quietly tell her.

Fuck. Maybe I wish I hadn't said that, but she hurts me and she doesn't know it. I'm strong physically but she guts me. What she does guts me, and her pain—caused by me—guts me most of all.

As she cries herself to sleep, her sobs softening gradually until all that's left is a hiccup in her soft breaths, I breathe her hair and hold her tighter than ever. I never ever want her to leave. Not even for a night to sleep in Diane's suite. I don't remember what I did when she left me, I was so out of it. But it doesn't matter, nothing mattered but that *she* wasn't with *me*.

When she's sound asleep, I start stripping her clothes, leaving her panties for last, pulling them down her leg and tossing everything aside. I stand up to strip myself too, then I get back in bed, naked.

I'm so fucking hard my balls hurt, but Brooke shivers in her sleep and searches for my body heat, innocently rolling in her sleep to press closer to me. "That's right, I'm right here," I say and wrap my arms around her. I drag my nose along her nape, petting her during the night, scenting and licking her. "I only love you. You're mine, and I'm yours. Nobody will ever have me but you."

❤ ❤ ❤

SHE'S TANGLED IN bed with me two mornings later.

Yesterday morning, she was quiet and angry at me, but this morning I've finally appeased her, and she's relaxed and in my arms. Her dark hair is spread behind her pillow and she's resting on her stomach, her face buried in my chest while I at last pull in a good breath.

Hell, I felt like such an unwanted piece of shit yesterday, every breath felt like I was pulling in water. I got punched last night at the fight so she would stop ignoring me and touch me.

She wouldn't touch me and I couldn't fucking stand it.

She had no choice but to touch me after the fight.

She was worried about me, tending to my cut lip up to the point she realized I took the hits on purpose. Then she was all fire and anger, ordering me into the shower so she could rub me with her oils after. I like to let her think she can order me around. But not this time. I carried her into the shower with me and told her she would fucking love me if it killed us *both*. Jesus, I'm so fucking greedy when it comes to her.

"You coming to the gym?" I quietly ask, massaging her butt with the palm of my hand.

She doesn't stir. Pressing against her back and scenting the back of her ear, I nip her playfully, then tongue her ear, and my cock hardens instantly, and a quick glance at the clock tells me there's time for that. "You're the most fuckable thing I've ever had the pleasure of seeing, touching, and sucking the hell out of," I rasp, nuzzling her.

She sighs softly. I force myself to get up and brush my teeth, then I grab my clothes from the closet and ram my legs into my sweatpants. She's still asleep, and I'm still hard, so I set my T-shirt aside, and go back to bed to wake her.

I pull the sheet down so the cold air makes her skin pebble and I can lick all those little cold bumps on her ass. I bite one cheek, then the other, sliding my hands between her legs to cup her pussy, growling softly when my cock starts pulsing, but when she doesn't squeal or so much as move, I frown and ease back to look at her.

Last night she was tired, and yet she still let me have her. She was languid as I fucked her, letting me turn her, suck her, finger and tongue her. She kept coming fast and hard for me every time, her eyes dewy and sleepy, watching me as I told her how good she felt, how good she smelled . . .

You're so hard for me, I love having you in me, she breathed, half-asleep.

I want to fucking live in you, I said, again and again, as I've said before.

She sighed and came, and after our fight, I still couldn't have enough, so after relaxing for an hour or two, I woke her up, scented her, and fucked her, loving how wet she was.

She's sleeping so soundly now I can't wake her again. Running my eyes down her curves, I make love to every inch with my eyes, then I pull the sheets and cover her back up, leaning over as I brush her dark hair behind one ear.

I press my lips to her ear, "Dream of us." Then I pat her butt again and stand. I bounce in place a few seconds to bring the blood from my cock back to my limbs and brain, then I head out to the kitchen to find Diane already on breakfast.

Pete is already in the living room, dressed and with the car keys.

I grab a green bar and a protein shake, tell Diane to feed my girl, and then we're off.

We're not a block away when Pete's phone beeps. He answers, "Yeah," and starts listening, his smile vanishing and his face paling by the second. My instincts shift into overdrive. My heart starts kicking harder and deeper.

BROOKE.

BROOKE.

BROOKE.

Pete swerves the car around and tosses me the phone as he speeds back into the hotel driveway. Diane's voice screeches out of the receiver before I even place it on my ear, "Get back here! Get back here *please!*" she begs.

I see red.

Before the car screeches to a halt, I yank open the door and charge out and into the elevator, my reflexes lightning fast. Pete slides in behind me, and neither of us says a word as I press the floor button over and over as we head up.

"REMINGTON!" Diane screams from the door when I charge out the elevator with Pete running after me. I charge past Diane and slam the door wide open only to see Brooke motionless on the floor, a puddle of water surrounding her, and soft crying sounds trembling out of her.

And there are . . . scorpions! All over her! Lightning fast, I charge over, grabbing and crushing them in my hands one by one. Stingers sink into my palms, but there's no pain. All my senses are honed in on Brooke. The way she's crying, the way she's trembling, everything I see making me half mad. I toss the last scorpion aside and pull her like a man clinging to life into my arms, and she's shaking and whimpering while I struggle to breathe through my nose, my body trembling with the need to fight and protect her, my system overloaded with adrenaline as a rage unlike any other starts bubbling in my veins.

"I got you," I passionately hiss as I wipe her tears, squeezing her to me. "I got you. *I got you.*"

If I lose her, it's over for me. I'm done.

"A woman just came and knocked! She said Remy had ordered the box for her!" Diane cries out between sobs.

I don't hear the rest of what they're saying. I squeeze Brooke closer to my body and bend to her little ear. "I'm going to kill him," I angrily promise her. "I swear to god, I'm going to kill him so slowly."

Pete is whacking the scorpions with a frying pan, telling me something which runs in through one of my ears, and out the other.

I'm too busy rubbing my hands up Brooke's arms and run my eyes up and down her body, inspecting her skin for marks. "Where did they bite you? Tell me exactly where, and I'll suck all the poison out."

"I . . . e-everywhere . . ." she says, looking helplessly up at me. God, I love her, I love her I love her and I'm sucking every drop of poison out of her.

"You shouldn't suck on these—let me have a look at her," Pete says as he comes over.

She's trembling so hard, I fucking can't let go, so I shake my head and tighten my arms around her and rock her. "I got you, little firecracker, I got you right here in my arms," I whisper fiercely. Brooke trustingly clings to me, and it guts me that I just left her, safe and warm in my bed.

Rage and impotence flood me.

"Rem, let me see her," Pete insists.

"No," she moans, clutching me. "Don't let go, don't let go," she continues to moan.

"Never," I promise in her ear, my heart crashing fiercely into my ribs. Never.

I need to protect her. I need to make it better. I need the poison out of her body if it's the last fucking thing I do.

"According to Google, they're Arizona bark scorpions. Venomous but not deadly," Pete says as he searches his phone.

"Hang on to me," I whisper to Brooke, and when her arms are tight around my neck, I lift her up and cross the room.

"Where the heck are you going with her, Tate?" Pete demands.

"To the fucking hospital, dipshit," I growl, angrily heading toward the elevator. I'll walk us to the hospital if I have to, but there's a familiar buzzing in my body, and I'm starting to believe I might even fly us there.

Pete yells after me, "Dude, Diane just called the EMT. Let's just take a fucking chill pill and give her some Benadryl."

"*You.* Take a chill pill. Pete," I snap back.

Fucking motherfucker.

Brooke is almost fucking convulsing in my arms. She can't focus. She's been stung by these asshole animals and I need her. To be. Tended.

"I'm awright," she says as she blinks dazedly at me, "I'm awright, Wemy. . . ."

My body temperature plummets. I look at her, and she's not only talking in a way that makes me want to kill something, but she's staring at my fucking ear like it's one of my eyes! "FUUUUUCK ME!"

The elevator doors roll open, and Riley steps off. "All right, what's going on? Coach is waiting at the gym, Rem. . . ." He sees Brooke in my arms, and his eyes widen.

"Live scorpions," Pete informs. "Venomous, but fortunately not deadly."

"I can't bweathe," Brooke says, looking at my ear again, as if waiting for my ear to explain this shit to her.

I can't fucking see anymore, my vision is blurred from my rage and impotence and I want to kill. Kill. KILL.

"The poison spreads through the nervous system, but it doesn't enter the bloodstream. Try to stay calm, Brooke. These bark scorpions are nasty suckers. Can you feel your legs?" Pete asks.

She shakes her head as she wheezes out air, and Pete leans over to inspect the damage. "Let me see that. . . ." I extend out her arm so that he looks at the stings, and I look directly into Pete's eyes, "I'm going to kill him," I tell Pete.

"It'll be all right, B," Pete tells her, watching me warily and staring into my eyes with growing alarm as he adds, "I've had the experience once. Awful, but you really don't die from a North American scorpion."

"There's a note! I turned the box over and there's a note!" Diane cries.

"What does it say?" Pete walks back to the suite's open door, grabs the note, and automatically reads. " 'You've kissed me. Now you've been kissed back by the Scorpion. How does it feel to have my venom in you?' "

My testosterone spikes. My heart jerks. My body tightens. Adrenaline shoots through my body and my mind snaps. My control, my fucking sanity. *Snap!* I'm going to kill Scorpion, and I want to dismember him before I do. Spreading his teeth across the floor. Pulling his brain out of his fucking head.

I'm fully engaged.

I'm going to dismember and get rid of the fucking threat. NOW!

Brooke moans softly, and I look down at her, pale, scared, and trembling, and my murderous determination grows tenfold at the thought of anyone, anyone, messing with my girl!

"Pete, I saw his goons downstairs in the lobby. I think he's here at the hotel," Riley says.

"The motherfucker is probably downstairs waiting for Remington," Pete murmurs, rubbing a hand across his face.

"Oh, he has it coming!" I thunder. "He's *already dead!*"

I'm going to make it slow. And painful. And I'm going to shove a burning firecracker up his fucking ass AND WATCH HIM EXPLODE!

Brooke. She's trembling. She's holding onto me, expecting me to protect her. He got to her in my fucking hotel suite! I will never fail to protect her again. Nothing will ever hurt her again. I am Remington Tate—Riptide—and I am HER MAN, HER PROTECTOR, and I am going to take care of this RIGHT. NOW.

Blood boiling, I'm touching the back of her head, and I look at her face, her glazed eyes and the tears on her skin, and I've never been more ready to commit murder, but I manage to speak softly when I tell her, "I need to do something right now. I love you. I fucking love you to pieces, and I'm going to come back and put you back together again, all right?"

She nods and trembles, and my gut is being cut on the inside, because I don't want to leave her either, goddammit.

"Why is she shaking like this, goddammit?" I ask Pete as I carry her back to the room.

He looks at me apologetically. "It's the nervous system being affected. She sustained several stings, so it'll be painful. While the EMT is on his way, let's give her some Tylenol."

Tylenol, yes. Tylenol and murder. My body is so wired and I'm single-minded. I feel like a robot who's just been programmed to kill, and the fact that he hurt my little firecracker was the trigger button.

Heart pounding, muscles tightening, system overworking, I carry her back to the room and set her on the sofa, inhaling the top of her head. Every minute that motherfucker enjoys life while Brooke has trouble breathing is penance. Every fucking bite I see on her skin screams at me to go hurt whoever hurt her.

That's right. I'm Death. I am fucking Death and I'm coming for him now.

"I'm going to go crush him now," I tell her. With all the love I feel for her, I'm doing it.

I'm charging off to the elevator and hear Pete yell after me. "Damn it, he's full speed ahead, Ri, go after him before he sees Scorpion or *any* of his goons— Diane! Get some cold compresses and wait for the EMT. We need to go get that man!"

Ha. They're not fucking stopping me. I head for the stairs so they won't find me in the elevator and run down several flights.

When I shove open the exit door into the lobby, I see them immediately. He's right there. Scorpion. Two goons. He's looking at me. I look at him and curl my fists. "You're dead, asshole."

He grins. "Your crowd is waiting," he says.

The elevators to my right *ping*.

Riley steps off, and he sees me.

"Rem," he says cautiously, holding the elevator door open as he spots Scorpion and his crew. "Rem, I can't let you do this."

"Don't make me break you, brother," I warn him, and that's when I feel a prick behind me.

The darkness pulls me, but I'm not going down. I'm not going to go down until Scorpion bleeds to death and Brooke is safe in my arms.

"Dude, you weigh a fucking ton!" Riley adjusts me as he and Pete start trying to get me up the stairs. "Good job, Pete, those assholes didn't even see you behind him."

"Fuck you," I growl.

God, fuck me. Fuck Pete. Fuck Riley. Fuck Scorpion I'm going to kill that motherfucker on the ring! I hope it's a submission fight and he's so fucking proud he won't submit and I'll just BREAK. HIS. FINGERS. THEN HIS ELBOWS. HIS FIBULA. TIBIA. HIS SKULL. THEN HIS NECK.

The guys are panting, floor by floor, and they both keep telling me to hang on while I keep telling them to take me to Brooke.

"Hang on, buddy," Pete says breathlessly as he helps Riley bring me back to the room.

"Need to see Brooke," I insist.

They get me on the bed and I hear Pete telling Riley to "Get the other side" and ask me what the hell he's going to do with me.

"*Brooke,*" I angrily tell them.

"She's coming, dude!" Pete says, laughing at my stubbornness.

They prop a pillow up behind me and I see her. Diane is helping her to bed, and I look worriedly at her.

My girl. God my girl hurt because of me.

"Okay?" I rasp out.

She smiles softly at me as she eases into bed and pulls the cover over us both, sliding her fingers into my hair.

"More than okay," she says, her eyes bright with love and understanding. All the tension in my body leaves me when she speaks to me. I was fighting not to succumb to the sedative, but her voice makes me unwind, and I succumb to her.

❤ ❤ ❤

BROOKE HASN'T RECOVERED from the stings, and I'm still black as fucking midnight.

She's been sleeping too much, and she spent the flight to Las Vegas sequestered in the toilet. The word pregnant has been popping out of Diane's mouth.

Pregnant.

Eight letters, one word that makes my chest swell, my cock hard.

"I'm not pregnant!" Brooke's been telling me.

She keeps denying it, but I swear to god I can almost smell it on her. I smell it on her and it makes me even *harder.*

While she takes a home pregnancy test, I've run around a worn path on the hotel carpet, but the urge to fuck is still acute. Now I'm shadow boxing between the bed and the seating area, trying to get rid of all this extra energy and pull the blood out of my cock. Pump, swing, pump. Holy shit, she could be pregnant. My balls draw tight at the thought and my cock jerks again. God, I hope she's pregnant. Now. I fucking *pray* she's pregnant. Sensing her all of a sudden, I turn around, and she's watching me with a lost, thoughtful look in her eyes.

"You check yet?" I ask impatiently.

She jerks at my voice and looks at me, looking thoughtful and delectable. Once again, my cock goes up.

"Brooke?"

She gnaws on the inside of her cheek and frowns, her expression uncertain.

"Did you or did you not pee on a stick, baby?" I prod.

"I did! I told you I did!" She goes back into the bathroom and comes out with a white stick. She looks at it, and I'm so restless, and so primed to mate, I continue pumping the air.

I swear if she's not pregnant, we'll remedy that soon. I'll keep fucking and taking and claiming her until she *is*. I want to be the father of her children. I want her to be mine. Every breath, every sigh, every moan of hers, *mine mine mine*. Her body mine, to have my children, to have me inside her. Mine to protect, to pet, to kiss, every inch mine to run my tongue over.

Feeling hot and hungry for her, I watch as she studies the test result, and I want it so bad, I'm running out of patience. "What's it say?" I demand.

"It says . . ." She stares down at the stick, then she sets it aside, and starts walking over to me, and she looks fucking adorable, and womanly, and vulnerable.

"Remington, don't forget this," she whispers, framing my face in her hands and looking into my eyes. "You're black right now, and I don't want you to forget what I'm going to tell you. I need all of you here *with me*."

"Hey." I frame back her face in mine, looking deeply into her eyes. "I got you."

"God, please do."

"Yeah, I do. I got you. Now what's wrong here? Hmm? If you aren't, then we figure out what's wrong with you. If you are . . ."

She runs over to get the test, then she returns and extends it out. "Two lines means, supposedly, that I am."

My eyes remain on hers for a moment. Does she want to be? Fuck, she better want to be. She *better* be.

I stare at the screen at the end of the stick and immediately see the double lines.

I frown because I need to be sure, but already, my insides are buzzing with pride.

I still see two lines.

More buzzing in my body, buzzing in my skin. I think I just grew ten sizes wide and high.

I lift my gaze to her, and she looks uncertain, as if she doesn't know whether to be worried or happy. "Come here." Unable to hold back my smile, I pick her up and lift her into the air, smacking a kiss on her abs, then I toss her down on the bed. She squeals and bursts out laughing as I fall on her.

"You're a crazy man! You're the only man I know who throws his pregnant girlfriend onto a bed!" she cries.

"I'm the *only* man," I correct her, "as far as I know. There's only one man in your world, and it's me."

"All right, but don't tell my dad I agreed so easily . . ." she whispers, rubbing my shoulders, gold eyes shining on me. I want this baby to have those eyes. That perfect smile.

"Brooke Dumas pregnant with my baby," I tell her. In case she didn't see the fucking test, now she fucking knows she's pregnant by me.

She grins happily, and that pure little grin feels like a kiss all along my pulsing cock. "My head is reeling. Kiss me."

I drop my head and trail my tongue in to mate with hers,

then I drag the back of one finger across her cheek. "Make it look like you," I whisper.

"You're the one who gave this to me," she counters.

"No, *you're* giving this to me."

"All right, we're both such giving souls."

She laughs, and I laugh with her and roll to my side, gathering her in my arms so I can kiss her all over. "You're mine now, from the top of your pretty dark head to the soles of your little feet." I caress her face and kiss her eyelids, and I'm so fucking delighted, I swear things are actually moving in my chest. "Don't even think about leaving me again or I'll come after you and so help me god, I'm going to tie you to where I am, and where I sleep, and where I eat. Do you hear me, Brooke Dumas?"

She nods breathlessly. "There isn't a single part of me that doesn't know I'm yours."

She seizes my hand and spreads it over the curve of her breast, right over her heart.

I clench her breast possessively so she remembers its mine, and I bend my head and kiss her. "*I'm so crazy about you,*" I rasp, and I drag my hand down her lovely curves and pet her.

PRESENT

SEATTLE

Gah!"

The only sound in the silent church comes from one of the front rows, and it is followed by soft laughter nearby.

"Rem, that boy is priceless. He already feels like he's the shit and he's not even one," Pete murmurs behind me.

I glance at my son and he's slapping Josephine now, saying, "Gah!" every time he hits her. Brooke says he'll be just like me, but I hope he'll be better than me.

The doors of the church swing open, and I straighten and stand in place, like I'm supposed to, the anticipation slowly gnawing at me. I rub my thumb along my ring when a figure in white steps forward—and my lungs empty in a whoosh. Fuck me, look at her. Only Brooke does this to me. The noise inside me stills and I feel whole and content, at peace, the instant my eyes lock on hers. And she's so fucking beautiful in that dress my collar suddenly chokes me.

Music starts playing. My bride's music.

When she starts walking toward me, I feel like every step

makes me grow inside my suit the way only she can make me, and I'm about ten sizes too large now and burning beneath the fabric. She didn't hide her face behind a veil. Every step, I see her smile. Her huge, wide, I-fucking-love-you-Remington-Tate smile.

This is my woman pledging her life to me.

This is me, pledging my life to her.

My eyes run over her face, and it's the same face I look for every morning in my bed, and every moment I'm in the ring, and every second in between. She's that girl, with the marshmallow mouth that looks soft and inviting, and those eyes, gold as a lioness's, and yet she tells me she's no longer a girl. She's a woman now. A mother. A wife. *My* wife.

The dress covers her completely, tight around her top and spreading wide at the skirt. She looks so fucking beautiful I want to mate her, take her, right now, slammed by thoughts of grabbing her into my arms, ripping off the dress's buttons and her panties, then spreading her open so I can claim my wife, every sigh of hers, every inch of skin.

I'm so fucking ready for this, I step off the platform to receive her a couple of steps earlier and I lock gazes with her father when I approach. He's unsmiling, his eyes wet, but there's no antagonism in his stare. "She's all yours," he tells me thickly.

I've already slipped my hand to her small one when I nod and murmur, "Thank you," then I bring her up with me to the altar. She stands trembling in excitement at my side, and I duck my head and lean over, brushing my nose against hers so she tips her head back to look at me. Our stares hold.

"Ready?" I ask when we hear the priest begin the ceremony.

"Dearly beloved, we are gathered together here in the sight of God to join together this Man and this Woman in holy Matrimony . . ."

BAD NEWS

Sometimes I wonder if it's me.

If there's something about me that repels the good. And the pure. Or if I'm just not meant to have a family.

Brooke is having trouble keeping our baby, and now we're flying in silence to Seattle.

I carried her to the plane; no Pete, no Riley, no Coach, no Diane flying with us. I want her all for me. All for fucking *me*.

I can't even talk.

I can't even fucking think.

My girl. Our baby.

Breathing slowly, I sit on the bench on the back of the plane and stare up at the ceiling, breathing in and out as I stroke my fingers down her soft hair, her head propped on my lap as she lies down the length of the bench. She's so sad and quiet I can barely take it.

The doctors don't want her traveling with me.

Brooke thought it so ludicrous, she laughed when the last one left our hotel suite, then she looked at me, not laughing anymore.

"You can't seriously be thinking of sending me back? Right? Reming-ton, I'll lie down. I won't fucking move. This is your son. He's going to hang in there! He will. I don't see how being sent away will stress me any less. I don't want to go home. I'll stay in bed all day, just don't take me back!"

My god, I felt like someone was whacking my chest with an axe, especially when I slowly spoke to Pete, who was quietly standing nearby, and I watched her face crumple when I told him, "Get the plane ready."

She cried all night, and all I could do was hold her. "You can't protect me from everything," she whispered, sniffing.

"I can try."

Now we're flying in silence, heading for Seattle.

Where I won't touch her, smell her, or see her.

Bending down to my lap, I kiss the top of her ear, her earlobe, the center of her ear, and there, I whisper that I'm going to miss her, that I'm going to need her to be good, to take care of herself, that I fucking need her.

She doesn't want to talk. She's sad and I don't even know how to make it better. She's my woman and how do I make her smile again? How do I protect her from the child I gave her?

Quietly, I pull out the extension of my credit card I just got her. "Use it," I whisper.

She stares at it in stubborn silence, but she doesn't take it.

"Brooke," I warn, placing the card into her palm. "I want to see charges. Daily."

She looks unimpressed by the fact that I want her to spend whatever she fucking wants, and put it on me. I smile down at her, while Brooke looks somberly up at me, not smiling.

Reaching up, she drags her fingers along my jaw. "When I came back, I promised myself I'd never leave you."

"I promised myself I'd never let you go. What else do you expect me to do?"

I brush her dark hair behind her face, surveying her for a moment. "We're going to be all right, little firecracker," I tell her. I glance at her flat little stomach and spread my hand out, trying to encompass as much as possible. "We've got this." I rub her gently and look deep into her eyes. "Don't we?"

"Of course we do," she says, but she studies me as if she's not certain. "It's just two months, right?"

I tweak her nose. "Right."

"And it's not like we can't communicate in other ways."

"Exactly right."

She sits up and starts massaging my shoulder. "Let your body rest. Ice yourself after your workouts. Warm up properly."

Fuck. Her warmth. The sound of her voice. I dip my nose into her neck and inhale, listening to her breathe me in. I pull her closer and lick her neck, then whisper, so she understands, "I can't let anything happen to you, Brooke. I can't. I had to bring you back."

"I know, Remy, I know." She runs her fingers through my hair and looks at me, as tormented as I feel. "We're going to be all right, all three of us."

"That's the point of all this," I whisper, reminding myself as well as her.

"And like you say, we've got this. We really do."

"Damn right we do."

"You'll be back before we even have time to feel sad or miss each other too much."

"That's right. I'll be training and you'll be resting."

"Yeah."

When we fall silent, we stay close, and she whispers, "I left some arnica oils in your suitcase. If you have any muscle soreness or any pain."

"Are you still seeing blood?" I ask, and when she nods, my concern and frustration feel like a spiked ball in the middle of my chest.

"Every time a cramp starts, I feel like it's going to come out of me," she admits.

Soothing a hand down her back, I press a kiss to her forehead. "I know it'll kill you not to run. Stay off your feet for me."

"Not as much as it would kill me to lose our baby," she whispers.

We ride in silence toward her apartment, and I scoop her out of the car and carry her into the building. She clings to my neck as we walk into the building, up the elevator, and into her apartment, and she feels so right in my arms, I don't even know how I'll let go of her. "Stay. Remington, *stay.* Be my male prisoner. I promise to take care of you all day, every day," she whispers.

I laugh softly, and I look into her laughing, pleading gold eyes, and I don't even know what to do with her, I want to sink in her and live in her.

She gives me a tour of her place, and then we go into her room.

I take in our surroundings as I set Brooke by the foot of the bed. Her room has earth-toned walls. Framed photographs of biceps, triceps, and abs. A nutritional chart, and a framed quote that says:

A CHAMPION IS SOMEONE WHO GETS UP
WHEN HE CAN'T —JACK DEMPSEY

There's a big wall with pinned photographs. And there she is, sprinting past the finish line with a number 06 in her chest.

I reach out to run the pad of my thumb down the length of her running figure. "Look at you," I say, turning. She's right behind me. Standing, like she shouldn't be. I scoop her up and set her on the center of the bed, brushing some escaped tendrils of hair behind her shoulder. "Stay off your feet for me," I chide.

"I will. I forgot. It's habit." She scoot backs on the mattress to make room for me and then she pulls me over her, whispering in my ear, "You should go or I won't let you leave me."

Instead, I cuddle her to me, my arms wrapped around her waist as I scent her, slow and deep, then I lick her slowly, then kiss her and murmur, "When you tell me you're in bed, this is what I'll picture. This is what you see." Her eyes glisten with tears as she quietly nods.

"I'll be back soon," I assure her, curling my palm around her cheek as one lone tear slides down her cheek. I try to smile. "I'll be here soon," I repeat.

"I know." She wipes her cheek, turns her head, and kisses the inside of my palm, then she forces my finger closed around her kiss. "I'll be waiting for you."

"Shit, come here." I crush her in my arms, and she trembles and starts crying for real.

"It's all right," I whisper, rubbing her back, but she sobs harder. I whisper *it's all right*, but the way she cries guts me. It's not anything close to right. She needs me. She fucking needs me and she will be here, without me, struggling to keep our baby. Our baby that might just end up being like me, and instead of making the woman I love happy, our baby will hurt her, just like I do. It pains me. Maybe the child I put in her isn't right. Maybe it's not strong. Maybe it's *just* like me, and everything I don't want her to have to struggle with.

But I'm so fucking selfish, I still want it.

I don't want her to lose it.

I want her, I want everything with her.

"You need to go," she whispers, suddenly pushing me away.

Fuck, I haven't even left and it already hurts as I breathe her in one last time and set my forehead against hers. I take her face in my hand and wipe her tears with my thumbs, rasping, "You okay, baby firecracker?"

"I will be. More than okay," she assures.

Her phone vibrates, and she checks the message, her eyelashes wet with her tears. "Melanie is five minutes away." Her voice cracks in the end as she turns her attention back to me. "Please go before I cry," she begs.

I curl my fingers around the back of her neck and shut my eyes closed as I lean my head on her. "Think of me like crazy."

"You know I will."

I lean closer. "Now give me a kiss."

She presses her lips to mine, and I spread out my hand on the small of her back, memorizing her, drinking her up because I'm going to be thirsty and there won't be water for me until she's home. With me. I feel a tear against my jaw and I lick it up from her cheek when we hear Melanie outside.

"Brookey!! Where's the hot dad and the upcoming momma?"

I curse and take another hard, fast kiss before I go, sucking on her tongue, taking everything I can, then I ease back and survey her pink swollen mouth and beautiful wide eyes, with the dilated pupils, just for me.

"You're everything I never knew I wanted," I huskily whisper, tucking her hair behind her. "And all mine, remember that tidbit," I add, forcing myself to stand. "Completely mine . . . Brooke Dumas."

She watches me back up to the door, her chest heaving, her heart in her eyes. "I'm pregnant with your baby, if there was any doubt about whose I was," she says, with a shaky smile.

"You're both mine." I point right at her. "Especially you."

When I turn, she calls me.

"Hey! You're *mine*, too."

Nodding, I pull out my iPod and toss it straight at her. "Don't miss me too much."

She catches it like she just caught my soul, holding it tightly. "I won't!" she cries, and I memorize every inch of the smile on her face. *Brand it inside your fucking skull, Tate.*

And I do.

It's still in my head when I meet her friend out in the hall. "Hey, Melanie."

She gives me the same doting look all my fans give me. "Hey, Remy."

My eyebrows furrow. "I want to be the first to know anything. If she's sick, if she's lonely, if she *needs* me."

She keeps nodding with that ridiculous smile. "Don't worry, I will call you or make sure she does," she assures, patting my chest with sparkling green eyes. "Now go." She pats my chest again, this time flattening her palms and pushing, to no avail. "Go! You sex god! I'll take care of your girl."

I grab her wrists, lower them, then force myself to head to the elevator. In the car, I'm drumming my fingers on my knees. In the plane, I'm flying with my headphones at my side, but no music. She has my music now. She's ALL. MY MUSIC.

When we land and I power up my phone, I get a message from her.

Call me tonight if you want to?

Hell, of course I fucking want to.

I'm still sweaty in the gym as I try to work out, but I grab my phone and call her, dropping down onto a bench while I suck up my Gatorade. No answer.

I call again.

No answer. After several tries, it vibrates with a text message.

My friends are still here. Maybe we should talk tomorrow?

I set my Gatorade aside to text. Same time?

Yes, any time

My thumbs are too blunt and big and I struggle to pound out Ok

Good night Remy

More struggling to write down You too.

Then I stare at the screen, but there's no more.

I can't sleep that night. I do sit-ups, push-ups, jump rope. I want her to marry a fucking champion, so I've decided I'll be training like one. Hours later, I stop working out, sit up on the carpet, prop my arms over my knees and hang my head between them as I think of the smile I'm carrying around, branded in my head.

I take a shower and play on my iPad, beating the hell out of some guy at chess at five a.m., trying not to think how much I'm craving her. The smell of her, the feel of her, the look of her. I move my pawns and in my head I'm thrusting her and making her moan. In the morning, I'm calling the florist closest to her apartment, but it's too early and they haven't opened.

During breakfast, Pete and Riley study my face. "Who are you calling and calling? Let Brooke rest," Riley says.

I sigh and put the phone down.

"Hey, look at me for a sec, Rem," Pete says, alarm in his voice.

I lift my head, and I meet his gaze so he knows I'm not fucking black. This time my sadness doesn't come from a chemical imbalance in my body. My sadness comes from my heart.

"Remy, here we go," Diane says as she comes up with my

breakfast, and she's smart, that one is. She seems to sense I'm not hungry and will give her shit about the food, and she's blended all kinds of things with egg whites in three huge glasses. I down them one by one. "Why do you keep redialing?" Pete asks, watching me. "I can do it for you, what do you need?"

"I don't want Brooke to miss me."

"All right, so what's the plan?"

I drag my hands down my face and growl, "I feel like I'm breathing under fucking water without her."

"Dude, she's a fighter, like you. They'll be all right. *Both* of them," he stresses.

He heads over to grab my iPad to check the store number. He pats my back before he calls the florist.

"I want hundreds of roses, Pete!" I yell as he walks around the living room, talking into the receiver. "I want them all over her apartment," I continue instructing. "All of them red. And I want every dozen to have a song so she'll think of me. I need her to think of me."

She does, think of me.

She calls and texts me, and I call and text her.

Every day I hear a report on what she did, how she is. The guys tell me it will get easier, but it doesn't. It gets worse.

It doesn't get any better until that fantastic day I finally get to go pick her up and bring her back on the circuit with me.

THE FINAL, FINALLY. My little firecracker and I made an agreement when she came back, and she better fucking stick with it. The thing is, Scorpion has blackmailed her sister back to his side too. Motherfucker.

Pete and I have planted a snitch, and we now know Scorpion

had something on her, which must've been why she went back to that asshole. But I'm not letting Brooke step in this time. Tonight I take care of it all.

This season hasn't been easy, but then nothing worthwhile ever is.

We're headed down the hotel elevator, on our way to the Underground, and I've barely been able to shake myself out of the deepest hole in the history of my lows.

I'm trying to pump myself up for the fight with some mashups as we ride down the elevator, but though my body feels ready, my mind is with my girl. As we shuffle out of the elevator and into the hotel lobby, I grab Brooke by the hips and pull her back to me, murmuring, "In my peripherals."

Her worried gold eyes meet mine, and I yank down my headphones.

"In your seat at all times, Brooke," I say, while winding my fingers into her hair, then I crush her sweet, hot, delicious fucking mouth under mine. She looks dazed when I pull her back an inch, and I set my forehead on hers while I keep my eyes on her. "I adore you with every breath I take—in every ounce of me, I adore you." Another fast, hard kiss later, I slap my favorite ass and whisper, "Watch me *break* him."

I play my music while we ride to the Underground. I need to concentrate, but I'm eyeing the back of her neck, the way her breasts rise and fall, and for a moment, I forward into the future, to the way she'll look at me when I ask her. The guys tell me everything is ready, and I just hope that she is. Ready for me. For all of me.

I'm winning tonight. Even if I have to kill for it. I'm taking it all. Everything I've never had, by force if I have to.

My championship, my woman, I'm winning, and when the

crowd is screaming my name, I'm taking the *yes* out of her mouth that I want.

When we reach the Underground, I keep my headphones on my head as I watch Brooke head to her seat. She ducks her head and spreads her hand over the mound of her little round stomach as she follows Pete, avoiding looking at me. God, she stirs up all my protective instincts and then some.

She's nervous.

I don't want her to be.

The last time she saw me in a final, Scorpion broke me. This time I want her to watch me break him. I want her to be proud. I want her to be proud of being with *me.*

I wait in the locker room—no other fighters here tonight. Just Coach, Riley, and me. They're arguing about something. I can see the tendons popping out of their necks while Coach tapes up my hands. I know it's hard for them to trust me when I'm pulling out of a swing. Maybe they think I'll do what I did last season.

No shit I'm getting Brooke's sister back again. But this time I'm the one who fucks Scorpion in every damn hole of his body. I get the girl, the championship, rescue the sister, and break the blackmailing motherfucker. All of which he can watch from his prime spot inside the ring—with me.

I turn up my music and tune into the rhythm of my heartbeat, the hard, steady pump of my blood reaching every inch of my muscles. I do a mental check, head to toe. Nothing hurts. I study my taped hands and squeeze my fists, popping out my knuckles. Every part of me is ready to fight.

I've been a sad, depressed fuck for weeks. Wondering if I'm good enough for Brooke, for our baby.

Tonight, I'll prove to myself that I *am* worthy.

Despite what every other person in my life has thought about me.

I stop my iPod when I see Riley lift two fingers in the air. Pulling off my headphones, I set them aside and stand to jump in place when I hear the voice out in the arena.

"Ladies and gentlemen, hello! Well, here we are this evening with you all! Are you people ready? Are you all READY for a fight unlike any other? *Unlike ANY OTHER, people!* Ringmaster?"

There's silence.

Breathing as I warm up, I twist my neck to each side, then forward and back.

"Sir, we won't need your services tonight," the announcer says.

The crowd lets loose a roar.

"That's right!" the announcer joins them as he keeps on yelling. "Tonight, there are NO rules, NO ringmaster. Anything goes. ANYTHING GOES, PEOPLE! No knockouts—this is a fight of submission. Submit!"

"Or die!!" the crowd screams.

"Ladies and gentlemen! Yes! It's a submission fight here tonight in the Underground! Now, let's call your worst nightmare into the ring! The man your daughters cry about. The man you want to run from. The man you *certainly* don't want to be up in the ring with. Our defending champion, Benny, the Blaaaack, Scorpionnnnn!"

I keep jumping in place and pumping out my arms, keeping my shoulders loose and my core tight.

"*Booooo!*" the crowd yells outside. "*BOOOOO!!*"

A few feet away, Riley stretches out my RIPTIDE robe, and I step up and ram my arms into the sleeves, tying it loosely around me.

"And challenging our champion tonight, we all know his name! We are *all* waiting to see if he's gonna bring it to this ring tonight. So . . . is he? Get rrrready to welcome the one and only Remingtoooooon Tate, yourrr Riiiiiptide!!"

I charge out the walkway to the instant chant of the crowd.

"Rem-ing-ton! Rem-ing-ton!"

The color red streaks across the arena as the fans stand to greet me. *"Remyyyyy, kill him, Remyyyy!"*

"Go, Rrrrrriptide!"

I leap into the ring and take off my robe, then I look around with a smile, sucking it all in, my fans' faces full of expectation, the way the arena looks in this season's final.

I will not fail.

I stretch my arms out and do my turn so that they can keep on screaming like they like to, feeding me, and the noise heightens as I start slowly turning around.

That's right, I'm going to break him tonight, and it's all for . . .

My eyes spot her, and I smile.

Brooke Dumas.

I have fought my life to control my mood swings. I have fought for my health, for the hell of it, and to vent. I have fought in anger, and tired, depressed, hungry, excited. I have fought to prove myself to my parents when they didn't care. I have fought to prove to myself I'm strong. But now I fight to prove myself to her. And I'm taking this one home.

The bell rings, and I lock eyes on Scorpion and leap into action. Going to center ring, I watch Scorpion jump around for a moment, then I hit him—fast and hard—one punch, two, three. He stumbles back.

"Remy!!"

Brooke is screaming at me, her voice loud, clear, thrilled. It charges me like a bolt of lightning. I drive my fist into Scorpion's jaw and knock him back a step, then I slam him again and knock him back yet another one.

"Go, REMY!!!"

"Kill him, Remy!"

"Remington, I fucking love you! Ohmigod, I love you!" Brooke screams.

Holy god, I'm so fucking wired to show her I'm the man, I'm the only fucking man for her, I drive my knuckles into Scorpion even harder, alternating between guarding, then hitting, guarding, then hitting.

The crowd loves it.

"Kill him, RIP! Kill him, RIP!" they chant.

The fight continues through the night, pausing only during small resting periods where we drop down on our stools and our coaches drill us with instructions.

I listen to what Coach says, pretending to listen, nodding. But it goes in one ear, and out the other. I know what I'm doing. Scorpion and I don't take our eyes away from the other as we head back to center again. I can see it, in his eyes, when he plans to move. We hit again, both of us landing hard punches. He clinches me, but I pull free and slam out my right hook. He covers and pounds my ribs.

My breath goes, but I quickly recover, going at him with my fastest punches, so fast he barely sees them coming. *Wham wham wham.* Soon blood starts pouring out both his nostrils, and his balance is rocking with my hits.

I know I have him, but the gleam in his fucking eye tells me otherwise. He doesn't plan to submit. Swinging out, he hooks an arm around my neck and pulls me down as he rams his knee into my gut.

He looks excited about that. But I don't think I'll let him land any more. Shoving him back, I drive my fists fast and hard into his body, slamming him like I do my hard bags until he's covering, ducking, trying to escape my payback.

I don't let him. I follow and pound him into the ropes.

He falls to his knees and spits on the ground, then he gets up and comes at me.

He hits my jaw, ribs, temple, slamming me into the ropes.

Fuck! I straighten and stalk him as he backs away, my eyes trained on his as blood trickles down my face.

I hit. He hits back. *Wham-pow-wham.*

In my peripherals, I see Brooke's sister by her side. Her sister who she loves.

Her sister who this motherfucker screws around with, which means he indirectly screws around with *Brooke.*

I start battering Scorpion until he's stumbling on each step—but he still won't fall.

He will.

He'll be falling at my feet and it's only a matter of three . . . two . . . one . . . Clenching my teeth when he doesn't, I grab him by the neck with one arm and spin him around to look at the girls.

"You think I wouldn't kill you in front of them? You think I wouldn't enjoy having them watch me break you?" I growl.

He laughs and I promptly break his elbow. He moans as I let go of his arm, and it drops at his side, dangling and useless.

He backs away now, and I corner him, slamming his head to the side, over and over. He rams his knee into my gut, but I recover and punch, left-right, left-right, until I drop him to his knees.

I won't be merciful. I grab Scorpion and pull him to his feet, forcing him to look at Brooke. Her sister is crying, her head down, and Brooke's cheeks are stark white, and the helpless fear in her gaze only makes my protectiveness rise tenfold.

"Look at her very well," I whisper with my lowest voice in his ear, "because what you see belongs to *me.* It's because of her that

I'm going to break every inch of your body, beat you to within an inch of your life, then I'm going to prolong your agony until the pain alone is what kills you. You think I won't kill you because she's watching? You're wrong. It's because she's watching that I *will* kill you."

He spits black blood to the mat.

I shove him away, pull up my fists and pop out my knuckles, ready to go at it again.

We don't lose time. We fight. I punch him, over and over, slamming hard and fast, all my power running up and coming from my gut, straight into my hit. I jab, jab, hook, until the sound of my knuckles meeting his flesh is replaced by the sound of his body crashing to the mat.

The chant rises up. *"REM-ING-TON! REM-ING-TON!"*

"Rip! Seal the deal, Rip!!!!!!!!"

I head over to his prone form, working some air into my lungs. Sweat drips down my chest and arms. I watch him crawl on the ground in an effort to avoid me. I keep approaching, my eyes on Brooke now, because that's where I'll see the victory, and not anywhere else.

"Go, Remy!!!!!" she says.

At my feet, Scorpion tries to move, and I swing my arm and slam him down.

The crowd roars. Bending over, I grab his unbroken arm and break all his fingers, then I move to his wrist, and I lift it up for the crowd to see, then I break that easily too.

A low sound rumbles up his throat, and he squirms on the mat. I slide my hands up to his elbow and I start twisting, wanting to make it painful, and slow. Oh, yes, fucker. It'll be slow.

He thrashes and sputters, and the bone is about to snap when I hear his coach yell out, and a black towel falls into the ring.

I see the towel and grit my teeth in frustration when I do.

"Booo!" the public shouts. *"Booo!!"*

Fuck me, I'm so wired, I don't think I can back off. I want his blood. I want to break his elbow, his shoulder, and then his goddamned face. I want him to pay for the little box of goodies he sent Brooke, and I want him to pay for what he did to her sister, and I want him to pay for what he did way back when that meant I'd never be able to box professionally again. It would be so easy to pretend I didn't see the towel, and just like that, I can twist his neck and he's dead.

. . . And I'd prove to Brooke that I'm a killer.

Only seconds before asking her to marry me . . .

Which isn't right.

With an inhuman effort, I let go and step away. Scorpion spits out blood and raises his head to look at me. I start walking away when I hear him, "Pussy, come and finish me!"

I do. I turn and slam my fist down, hard enough to knock him unconscious.

"RIPTIIIIIIIIIIIIIIIIIIIIIIIIIIDE!" the announcer's yell reverberates across the arena.

The crowd stands with a roar, and I immediately search the stands for Brooke. I'm fucking hungry for her. For the acceptance I see in her eyes, the joy. I want to see that she's proud of me, and I want her to know I would kill him. For her. I would maim, destroy, do anything, for her. But I also won't. For her.

Her lips are curled into the sweet little smile I like, but her forehead is puckered, and she's crying softly in her seat, the only person in the arena that's not standing.

I'm barely aware of my arm being raised as a kernel of fear settles deep in my gut.

"The winner of this season's Underground Championship, I give you, REMINGTON TATE, RIIIPTIDE!!! *Riiiiiiiiptide!!* Riptide . . . where are you going?"

Something's the fuck wrong. Something's the fuck wrong and the instant it hits me, I leap off the ring and charge for her, kneeling at her feet, wrapping my sweaty, bloodied arms around her.

"Brooke, oh, baby, she's coming, isn't she?" She nods, and my heart has never pounded so hard as I wipe away her tears, murmuring, "I got you, all right? You got me, baby, now I got you. Come here." I scoop her up in my arms, and she cuddles into me, so vulnerable and sweet as she cries into my neck.

"He's not . . . supposed . . . to come yet. . . . It's too soon. . . . What if he won't make it . . . ? "

The crowd has flocked around us, but I tuck her head under my neck and use my shoulders to bulldoze past the fans, determined to get us out of here as fast as I can as hands reach out to rub me. *RIPTIDE, YOU ROCK! RRIIIIPPPPTIIIDE!*" they scream.

White roses start raining over us from the stands when the announcer speaks.

Fuck this is all wrong. I'm supposed to be on my knees. She's supposed to be happy tonight.

"At the request of our victor, who has a very special question to ask . . ."

I spot the exit when the music starts playing in the background, and my heart starts pounding in a way it doesn't even pound when I'm fighting. Brooke's confusion seems to grow, and the chorus that asks what I've wanted to ask her from the moment I held her in my arms, kissed her for the first time, and introduced myself to her, plays out loud.

She was mine then.

She. Is. Mine.

She will be mine.

"Wh-what?" she asks me in confusion.

Pushing out through the exit, I tell Pete, "Pull the car

around," and I keep walking until Pete screeches to a halt before us. Brooke's sister climbs up front.

I tuck Brooke into the back, and she keeps looking at me expectantly, watching me close the door as Pete drives us out of there. I hold her face between my hands, and my heart is still galloping.

This is it.

This is what I want most in the world.

I feel like I've been waiting since before I was born to ask her. It's like asking her to jump off a cliff, with me. It goes against my instinct to protect her, but my instinct to claim her overrules anything else. She's mine, my girl.

Her eyes hold me, hot and pained but shining expectantly, and I hear the need in my voice when I speak, "The song was supposed to ask you to marry me, but you'll have to settle on me doing the asking . . ." She stares at me, her lips apart, and she's trembling so hard, she doesn't know my hands are trembling too as I squeeze her face between my hands. "Mind. Body. Soul. All of you for me. All of you mine . . . Marry me, Brooke Dumas."

"Yes!" she exclaims, sobbing and grabbing my jaw and pressing her lips to mine, no hesitation in her answer, no worry, no concern. "Yes yes yes!"

"Fuck baby, thank you," I murmur, my throat tight as I pull her to me and she buries herself against me. She can't see my face, and I exhale a breath against her hair and hold her, my adrenaline starting to crash almost instantly. She moans in pain and I quietly rock her, whispering in her ear, "Tell me what to do."

"Hold me," she says, groaning softly, then breathing fast, "Stay with me, don't go black, stay with me."

I nod and hold her, but I start to worry when she keeps moaning in pain.

Don't fucking go black, asshole!

When we check her in, I'm trying to calm down, but she's moaning and grimacing and I can't stop thinking I'm the bastard who knocked her up.

I try to think of the look of happiness on her face when I proposed. I try to hang onto it and remember what she's told me before. We want this. We want a family. We deserve it like anyone else. I try to think of that look of happiness when she's on the delivery table, pushing.

Holy god, I don't even know how I'm in one piece.

I hold her hand as her cries tear through my ears and split me open.

I brush her hair behind her face and watch her chew on her lip as she pushes, while I quietly beg myself to please just hang tight and not let my daughter first meet me when I'm black.

It feels like forever by the time Brooke lets go a sigh and drops back on the table, suddenly relaxed, when I see the doctor holding a squirming, wet, pink figure. "It's a boy," he says, and a soft cry follows.

"A boy," she gasps, delighted.

"A boy," I repeat.

"Breathing on his own. No complications. He's preterm—we still need to incubate," the doctor murmurs.

"We want to see . . ." Brooke cries.

She lifts her arms and they tremble as she waits for them to clean the baby, and it howls in protest, and then, the nurse brings it over.

I'm staring in disbelief as Brooke holds it . . . not it . . . *him*. Our son.

Our son who stopped screaming when they placed him in her arms.

She ducks her head, her hair tangled, a sheen of sweat across her neck and face, our son wrapped in a small blanket and in her arms, and my body loosens as I bend my head to her, and to him, as a whole truckload of protectiveness, and love, and pure raw happiness slam into me.

"I love him, Remy," she whispers, tilting her head to me, and I feel so fucking grateful for her giving me this, I just need to kiss her, feel her whisper against my mouth, "I love you so much. Thank you for this baby."

"Brooke," I rasp, protectively wrapping my arms around both of them. My throat is raw, and my eyes are killing me, and I've never had something so perfect, pure, and precious in my life than my little firecracker and a little part of her, with a little part of me.

"If he's like me, we will support him," I whisper to her. "If he's like me . . . we'll be there for him."

"Yes, Remy," she agrees, looking at our son, and at me, her expression so loving I feel renewed by it. "We will teach him music. And exercise. And how to take care of this little body. It will be strong and astound him and maybe frustrate him sometimes too. We will teach him to love it. And himself. We will teach him love."

I wipe the moisture from my eye and tell her *yeah,* that *yeah, we will,* but I won tonight, and I still wish I felt worthier and I were different. I wish I were perfect for them. I wish I were perfect in every way so they'd never shed a tear for me, worry, or stress because of me. But I love them more than anything perfect ever could. I love them more than anything perfect ever will. Nothing perfect would kill for them like I would, or die for them like I would.

Tears are streaming down her cheeks as she stretches out her arm, and I realize I stepped back like some pussy afraid to be rejected by them.

"Come here," she whispers, and I come and bow my head to hers, and I'm not sure if the wetness on my jaw is mine or hers, but it's taking all my effort to hold myself under control. "I am so in love with you," she whispers as she nuzzles me, caressing me in a way that makes my eyes burn even harder. "You deserve this and more. While you fight out there, I will fight for you to come home to *this*."

I growl, angry that I'm crying, and then wipe my tears and kiss her lips, rasping, "I fucking love you to pieces. To pieces. Thank you for this baby. Thank you for loving me. I can't wait to make you my wife."

PRESENT

SEATTLE

The way my wife looks today.

The way my wife smiles today.

The way my wife nuzzles our smiling son as she says, "Good-bye, Racer, be good with Grandma and Grandpa. . . ."

"Gah!"

I pat the top of Racer's round little head and kiss his chubby cheek. "That's right, devil, you heard her."

"Leave him to us," Brooke's mother tells us outside the church, while the team looks on from a couple feet away. Brooke's sister, Nora, is clutching the bouquet she just caught to her chest, and Pete looks ready to puke at her side because of his feelings for her. Coach is grinning like he never does, while Diane is standing with her arm linked to his, and Riley can't stop glaring at Melanie's new boyfriend, who clearly doesn't give a shit.

Me . . . I've had it with the suit, with being kept away from my bride in our own home, with kissing her meekly by the altar and without using my tongue and my teeth or putting my hands on her ass. As Brooke waves to Melanie and yells, "Racer, Mommy loves you!" I pull her into the back of the limousine and reach around her to slam the door, and I finally have her all for me.

She turns, panting, to look into my eyes, her cheeks blushed pink, her eyes sparkling in excitement, and no, I will never forget today.

I reach for her while she simultaneously tries climbing on my lap and I grab her waist to help her, but she squeaks as she tries flattening the billowing skirt of her dress and we fail to get her comfortably on top of me. "I loved this dress until this moment when it won't let me get close to you," she complains.

"Shit, I'm so hard for you, come here." Sliding my hand under the fall of her hair, I grab her by the neck and dive hungrily for her lips, kissing her, my tongue anxious to be touching hers. I want more. And she instantly gives me more, thirsty for me, moaning softly.

Keeping our mouths attached, I gather her closer as she strokes my hair. "I can't wait," she breathes. "For you to tear this dress off me."

"I'll send those fucking buttons flying." My mouth waters as I drag my thumbs down her cheeks. "And I'm going to feast on you like a fucking banquet."

"Oh yes, please." She sets her nose on mine and sighs, her fingers playing in my hair. "We've never left Racer for more than two hours before. I feel like a bad mother."

I shake my head, nuzzling her as I do. "If we don't want to leave him and go on a honeymoon yet, you at least have to let me steal you for an evening." I kiss her jaw. "You're the most tender, playful mother I know, Brooke."

She laughs. "Oh, and how many do you know?" she teases, reaching up to poke both my dimples. "To compare me to?"

Really? I know none. But the mother of my son.

God, they're so fucking perfect, and they're both mine.

I sometimes watch them from across the room, and my chest swells as they play around with each other. Brooke has a canny sixth sense that always knows when I stare. She always looks up, her eyes warm and sparkling with happiness at me, and I come over and pull them close to me, kissing and nuzzling them both.

"I know my mother wasn't like you," I whisper to her now, kissing the tip of her nose.

"And you, there's no father like you." She caresses the bow at my neck. "I love you so much, Remington." She presses her face into my neck and tries getting closer to my side, dragging in a deep inhale, her voice thick, "You look so hot in that tuxedo, I'm dying to have you all to myself."

"I get you all for me too." I tighten my arm around her waist as I buzz my lips over her hair.

Maybe taking a honeymoon currently is impossible, especially when neither of us wants to leave Racer, but I need my wife tonight.

Quietly I kiss her forehead and her nose. Running my eyes over her features, I tip her head and scrape my thumb across her lips. "I need this," I rasp, and set my mouth on hers.

She rubs my tongue to hers and sighs as I slip my fingers into her hair and loosen the crystal clips scattered throughout. Pulling each raindrop-shaped crystal from her hair, I tuck them into my jacket pocket while I slowly savor her mouth and kiss her all the way to the hotel, until neither of us is breathing right by the time we arrive.

The moment we walk into the lobby, a dozen curious stares land on us, and they're soon followed by claps and cheers as I take her by the hand and lead her to the elevators.

"Many years, man!" someone shouts.

"Cheers to the bride and groom!"

Brooke laughs, and I'm chuckling too as I pull her into the

elevator with me and then bury my face in her neck, smelling her as we head to the top floor.

"I want to eat you," I growl, sliding my fingers under her hair again. Her eyes darken as she reaches for my free hand and spreads it over her heart.

"Are you going to kiss me here?" She forces my fingers to curve around the round flesh of one perky little tit.

I nod.

Then she lifts that same hand to her mouth and sets a kiss on my palm. "And here?"

I nod again.

Her smile matches mine in mischief as she slides my hand down her abdomen and to the bell of her skirt, then she laughs and pushes up on her toes. "What about . . . there?"

I tip her head back. "Your pussy is getting kissed tonight for sure."

Her lips curve in pure delight and I have to take them and kiss her, stopping only when we hear the *Ting*.

When the doors roll open, I scoop her in my arms and she squeaks in surprise as I head to the double doors down the hall. "Remy!"

"This is what husbands do the first night. No?"

She links her fingers at the back of my collar and nods.

I duck my head low to whisper in her ear as we reach our door. "As your husband, I do whatever the hell I want," I say, sliding the key into the slot while I add, "And right now, I'm going to do *you*." I push open the door, take us inside, and kick it shut behind me, then I set her to her feet, facing the room.

I click on the lights, and Brooke lets out a soft, surprised gasp.

Rose petals of every color are littered across the carpet. A hundred vases are scattered throughout, bursting with red bouquets, white bouquets. I wanted a fucking rose garden for my wife, and this is what the guys could help me do.

As Brooke stares quietly around, every inch in the room is either green, yellow, white, red, pink, some roses in buds, some blooming, some with stems, some scattered on the furniture without them, I quietly come up from behind her and set my headphones on her head, and click Play on my iPod.

"Everything" by Lifehouse begins. A hand flies to her chest when she starts listening, her pink mouth opening slightly and her eyes instantly tearing.

My chest swells and my throat feels itchy, my eyes stinging like the day Racer was born, and in that one instant, only hours after Brooke accepted to marry me—they became my family and the center of my world. Now my wife stands in this room I filled with roses for her, and I have. NO. WORDS. No fucking words to tell her. The way I need her. The way I want her. The way I love her. How every day I wake up a happy man, and go to sleep a happy man, sure that I can't love her any more than I already do. But every day, the impossible happens, and I love her more. Her smiles, her strength, her dedication to our son, to me, everything about her is perfect for *me*.

She starts sobbing softly as she keeps listening to the song, clutching her stomach as if it hurts to hear the lyrics.

You're all I want, you're all I need, you're everything . . . everything . . .

My eyes burn as she cries softly, and I'm flooded with tenderness as I step before her. I lift my palm to catch the tears of one cheek, and press my lips to the other, kissing her tears dry. "No crying," I murmur into her skin, and she squeezes her eyes shut as more tears fall, her arms trembling as she wraps them around me.

"No crying. I want to make you happy," I murmur, pulling

off the headphones and tossing them aside as I repeat it in her ear. *I want to make you happy.* She shudders quietly, sniffing, and I frame her face in my hands so my thumbs can dry the rest of her tears as I look into her eyes. The only eyes that really see me. The tender, hungry, and passionate gold eyes of the woman I love. I caress my thumbs on her cheeks. "Not just happy. I want to make you the happiest woman alive."

"I am," she says, sniffling, wearing her heart in her eyes as she looks at me. "It's why I'm crying."

With a soft groan, I pull her to me and go kiss her ear. "Every day you make me the luckiest man alive," I whisper, sliding my fingers up her back and tracing the buttons of her wedding dress, impatiently popping them open, one by one. She nuzzles my neck and kisses my throat when suddenly, she pulls away from me and starts backing across the suite, a new playfulness in her gaze.

"You want me?"

One of my eyebrows shoots up. "You doubt it?"

I start following, my hunter kicking into gear, all my instincts rearing up and priming my body to chase and catch her. I'm not about to let her get very far. "Come here," I growl, reaching out and pulling her close. She lets out a squeak a second before I kiss her, hard and deep as I run my hand down the buttons on her back, grab the fabric, and rip it. Buttons fly, landing over the rose petals on the floor. She moans when I slide my hand through the tear and touch soft, bare skin. "Hmmm." I lick up her neck as I pull her arms out of the sleeves of her dress and yank the top down to her waist.

She pulls off my bow tie and slides my jacket over my shoulders. "I'm so ready for you, you can consider all day foreplay," she says.

"I don't think so," I laugh, then I pin her hands at her sides and lace my fingers through hers, keeping her fingers from going anywhere as I kiss her mouth, slow and languorously. "Let's start stripping you."

Grabbing her by the hips, I prop her on the back of a couch and push her skirt up so I can reach one silver glittery shoe. I unbuckle all the little line of crystal buckles, then I toss one shoe aside and work on the next. Once it falls next to the first, I run my hand up her stockings and find the perfect spot to rip.

She gasps in delight as I rip and pull it off her leg, baring her skin from the tip of her feet, up higher. I lick her toe, then trail my tongue up the arch of her foot while my hands slide up her lean, long legs to tug the rest of her stocking free. I hear her start to pant, and when I've bared all her legs under her dress, I have a perfect view of the damp spot on her panties as I suck one pink-painted toe. My eyes blur from the force of my need, and I part her thighs and hear her catch her breath as I release her foot and bury deeper under her skirt to lick her over her panties.

"Remy," she groans, as I lick the damp spot on the lace. She's never worn lace before and I can see her pussy lips, pink and snug under the material. Groaning low and deep, I urge her legs wider apart and give her one thorough lap of my tongue, then I emerge from under her skirt, and rise to my feet, so fucking hot I'm about to turn to cinder.

Brooke's chest is heaving and she's leaning weakly backward, looking dazed and in love and beautiful with the top of her dress pulled down to her waist. Her body is twisted at an awkward angle as she braced herself, her dark hair falling behind her, and she's catching her breath from the licking I gave her. Her round, pretty tits are as juicy as they've ever been, her nipples jutting out and almost screaming for my mouth. "Remington," she says, almost pleadingly.

My body tight with desire, I scoop my arms beneath her. "You get a bed tonight, Mrs. Tate," I whisper.

"Mrs. Dumas-Tate," she says as she opens the top buttons of my shirt and drags her lips along the stubble of my jaw.

"Whatever. You're mine."

She agrees with a sound against my throat, and a lick of her tongue. My blood is bubbling with need as I set her down on the bed, then I get busy stripping off my shirt. While I get rid of the cuff links and jerk it off my shoulders, my eyes run over those full breasts, fuller than ever, her nipples larger for my son to suck. And me.

I'm burning down to the pit of my stomach.

Beneath my zipper my cock is fully hard, and all I have to do is jerk open my pants button and it explodes through the zipper. Brooke is trying to squirm out of her big dress and I decide I need her naked before I do anything else.

I reach out and pull the skirt and she squeaks and laughs when the fabric tears again and now easily slides down her body. "Oh, I knew this dress wouldn't survive you, I *knew* it!" she cries happily.

We laugh together, and as soon as she's in nothing but panties, scooting back on the bed, I finish stripping and then stand there, at the foot of the bed, naked and so fucking hard I can barely see straight, and I look at her with my heart pumping in my chest and my skin buzzing from her nearness.

I look, and look and look. At my bride. My woman.

She grows impatient and crawls over to me in those wet lace panties. She kisses the length of my cock, the tattoo behind it, up the squares of my abs, up to my neck, and works her way to my lips. "I'm so hot, I'm shaking for you." She caresses my cock.

I fist her hair in my hand and draw her back an inch, slowly dragging my tongue along her lips. "Then give me." She smiles against my mouth and then moans and opens up so our tongues meet, and I lay her back on the bed littered with rose petals. Grabbing a handful of rose petals on the bed beside us, I flatten her on her back and raise my fist above her to sprinkle the rose petals over her.

She catches her breath as they fall on her body, her hair splayed dark behind her as she runs her fingers up my biceps, my shoulder, caressing me as I caress those rose petals and drag them up and down her body.

A mew leaves her lips and her eyes drift shut, and I keep dragging all the petals under my hand up to cup one tit, rubbing the petals over her nipples. The room is fragrant of rose petals but Brooke smells best of all. I know when she's completely wet and ready for me, and she's ready now.

"Remy . . ."

Pulsing to bury myself in her, I stretch my body out next to hers and take her in my arms, and whisper against her mouth, "It's our official wedding night."

"Yes." She rubs her hands up my chest and looks at me with half-closed eyes.

"And I want to make it last." I press my lips to her several times, without tongue, kissing the corner of her lips, the top, the bottom . . . then the center. "I want to freeze you right here," I huskily murmur, "in my arms, where nothing can touch you but me." As I drag my hand down her side, she shudders, letting me pet and kiss her, and she kisses me back with slow, wanton thrusts of her tongue. "Nothing, just you," she agrees.

"That's right," I rasp.

"But I'm so wet," she breathes.

"And you know I like it," I murmur, petting her pussy with my hand before I ease her on top of my body so that she's splayed above me and I can kiss her and grab her ass, and feel her pussy close to my cock while I have that juicy ass clenched in my hands and our mouths won't leave the other alone.

She grows restless as we kiss and starts rocking her body, and I roll her to the side so I can ease a hand between our bodies and pet her pussy over her panties. I kiss her shoulder, then go downward, up the rise of one breast, to a puckered pink nipple. I drag my tongue out to lick it, then I head down to her navel and taste every inch of skin I can, feeling how her abdomen rises and falls as she pants but lets me do whatever I want with her.

She buries her face in my hair as I nuzzle and lick her belly button, and she grabs a rose petal and drags it over my shoulder, silken smooth as she trails it over the muscles of my back. Rising, I grab another fistful of petals and drag both hands over her body, so she feels all of them against her. "I love you," she says, looking into my eyes, watching me cup her face. "I know," I rasp. "And I love you."

Our bodies are so hot, we're perspiring and damp as we keep petting. She knows each of my muscles, but it always feels like she's memorizing me. I know every inch of her body, but I want to live in every inch, kiss, lick, eat, bite, every inch.

I do, and then she's writhing and fisting her hands in my hair, mewing, "I'm going to come."

"Yes you are," I murmur, and I seize her by the waist and I drag her down to my erection, watching the little pulse flutter at the base of her throat as she takes me. Groaning, I duck to dip my tongue into the crevice at the bottom of her throat as the head of my cock goes in.

The breath ripples out of her lips, and she grips my biceps and mews softly.

"Do you like it?" I rasp.

"I like everything you do to me."

I lower my head and bite her near her shoulder, the sweet, smooth curves of her bottom in the cup of my hand as she slides lower and lower. She tries to go down the last inch, and I stop and lift her so I can lick her nipple.

I give it a good, long lick, then I blow air over the puckered tip. Her eyes pop open in surprise, and she shivers and starts rocking against me. "Remington," she pleads, tilting her hips to my erection.

I roll her over to her back. "What do you want?"

Cheeks flushed with arousal, her eyes are brilliant gold. "I want my husband," she says, sliding her fingers up my pecs. "Right now. All of him."

I take her legs and part them open as I bend over, the damp spot between her legs driving me wild. But first I move my mouth down her thigh to kiss the scar on her knee, then I work my mouth back up. "You want his cock but what about his tongue." My mouth hovers above her pussy and I lick the damp spot.

She gasps my name and grips the back of my head, cupping me. "Yes," she breathes, moaning.

"Where do you want it," I murmur, and I slide a finger into her panties and then into her sex while I roll her clit with the tip of my tongue, nothing but that thin, wet fabric between us. Her folds are slick and swollen. I insert one finger, then two, as I push my tongue over her clit. She comes and drenches my fingers, and I pull them out and make her suck them.

With a hungry noise, she pushes me onto my back. I fall willingly and pull her on top of me. Her thighs straddle mine and she moans at the contact of our skin. She rubs her sex against my dick through the underwear and caresses her fingers up my chest. I groan and sit up to squeeze her breasts in my hand, a primal nature to conquer and roll her around and fuck her coursing through me, winning over. I roll her over, then reach between us to play with her pussy as I lick one nipple. She tastes as good as she fucking smells, and I bury my head in her neck and inhale as her thighs spread wide beneath my weight, and I hold her lingerie open so I can tease her folds with the head of my cock.

She moans again and rocks her hips. "Oh yes." Her legs spread wider open beneath me, hot and inviting. She tilts her hips and sinks her nails into the flesh of my back. "Remy," she tells me in my ear, reverently, as if I'm her god and this, us, here, is our real church.

"We're mating all night," I tell her, looking into her face and rubbing the head of my cock along the fleshy part of her lips.

"All night," she agrees.

Gripping the lace between her legs, I rip open her panties. "I'm coming inside you."

"Yes."

I pull her arms up and shove up inside. "Inside my wife."

"Yes," she pants against my ear, thrashing as I fill her. "Oh, *yes*."

Pinning her down by the hips, I groan and start moving in her, our bodies hot, slicked with sweat. She moans, I groan and pulse inside her, our bodies moving together, fast and hungry for more, slapping as she tilts her hips upward and I push downward, wanting as close as I can get.

I tongue her ear, her neck, then her nipples, one at a time, my hands rasping up her sides, her fingers gripping me closer, her lips in my ear as we lose it, out of control.

I love you, she gasps

No, fuck, no, I love you.

She thrashes and shudders beneath me, coming fast and hard, and as her pussy clenches my cock, I start ejaculating inside her, clenching my arms around her shaking body and letting her take me with her. I growl softly in her neck, biting the curve of her neck as I go off inside her for a third time, and she moans in pleasure until we're both panting and sated, my tongue rubbing out the spot I just bit.

I shift to spare her my weight when she whispers, "Don't pull out. Please. I need you in me."

I roll to my back and bring her with me, and she sighs and cuddles, catching her breath while I slide my hands down her body and to her ass. I nudge her head back with my nose, murmuring, "I still want you," and when she looks up, I take her mouth and start kissing her, using my hands on her ass to start rocking her over my cock.

With a guttural sound in her throat, she grabs my hair and pushes her tongue hungrily against mine, starting to ride me.

"That's right, baby," I croon, grabbing her hips and moving her on me, sucking her tongue, nipping at her bottom lip. "That's right, take me, ride me, show me how much you need me."

She sits back and rides me harder, and I rise up to feast on her tits and clench her ass cheeks as she moves recklessly on me. "Remy," she gasps, and I know she's close. She's hot and wet and tight as fuck around me, and I groan as my body tightens and the pleasure gathers at the base of my spine.

I stick my tongue into her mouth with a heavy groan, and we kiss and caress each other until we come. When she sags against me, she keeps me inside her and tucks her face into my neck, and I bury my nose into her hair and smell her. We don't speak for some time, but we don't need to. I know her, and she knows me. I'm inside her, and she's wrapped around me. Our bodies say it loud and clear.

We lay in bed for a while, quiet. Brooke alternates between kissing my throat and teasing a fingertip round and around my nipple, while I smell her hair and neck, and quietly pet my little firecracker.

PRESENT

SEATTLE

Brooke

I wake up snuggled into his hard body the next morning, and he smells like he does, and he makes me feel like he does, and I realize I still haven't shown him his wedding present. My tummy grips with nerves and excitement when I remember I haven't showed him my wedding present. Butterflies.

He always gives them to me.

I feel like a virgin every, single, time, he touches me, and kisses me, and makes love to me.

Quietly and with a chest overflowing with happiness, I look up to find him with his eyes closed, but a smile on his lips. I smile because I know he's awake . . . as relaxed as I am. "Mr. Remington Tate, you got yourself married yesterday," I whisper as I run my fingers up the hard muscles of his tan chest, up the thick tendons of his throat, his scruffy jaw, those beautiful dimples, teasing past the closed eyes, and to the standing-up ends of his spiky black hair, caressing him quietly while inwardly I'm swooning.

Watching him waiting for me at the altar yesterday, as I walked slowly—painfully slowly—up to him in my father's arms when all I wanted was to run; he took my breath away.

Remington in a black tuxedo, his hair as dark and spiky as ever, his broad shoulders filling his jacket, fitted to his narrow waist and hips, and the way those dancing blue eyes watched me as I walked up to him . . .

Nothing existed as I stared into his eyes. Nothing ever exists for me when I stare into those eyes. It's not the color, or the hue, it's what I see in them. Every marvelous, complex thing that makes up Remy.

"Our baby will be six months soon, and you still give me butterflies," I whisper quietly.

He's a man. He might not know about butterflies, but I know enough for the both of us. And I've got a zoo full of them right now as he opens his eyes and looks at me. With those same blue eyes I want to stare at all day.

He angles his head to mine and feathers a kiss across my lips, and warmth surges through my being as his rough, delicious voice ripples through me, "You're mine. My obsession. My dreams. My hope. My heart," he whispers, his rough hands running up the sides of my body like they did all night.

"Tell me I'm your Real again, Remington," I plead, trailing my fingers up his jaw as he looks at me.

"You're my Real, little firecracker. You're my everything."

My stomach tightens when I remember the song he played me. The suite still smells of roses. I've heard the guys banter with him, telling him to get me something other than roses, something less old-fashioned. He won't budge. He doesn't care what anyone thinks about it, only what he believes they mean, and he uses them to talk to me. To tell me he loves me.

Remington is big on actions, even if he might not know it.

He's always proving, in so many ways, who he is, and what he feels. And I've done something . . . that I hope talks to him. Just like his roses and his songs talk to me.

Tummy clenching in anticipation, I turn to the nightstand and get one of my hair bands, which I tie around my wrist when I don't use it to pull my hair in a ponytail. "Will you help me put this on?" I ask, passing it back as an excuse.

He sits up and lifts my hair, and I love how he lifts my hair with one hand while apparently trying to figure out how to use it with the other.

Then the movements stop, and a complete silence falls.

I hold my breath as he sets my hair band down on the mattress, and then he brushes my hair aside to reveal the back of my neck with both hands. Ever so slowly, slowly seducing my body, my mind, and my heart, like only he can, he traces the curve of my nape with the rough pad of one of his fingers.

Delicious tingles run through my body as he lowers his dark head to my neck, the deep male pleasure in his voice unmistakable. "What's this," he murmurs, licking it softly.

I feel his tongue rasp over my skin, and my heart flutters for him.

"Whatever it's on, it means it's yours," I breathe. He buries his head in the side of my throat and smells me, murmuring, *"That's right,"* then he turns me around by the chin so he can take my mouth and kiss me, long and hard. Remington Tate. My love, my husband, my baby's beautiful father, kissing me gently as his fingers trace the tattoo on the back of my neck that says simply

REMY

ACKNOWLEDGMENTS

Thank you to my beautiful husband and children, for being patient with me while I sat down and lost myself in this story. Without your support, I could not move a pen. I love you!

And to my parents, for patiently spending days and weeks without hearing from me and still loving me. I love you both so much and I promise I'll be better about calling.

To Adam Wilson—Adam, I don't know how you managed to get married to the love of your life while managing to edit and put *Mine* out on time for the readers, but you deserve a red cape and I have no words to thank you for all you do for me.

To Amy Tannenbaum, who is there for me through thick and thin, always with invaluable advice and a helping hand. Another red cape to you!

To my amazing publisher at Gallery Books, Jennifer Bergstrom, and to Lauren McKenna, two fine ladies I only recently met and can't wait to meet again. Thank you for being Team Katy too! To Jules, Kristin, and Enn, the best PR team I could ever have; I'm blessed to work with you. To my copy editor, for the fantastic suggestions and also for forgiving me when I get stubborn and want to leave my sentence raw. To Sarah Hansen for another kick-ass cover—your talent knows no bounds. To my proofreaders at Gallery, and to Anita Saunders, thank you for spotting all the little details I can no longer see and for helping to make it shine.

To my author friends who read, suggest, cheer, and support. Writing is a lonely business and you get so much more done when you have understanding friends who can push you through a little hump!

To Kati Brown, you deserve special thanks and love from me. Your input on this book was golden. Thank you, Kati!

To all the bloggers who *Real* introduced me to, I can't even explain how much I appreciate you!

To Dana and the Scaries, you are treasured by me! Dana, you are PRECIOUS!

And especially, to everyone who has suffered, or suffers, from any form or shape of mental illness, and to anyone whose loved one suffers from any form or shape of mental illness, I do believe there is light in the dark, and I hope you find yours.

Friends, author friends, bloggers, and readers. Thank you for loving Brooke and Remy like I do.

Xoxoxox!